# TEWODROS
# **THE  KING**

Ravi Faiia

*For St. Anne*

Tewodros The King
Copyright © 2020 by Ravi Faiia

Cover photograph copyright Santha Faiia
Cover design by Lawrence J. Pearson

# PROLOGUE

Only his own hand was worthy to take the life of Tewodros.

He was pure, more than any other prince. Not once had the monks pampered him as he waited in a cave for the crown. Their discipline was his discipline as they sought to keep evil at bay, not just the rivals to the throne who might attack the prince, but to keep it from their thoughts and minds.

Two hundred feet of sheer cliff dropped away from the mouth of this cave in the central highlands, commanding the great rift valley that had cradled man from his earliest steps on the earth; that to the south carried wildebeest in thundering droves across the fertile savannah; and at its northern end pointed towards the land where Jesus had walked while a great empire had been born into legend here. This was Ethiopia, where the cold winds whispered on the plateau even as the sunbaked riverbeds parched in the heat, and where the valley it wore across its shoulder was the crack left by a giant in ages past, whose great adze had sought to splinter Eden, this paradise, asunder from the African continent and set it floating in the sea; a holy land set apart for wise kings to rule.

On a clear-skied morning in the thirteenth month, the month being intercalated by the Ethiopians so their time could track the year set by the sun, the prince dangled his toes over the abyss and marveled at how quickly the morning climbed. When he was a child, he had glimpsed for a moment the fractured fate of a man who fell, before the monks pulled him away, but he had no fear of the cliff's edge, and no concern for the consternation of his caretakers.

He gazed out to the stark escarpment facing, looking for the lammergeiers that he fancied gave him portent of news from the great beyond. In the heights above he saw one of the wheeling birds of prey had caught a rabbit, a tiny speck falling slowly as the vulture dropped its victim's bones upon the rocks, and plunged down to feast on the sweet marrow dashed free.

Yohannes, a monk and tutor to the prince, had shuddered once at this brutal practice. In his own subtle way Yohannes had imparted his belief to Tewodros that a gentle rule would stabilize the country, following the bloodshed that had unified the empire. A primacy of peace, he called it. But Tewodros would not abhor the smashing bones, as he could only admire the lammergeiers' ingenious use of what tools were present to extract the maximum from their dead prey, wasting nothing.

He could think no ill of the high-flying and free bird, linked in his mind to word from the broad country outside the cave, where he longed to spread his own wings someday. The monks guarded him from the outside world, with the sheer cliffs for help, but they were also charged with keeping Tewodros from leaving, and they isolated him from the royal court. His father Kassa was the negusa negast, the king of kings, ruler of an empire where the nobles beneath him would never cease to look for their own aggrandizement, and even his own son's ambitious machinations might pose a threat.

The sun's brightness was dimmed for an instant, and Tewodros looked up from his prison to realize that the shadow of a lammergeier had passed across his face.

Yohannes stood beside him, witness. "In the East, this bird is rare," he told Tewodros. "They deem it a symbol of good fortune."

"With so many of them in our lands, good fortune must fall upon Ethiopia more than other empires," said Tewodros with a friendly nudge to his tutor.

Yohannes smiled a bit and went on, looking at his pupil from eyes that seemed to know everything. "They also say that when its shadow falls on one, he will be lifted up to rule over others."

"Then I will be the king," said Tewodros softly, of a sudden more serious. In the distance he perceived a rider's figure cantering down the valley. The raptor's portent had spoken true, as the rider was a messenger from the king of kings.

* * * * *

The jungle was swaying as if alive to the beat of the workman drummers. The dull thumping paced the line of men tasked with beating the bush, emitting noisome shouts to scare and flush the game inexorably towards where the hunters stayed waiting. Fully four-score men had been deployed to aid the encounter between the master of the wild, and the representative of the ruler of the civilized, the Viceroy of India's general. Most of the men were fanned out across the square mile where fresh tiger prints had led that morning, the ones with drums feeling only slightly more nervous than the ones armed solely with two-foot wooden clubs, or, if lucky, a dull machete. It paid at all costs to keep the next man over in sight at all times – to hold the line almost in a military sense so the tiger in being driven away from the ruckus of one beater would always move in the same direction, and not towards the practically defenseless foot soldiers.

Of course, as the men flanked the area where the tiger was supposed to be, at a certain point each flank was pushing the tiger towards other lines of men, with the hunters positioned at the only quiet outlet. Each part of the line had to count on the others to correctly triangulate by listening to the drummers and keeping a steady course, such that the tiger would never be cornered and see its only way out as through an unlucky man, who would be torn by tooth and claw or, if he ran scared and let the tiger pass by, beaten by the rajah for spoiling the hunt.

Jeevan was a veteran of three hunts, but each time had managed to be peripheral to the real action, for which he thanked his lucky stars. There was no glory to be had by him from a successful hunt, and only risk of mayhem if the endeavor went awry. "I hope this British big shot can shoot straight," he muttered under his breath. The general's name was Napier, which had sounded to Jeevan like "no love" in Hindi, and seemed appropriate. His friend from a neighboring village had been the victim of the errant shot of a spoiled rajah in the past, maimed not by the bullet but by the angry prey it had missed, who had encountered the hunters head on and then turned back unscathed to tear through the beaters and escape. The beast had simply batted Jeevan's friend aside as a hindrance in its path, but the claws had cut deep and the infection had claimed his left arm. Jeevan wondered if it was the same animal they were after now. Their territory ranged quite far and this was only six miles from where his friend was mauled.

Jeevan stubbed his toe against a root and cursed, returning to a better awareness of his surroundings. The trees shot straight up here, the canopy not too high as this was new growth, but the length of bare trunk before the leaves were splayed to catch the sun made them seem tall. A few birds flitted from branch to branch, secure in their perches and unperturbed by Jeevan below. There was some dry, thigh-high grass in places, dead branches in others and the corpses of creeping vines, then the stands of thorny bush that sometimes sprang a startled deer; that Jeevan hoped did not hide a surly rhinoceros. Those at least he had some confidence that he could dodge their clumsy, armored charge, though this theory had never been proven.

He noticed the pain in his back that flared up almost every night during his farming days was totally gone, and his sandalwood arms much lighter now that he spent less time in the merciless sun. Those things were good, but he was not so sure going for a soldier had improved much else in his life – he answered too many masters now, instead of just the wolf of famine at his door. He became absorbed in tracing the outline of a burn on his forearm from when he first learned to use a rifle; in those days he had truly missed the rice paddies. Jeevan physically shook his head back into focus, his mop of jet black hair flopping back and forth across his unusually young-looking face. This was no time to let his attention wander.

The terrain was quite flat and no river was near, so the men made good progress. It had not rained in some days, so the crackling helped Jeevan announce his presence to the wildlife, but the dust rising from his steps obscured his vision now and then. The breeze moving the trees did not reach the men underneath and despite the dryness he felt a sweat break out. His palms had to grip his club more tightly as his voice began to feel hoarse from the constant shouting. A small knoll to the northwest indicated the hunters' position. They were getting close and Jeevan's insides involuntarily tightened as his line approached the outlet.

Jeevan looked right and froze – he could no longer see his fellow beater who had been there two steps before. As if on cue the shouting paused, and in the moment of stillness between the drumbeats he could hear a leaf rustle, and a twig snap. A feeling of awe came upon him before his senses detected anything more, time slowing as the next drumbeat seemed long, lower, drawn out. A flash of orange and black, susurrating grass and he caught the twitch of a tail clearly before the signs were gone again. Another beat or two before his breath became unstuck; he had seen the tiger pass and it had escaped the net of men.

The fellow to his right stepped into view again, but Jeevan had been the only one to see the prey. Time snapped back into motion as he passed the news to his neighbor with flailing arms, pointing in the direction where the tail had disappeared. A chain reaction spread down the line like fire, the noise now becoming confused. The beaters had to swing around quickly, or there would be hell to pay with the general. As much as Jeevan feared the tiger, there was something much more dangerous waiting on the other side of that knoll.

* * * * *

The invitations to the coronation went on their speedy way to the four winds, whence all manner of dignitaries, commoners and the king of kings to be would converge at Magdala, Ethiopia's capital city, at the appointed time. Some of the letters had gone down the green ribbon of the Nile that wound through the desert from Ethiopia, then been tapped out by telegraph in Cairo to the exchanges in Europe. One in particular landed in London and assumed its paper form once more. On its way through the Sahara it had been a grand parchment addressed to the Queen of England and bearing a royal seal; now it was just a simple rag of a notice, finding its way through the maze of Whitehall to a stack of dispatches on the Africa desk, where the under-secretary to the assistant secretary to the Foreign Secretary would deign to read it. He was, at least, the head of the Africa desk, Mr. Mark Glendon.

Glendon stooped in this particular morning in his crumpled jacket with the sleeves just too short, his rangy stature made less impressive by the slouch that took two inches off his height, and his eyes cast down to the marble floor. He quickened his pace past the more important offices of European relations, where the politically better-connected snickered at his passage with snide jibes about his ill-disguised ambition. "The fool thinks Africa is the next India," one said. Glendon heard another mutter, "you know his middle name is Antony. Mark Antony Glendon," and a third rejoined, "sits at home imagining himself married to Cleopatra and ruling Egypt, I'm sure."

They were just like the boys had been at school, where he was only able to walk the same hallways because his father was a groundskeeper and had the tuition costs waived, and they had let him know every day that he didn't belong. "You be smarter than all them lads," his father would say in his thick commoner's accent, but Glendon hated that the old gaffer was a nobody, and ran from his family just as he ran from the childish taunts. And so he burned to be a man of consequence, but he saw Africa as he saw every other dry tool of government – dispassionately, as a means within his reach to further his climb through his structured, stratified world. Thus it was that he grasped the Ethiopian invitation too tightly in his hand, and saw an opportunity.

As he stumbled towards his chair, the break he had been waiting for set his limbs aquiver. The imbeciles at the Europe desk were too caught up in their games of influence-brokerage to see that the next power struggle among the white races would be for control of that dark continent, where Britain, if she could plant her seedlings now before the focus of others was trained southward, could control the eastern seaboard and connect the Cape to Cairo while the French sweated over the useless western deserts. Too soon from now the Suez Canal would open under French ownership, and the rush to the Horn of Africa, the gateway to the Red Sea and from there the Mediterranean, would begin in earnest. A change of power in Ethiopia was the perfect inflection point for Britain to make its move.

Glendon knew he would be given only the most junior of diplomats to carry out his requested mission, but that was the perfect cover. Britain could be the one nation in attendance at this coronation, presuming any others would even attend, that came with a treaty in hand to establish commerce between the two nations. Britain was just becoming a Roman backwater when the legendary king Ezana of Axum ruled Ethiopia, but now it was the empire of Queen Victoria that looked down upon the rest of the world. That great emerald in her crown, the Indian subcontinent, would provide wealth and armies unparalleled in history to wreak her will upon the world. He cradled his round head in his hands and massaged the wispy, blond hair as he pondered how to convince his superiors first, to take a meeting, and second, to see the future of Africa as he did.

PART ONE:
KING OF KINGS

*Chapter One*

*"Much have I travell'd in the realms of gold..."*
*- KEATS*

Tewodros closed his eyes at night and opened them to the morning as if only a split second had passed, the way small children do. The smoke from the cooking fire preceded the dawn, its tendrils acrid in Tewodros' nostrils as he felt his way along the wall to the cave mouth. The smoke mingled with the mists that hung enveloping the cliff, and he squatted to breathe the fresh, moist air, his mind still empty with the newness of waking. The sun began to burn the mist away, and the cave was clear before the valley floor. Tewodros looked out upon a sea of cloud beneath and dreamed of sailing its soft billows in a coracle to a further ocean.

The youngest monk Asfaw, who naturally gravitated towards the prince, broke Tewodros' reverie with a call to breakfast. The prince took his portion of the strong, bitter coffee, drunk with ceremony by the circle of men crouched in silence together, and watched the sleep slowly fade from the countenances of his companions. Then it was morning prayers, a chanting affair where Tewodros skipped ahead in his mind to the rote words that were sure to come next, and was always bored by the end. The drone of voices eventually ceased, replaced with laughter as Tewodros teased the older monks for their aches and pains as they began to stretch for morning exercises.

Tewodros' limbs were supple and strong, his lithe muscles a surprise next to the smooth skin of his young, delicate face, with braids in tight rows on his head and hanging down the length of his neck. With such cramped quarters, the monks had to devise ingenious ways to raise the heart rate, and Tewodros took turns with Asfaw to raise himself from a squat with the other sitting on his shoulders. Tewodros felt such camaraderie with his seniors that he would not hesitate to race them up and down the ropes thrown from an overhang, his arms burning as he whooped, "come on, slowpokes!"

There were combat lessons too, and here the cave walls improved the training ground as Tewodros learned to maneuver around an enemy in a close environment. He puffed air out of his cheeks to stay focused while Asfaw came at him with a spear, and he swung his heavy club to parry the blade. Asfaw brought the shaft overhead for another feint, but Tewodros dropped his club, ducked and drove his shoulder into Asfaw's stomach, feeling the soft belly give as he wrapped his strong arms around his friend and twisted his hip to fling Asfaw to the ground. Before Asfaw could say "ouch" the prince stepped on the spear and picked up his club again, grinning as he forced the monk to surrender. "That was fun," he said, but secretly Tewodros longed for the practice of shooting, spear-throwing and most of all horse-riding that would give him the full complement of battle skills he might need someday. He sat back to watch the next pair tussle, and daydreamed of the wind in his face as he brandished a rifle at the head of a charge of horse, and of what he might say and do when it came time to play his part in weighty matters.

Yohannes with his pacifism never joined in the combat exercises, though he competed as well as any of the men in the calisthenics despite his white hair and age-furrowed brow. "Yohannes, why don't you join us in training to fight?" Tewodros asked, knowing already the rhetoric that always followed his question.

"God is my only fortress," Yohannes responded with his arms crossed, wearing his dark habit with the rope belt tied at the left and the hood thrown back, never changing.

Sweat glistened on the prince's skin as he made his way to the dark recess in the back of the cave to perform his ablutions. The freshwater spring was carefully rationed, but the monks would always insist that he be spotless and clean for the daily eucharist. He even remembered today to reach behind his ears and scrub.

He smelled the frankincense and scurried to take his place at the mass. Even a small amount of the precious sap burned to bless the occasion filled the cave with pungent reverence. The abbott Gebrewolde, eldest and leader of the monks, opened a blackened leather-bound Bible written in the ancient Ge'ez script that Tewodros had still to this day never dared to touch, so precious did it seem. The liturgy varied according to a preset order that spanned the years, and Tewodros had been through the full cycle four times that he could remember. Different prayers would strike a chord with Tewodros on different days, as each time one facet of God was enough to fill his contemplation. Today it was the simple Glory Be, and a passing sunbeam at the right moment raised a hallelujah in his chest. "And ever shall be, world without end," came out ecstatically. He felt the usual eagerness to take his piece of broken bread and commune with his fellows and the whole church militant, expectant and triumphant. The dry crumbs slowly spread over his tongue, and he waited to swallow until he had reflected on the meaning of this feast. No matter how tired and hungry from the morning's exertions, Tewodros was always satisfied when the spiritual exercise was done, and barely felt the need to turn to more than just coffee to fill this belly.

Injera, the bitter spongy bread made from grain unique to Ethiopia, was invariably the meal. Tewodros' favorite side dish was the split yellow peas, an ample store of which was kept year round, and a touch of which always stained some part of his woolen robes. He reached for an extra handful, feeling the lentils mush between his fingers. "Simple tastes for a simple man," Gebrewolde joshed him, smiling as the prince devoured his food. Tewodros never felt a monk to treat him any differently than his fellows, but when the prince had left the meal, Gebrewolde let his admiration show. "He is mature beyond his years."

"I know," Yohannes replied, "but perhaps it would be better if there were more young, brash, headstrong men than just Asfaw, to lead him to form bad habits."

"Ah, you think an outlet now for his rasher tendencies would calm his fire?" said Gebrewolde.

"Exactly – mistakes are best made before he takes on greater responsibilities."

"Yes, with all of us, he has no end of examples to follow in never making a mistake," Gebrewolde was back to half-joking, but the abbott considered Yohannes to be the wisest monk he had ever met and could not think of a single error in his ways.

"I have to go start the lessons," Yohannes rolled his eyes. "I wish we had a better view of the changes going on in the world outside. Tewodros learns so quickly, he needs some newer knowledge."

"Off you go," said Gebrewolde. "I don't think it's a bad thing for us to nurture his conservative streak – God knows the ways of us old religious change as fast as the mountains grow."

Tewodros sat waiting anxiously for his lessons to begin, as he would have Yohannes all to himself. His connection with his tutor felt stronger than with any of the other monks – only on the back of this man's experience could the prince's imagination take him to the places where his heart wished to go. Yohannes alone had traveled across the sea, tracing the route of the Queen of Sheba as something of a pilgrimage before he came to rest in the monastic life. There was something mystical about the man, thought Tewodros as Yohannes pushed aside the Bible and the two books of commentary that formed the entirety of the cave's library.

Yohannes delivered the lesson almost as a griot, entirely oral, from memory, interweaving his understanding of philosophy with his recounting of tales from experience and from other tellers. He spoke of how the Queen of Sheba convinced King Solomon to take her son by him, Menelik, into his court to prepare the young man for a future as the ruler of Ethiopia. "Tewodros," he stressed, "Menelik did not earn his place in history simply by his lineage alone. He demonstrated his merit to stand out from among Solomon's hundreds of descendants, and founded his own kingdom by righteous faith and good works."

"It is as you taught me – the role of the king is the first servant of his people," said Tewodros to his tutor's approbation, but the prince also truly believed what he was saying.

"Speaking of servanthood, it's time for your duties now. And don't forget we are debating later," Yohannes admonished. Tewodros stood up and realized it was his turn to muck the latrines. He gritted his teeth and walked over with his bucket and swab, almost heaving at the smell and trying not to curse when his foot slipped on the wet rock. His mood was thoroughly dampened until he looked over his shoulder and saw the wizened Gebrewolde resting his aching knees while the younger men took care of the chores, and it actually felt like some reward.

Today's debate was meant to increase the interest and impact of Tewodros' lessons, but it almost made him dislike the learning when he had to stride up and down in front of all the other monks to argue his side.

The older monks would always slap their palms together to emphasize a particularly strong point, but Tewodros was usually not sure enough of when he had a winning argument to know when to slap. He had prepared thoroughly for today's issue of tariffs on Somali livestock, but Yohannes was his opponent and would be a tough one.

Yohannes took the first turn and the job of justifying the existence of the tariffs. "The Ethiopian people treasure their cattle," he declared, head down and hands clasped behind as he slowly paced. "The nomads who live on blood and milk alone have learned to manage their herds in a way that preserves their wealth, preserves the grazing pastures, and preserves the way of life of thousands of years. If we reduce tariffs," he paused for dramatic effect, "the Somalis will send their kine to flood our markets, and the value placed on each head will diminish. What then?" Yohannes looked around with widened eyes at the audience. "A young man looks at his father who spent all those careful years nurturing a few beloved bovines, which can now be had in the market and slaughtered for a feast if only he can scheme up a way to earn the thalers to buy them. He stops paying attention to the cows he is supposed to be guarding and dreams up some winnings at gambling. How many fine cows he will have, right away! A fatted calf for any occasion! What a pretty wife he can attract with his noisome feasts, and why should he sit here with a grumbling belly and only milk to fill it when his foolish fantasy waits at the nearest town, where markets and gambling dens sprout from the earth with no hard toil?

Before you can blink, all the young men will think this way and what then?" Slap! went the hands of Yohannes. "Ethiopians! Our way of life is gone."

Murmurs passed through the watching monks. "Lower tariffs – beginning of the end." Nods of agreement. "Tough for young Tewodros to top that one, eh?"

Tewodros took a brief time to think, gulped, and took his place in front of the audience. "Why do we stick to this tradition of milk and blood?" his voice seemed plaintive and soft. "I think it is not such a wonderful way of living. I think we can seek something better for all Ethiopians," his volume grew, and he turned from looking to the side to looking at the monks. "Listen: the khat plant the Somalis love to chew grows rampant in the pastures of our nomads. If we accept Somali beef without duties, they will reduce their tax on our khat," he waved a finger in the air. "Our young men can better spend their time tending crops, and we know the Somalis with their wandering ways will always wish to move only with their herds. What we grow better than them, let us grow, and for sending them our khat we will have all the cows we could ever want. The Somalis will not stop raising livestock, and if we keep our high tariffs then where will the cattle go? To Yemen for the desert tribes to enjoy! And the Ethiopians? Shall we not eat meat!?" Slap!

"I like meat!" declared Gebrewolde, and forgoing the usual rapid exchange of questions and rebuttals back and forth, the debate devolved into some chuckling and a smiling announcement by Yohannes that he admitted defeat and was too tired to argue with his pupil today. In reality he did not want the prince to become too wedded to one side of a sensitive political issue too soon, and he could not tell how strongly Tewodros felt the words he had spoken with passion. "Next time I'll keep the easy side of the argument for myself," Yohannes said with a straight face, and was promptly teased for not only losing to a young idiot like Tewodros, but being a sore loser to boot.

As soon as the debate was over the routine part of the day was done, and it was time for Tewodros and the monks to relax. Gebrewolde produced the gebet'a board to pass the time, a game involving pebbles that represented cows, and a wooden surface with hollowed-out depressions that represented fields. Like in many villages, the monks had made their own intricate rules up and this particular game was played nowhere else. Tewodros threw the tiles when it was his turn and hoped for good luck, but knew he was no match for the others in haggling to increase his pastoral wealth.

"You're a terrible bargainer," Asfaw remarked when Tewodros handed over several pebbles to Gebrewolde, naïve to the strategy of the old hands.

Tewodros enjoyed the play nonetheless, though in many years he had only won three times and each time had crowed for a week about the accomplishment. This time he could see he had no chance, so he took another sip of tejj and felt all the more mellowed by the honey wine that never seemed to result in disgraceful drunkenness. While any of the monks would be able to find smoky wild honey to make the brew, Asfaw had a connection to a nearby apiary and brought back the more consistent product of kept bees to ferment in gourds. He was perhaps the most indispensable inhabitant of the cave, as far as the prince was concerned. Supper was informal after the game, and Tewodros always enjoyed the leftovers from lunch since the mess of chopped up injera had had more time to soak up the sauces of the day.

When the sky seemed painted in early evening they retired, and Tewodros asked Yohannes in the fading light if he might tell a story of his travels. The prince settled in with sparkling eyes to listen, as he learned the most from knowing other lands and ways that put his Ethiopian experience into perspective. It was his favorite time of the day when he could escape from life into his tutor's tale, and it was his favorite part of the religious brothers' personalities that they all had a sense of humor. A monk joked, "I hope this one is better than the tall one you told about the talking mule in the Hijaz," while another shot back with a reminder of the talking donkey in the Bible as proof of the verity of Yohannes' tale. "Or how about the one about the sheikh who kept a tame leopard on a chain, that ate dates from Yohannes' hand? As if you could tame a big cat like that!"

Yohannes cut off the playful bickering, promising to tell them of an event that was both fascinating and, he assured them, entirely true. "It was my first time through the Yemen and I was full of wonder as I laid eyes on a great city in the distance," began the erstwhile traveler. "There were buildings sprouting from the very earth, straight-sided and tall as the hills behind them. As I came closer I could count rows of windows, one row on top of the other, stretching up a full six or even eight high and seeming to scrape the sky. It was one of the Hadhramaut's famed cities of mud. Imagine, they took dirt and water and strengthened it with straw to create these monstrosities that make our thatched tukuls look like mere mushrooms on the forest floor."

Tewodros could see tukuls far down the valley when he looked out, and yes, they did look like mushrooms.

"Perhaps to impress me further my hosts gave me a room on the seventh level, and I could not decline their hospitality – one never declines hospitality from the Arabs." Tewodros nodded, as this tidbit was already filed away on a checklist in his brain. "I only hope my trepidation did not show. I have seen how sturdy are the stone stelae and castles we have in our country, but I had little faith that something that tall and made of mud could stand secure." Tewodros had no memories of seeing the palace in which he was born, and could scarce think of how these tenements must have appeared as he kept his gaze fixed on the storyteller.

"I approached the square cut window in my room where the sunlight beckoned and was dizzied by the view! The people moving in the street below were so small, like ants going about their business. In the morning I could not wait to get back to solid ground. I was just on my way to see the emir of another region when I felt a drop hit my head – splash!"

Gebrewolde interrupted the story. "How can it rain in the desert?"

"Even in those arid climes, it rained from time to time and when it did, the most beautiful carpet of blazing red flowers and soft green grass would bloom across the hillsides, only to disappear again two weeks later." It was dark now and the monks pictured what Yohannes was painting. He continued, "but rain of this kind was something the city's inhabitants had never seen. Compared to the drizzle they knew, these fat drops were something new and alarming."

"They must have done something sinful – these drops can only have come from the hand of God," Gebrewolde interrupted again. The other monks shushed him, "let Yohannes finish the story."

"Not wanting to get wet, I followed the other people in the streets who began rushing into the buildings for shelter from the freak storm, almost making up their own human deluge. Outside the window the color of the buildings was turning from dunnish yellow to dark and angry brown, in jagged patterns where the rain hit directly and where it flowed down the sides. Some were upstairs to watch the lightning bolts on the plain from the higher vantage points, but I stayed on the ground floor, breathless with the other inhabitants. Rivulets began to run in the streets and finally I looked up and noticed that the angle of the ceiling had changed.

"I saw the east wall was sagging, bending almost, with an ominous protuberance forming in its middle. I realized at the same time as the whole room of people that the mud was melting. The shouts began and everyone pushed for the doors, and those on the higher levels began their own stampede down. A few even jumped from the windows, but their landing was on soft mud.

"We ran for the stony hill behind the city, our feet splashing in the flood and heedless of the soaking we were enduring. From up there we saw chunks falling from the ruined city as it sagged into a river of sludge on the plain, moving with interminable slowness but still carrying away animals that were too dumb to join us on higher ground. Praise God, I believe every person made it out alive." Tewodros exhaled with relief, so engrossed he was; and wondered how Asfaw next to him had managed to nod off. Yohannes did sometimes have a ponderous way of speaking.

"We slept a whole sodden night on that hill after the rain had stopped, a mass of refugees, and in the morning the mud was already beginning to dry into a new, corrugated plain. I was amazed to see the residents already planning their neighborhoods anew and forming work groups to produce new mud bricks. No self-pity, no wallowing, just back to work and rebuilding their lives." Yohannes would usually find some way to end his story with a moral. This had been a good one, so the monks didn't mind; though each did wonder if this were one of Yohannes' taller tales.

Gradually each man found his rough sleeping-place, and Tewodros' long day melted away into the cave floor, eyes and chin drooping and his waking energy dying with the embers of the fire. He closed his eyes, and when he opened them again the king's messenger was on his way.

*Chapter Two*

Mark Glendon's career would live or die with the good will of Assistant Secretary George Matthews, to whom he reported. Glendon was confident he could convince Matthews of his plans for the Ethiopian coronation, but he would have to rely on his superior's connections to secure the diplomats needed for the mission.

Just the evening before, Matthews had been a guest at the Trafford family residence, a house near Regent's Park with a carved façade and a mews behind. Matthews and the Trafford patriarch were old Harrovians and had just finished catching up on whom from school they had seen recently, while the other guests ebbed and flowed in noise and person all around them. "Come, George, let's have a pipe in the withdrawing room before my wife causes me to entertain one of our drearier neighbors."

"Tired of telling stories about the textile business, eh John?" said Matthews in his typically wooden tone, that went with his tree-like appearance as solid, rough and imperturbable.

"I used all my good anecdotes already once today," the host replied, "and I don't feel like telling them again to someone new. We have too many parties," he shook his head and realized he had begun talking to himself. He turned back to Matthews. "That chap there," he nodded, "the Greek, he owns the shipping house of Schilizzi," and seeing that Matthews was not suitably impressed, went on. "A very respectable merchant family from the island of Chios. They've got a tramp steamer I can charter to go from Bari to Alexandria. Have to get several bolts of fabric to Egypt, you see, and I can't get my cargo on any of the regular ships on such short notice; they're full up."

"We haven't much pull in Egypt at the moment," remarked Matthews.

"Quite right, you've got plenty else to worry about at the foreign office," said Trafford. "I say, do you need a good hand over there by any chance? Paul's not taken much to the family business, I'm afraid."

Matthews looked around and did not see Paul, that estimable scion of the Trafford family at the party; he must be out at the clubs as usual. "Yes, John, there's always something coming up – is he willing to travel?" Trafford had given Matthews' son a post in his firm to get the boy started, and Matthews owed him one.

Paul Trafford only dimly remembered somewhat drunkenly telling his father he wanted to try his hand at international diplomacy. When he was referred to a Mr. Mark Glendon from the Foreign Secretary's office, the chap in charge of African affairs, he thought regardless that it sounded like quite a lark and brought along his two best friends, James Johnson and Philip Boyle. The three had bonded over their collective lack of interest in the daily London life of spoiled sons who did not have to work, and had no inclination to. They found they made quite good sixth, seventh and eighth batsmen at their cricket club, pairing well as they piled up runs, and even better as they appraised each others' fashion choices on a trip to Savile Row.

Glendon had instantly perceived from watery blue eyes that a combination of connections to the right society, and that same society needing respite from their boorish presence in the gentlemen's clubs had resulted in their selection as emissaries to Abyssinia, to represent the British crown, and he inwardly sighed in dismay, with a sting of jealousy besides. The disappointment on his face did not register with the three British envoys-to-be, who were tickled to a man at being foisted upon this unsuspecting civil servant. "In the Horn of Africa," Glendon had explained, "where the Blue Nile rises."

"Source of the Nile…jolly good bit of adventure, that!" remarked Boyle, to Johnson's nods and grin.

"And this treaty," Trafford had inquired, "how are we to know what you would like it to say when we make dealings with this Emperor fellow?"

"There will be no dealings!" responded Glendon snappishly, and then smoothed his coat as if to brush away the peevish feelings that threatened to get the better of him. He had determined with Matthews, that given the training and expertise of the envoys that would be sent, they could only be trusted to deliver a predetermined document to be signed as is. "If they do not accept our terms, you will do your best to convince them of the merits of a British partnership. While this is very important to our foreign interest, it is only worth having if we can achieve an exclusive treaty that blocks the continental powers from establishing a similar relationship with Ethiopia," Glendon explained, moving his hands aggressively as if that would help.

"I say if we bring enough good gin we'll have a round or two of drinks with this Emperor fellow and convince him of anything!" declared Johnson while Trafford laughed, "ha, ha."

Thus it came to pass that when the Evangeline made its lazy way across the eastern Mediterranean towards Alexandria, three Englishmen were also on board. It just so happened that the senior Trafford had chartered the ship at the exact time that his son needed passage to the same destination, which Glendon had taken as a fortuitous coincidence, but one that marked his dubious emissaries as meant to be.

Now on the ship Johnson took yet another draught of gin with tonic as the three envoys played cards with Pierre something-or-other (Trafford had no idea how to spell or pronounce his last name). They had met in Paris, introduced by a French acquaintance that knew of his own countryman also going to Ethiopia for the coronation.

"Are we sure we should have this bloke following us around?" Boyle had asked his colleagues. "What if he's just come to spy on us and find out about the treaty?"

"We shan't mention it in front of him," Trafford had replied in hushed tones, feeling that he was engaged in a grand game of subterfuge against the cunning trickery of French espionage.

"In fact," joined Johnson, "perhaps it is better to have him close and we can ascertain the French plans for attending the coronation." In the end, it was better that they had a fourth to play bridge, as there were many hours to while away on the Mediterranean passage and no such game that three could enjoy so well.

"Come on Pierre, it's your go," said Trafford for the umpteenth time on the voyage.

## Chapter Three

"Let the ropes down!" cried Gebrewolde, feeling the energy of the bustling monks around him as they anticipated a visitor of interest. The messenger Ghannatu, a somewhat portly man with a jolly face, peered up at the dizzying rock face above him, extending up to the dark eye of the cave's mouth and again just as far above it to the top of the cliff, and wished he could close his eyes; wished he had eaten less for breakfast with each step up the woven ladder. His hardened feet felt nothing of the rough rope but the exertion was beyond his custom, and he had to suppress the urge to puff and blow in front of the monks he greeted at the top.

He paused, as if for gravity, before declaring "the negusa negast has sent me," all the while inching away from the cave's edge he could feel behind him. "I must speak with Tewodros."

"My friend, there is time, first sit and enjoy some coffee after your long ride," replied Gebrewolde. "I am Gebrewolde, welcome." Others chimed in with exhortations to "sit, sit," and "coffee? water?" while all Ghannatu really wanted was tejj and a nap. Though he had endured a lonely ride on his way here, it still did not whet his appetite for socializing.

"I am Ghannatu. Some coffee, please, thank you, wonderful, thank you." He was hustled to a cushion, smiling weakly and nodding all around. He sat in the main chamber of the cave, an almost circular room with a high ceiling that had been carved in some places to give the impression of a dome, and with some simple paintwork to suggest pillars. This was the room that received the light from the mouth of the cave, and was where the monks held their meals, their masses, their debates and any other social gathering. Towards the back of the central chamber was a fireplace, and beyond it the kitchen area with more fires and the water source behind.

Branching off from that first fireplace, to the left as one approached the kitchen, was another large chamber where the monks slept. Just visible from the main chamber were some headrests and personal effects in neat rows marking each man's place. Opposite the sleeping chamber another, narrower passage led to a dead end, but with some alcoves along it where monks might meditate in more solitude. Before entering the cave, Ghannatu had seen a small ledge leading to another hole in the cliff; he would later find this was a second cave that held the latrines and a rather bottomless pit for disposing of waste. Cramped quarters all round, thought Ghannatu as he sat by the abbott and adjusted the crossing of his legs.

Gebrewolde finally called out, "Tewodros, come here, sit by me. This is Tewodros. How was your ride?" he asked Ghannatu, ever the host even though he knew the prince was ready to explode for wanting to know what news the messenger brought. Unfailingly polite, Tewodros waited until coffee was drawn, had cooled and sips were taken, before choosing an opportune pause in the small talk to interject his own question. "My father – how is he?"

Ghannatu had known the king, Kassa, since they were boys together in the mountains, and had not been forgotten when positions were given out in Kassa's administration. In the past three months he had only seen the king once, but the prince's eager face needed an answer. "Bless the king, he looks well; as well as I have seen him since you were born."

"What is he like?" Tewodros, eyes aglow, had never had the opportunity to speak to anyone who knew his father well.

Ghannatu was not sure how to take the question. "The king is a great man." He looked around while the monks looked primarily at the floor. He was a simple messenger, not a diplomat. "He has sent a message for you, Tewodros. The king of kings has bestowed peace and prosperity on his empire, and feels his magnanimous service to be complete. He wishes his son to learn the workings of government and will act during that time as regent, but will prepare for the coronation of Tewodros immediately. He wishes Tewodros to meet him at the springs of Sodere, on the first of Maskaram, the first month." He recited the words perfectly.

Tewodros had often thought of becoming king, but now it was real and something in him quailed. Seeing shock and a curious disappointment written on his student's bright face, Yohannes swiftly broke the meeting up. "Let's discuss this when dinner is ready. Our guest has ridden far and should rest, and we should consider this weighty matter before words are spoken on it." Before Ghannatu was able to move away from the breaking circle, Yohannes caught his ear. "My friend, the poor boy has not seen his father these many years. Please, if you can, give him something to satisfy his need to know the man, lest he meet the king as a total stranger. Now, rest and be refreshed." Yohannes guided Ghannatu to a quiet alcove.

The monks moved to their stations for preparing the meal, and Tewodros fell into step to draw water for boiling. His motions were robotic as he reached for a gourd, unwilling to free his mind to think and relying on his routine to keep his world from imploding. Halfway to the spring, he suddenly felt Gebrewolde's hand on his arm. "It is unfitting," the old monk said, some of the usual kindliness in his eyes replaced by an uncertainty as to how he should treat the king-in-waiting.

Yohannes found his young charge pacing to and fro, his earlier look of shock becoming chagrin. Tewodros stopped when he met Yohannes' steady eyes. Words did not come as he obediently followed Yohannes to the empty sitting area. "Gebrewolde will not let me help with the meal," was the first thing he blurted.

"The king is the loneliest man in the empire," replied Yohannes. "You have not felt this until now, but you are a man set apart. In a way it is akin to holiness, but thrust upon you so that you must rise to deserve it."

"I didn't ask for this!" cried Tewodros. "Why must I be king so soon?"

37

"I know you feel a great unfairness, Tewodros. I did not expect this to come at your tender age either, and I have not even begun to prepare you for it."

"What do I do? What if I cannot do it?"

"Tewodros, you always knew this day would arrive, just not when. You always knew in your heart that you would be king. And what desires of yours are they that reach God's ears? If I were to guess, they would be to leave this cave and take on the whole world. They would be to meet your father and know the man. Your wishes have come true, though the price is that you take your crown as a man so young."

"Yohannes, if I must leave this place, you must come with me. If I am to be king I can decree such things, is it not?"

Yohannes chuckled. "Try never to decree what another man's path must be, even though yours has been decreed for you. Always give him the choice, and inspire him as far as you can in the right direction. As for me, I would willingly follow you wherever you go. Let us take some rest before dinner; there will be more time from now to talk."

Yohannes moved off to check on Ghannatu, anxious to maintain the highest hospitality. The messenger was trying to work some of the knots of travel out of his old legs, and looked up at Yohannes hopefully, "perhaps, if it is not too much trouble, I might have a bit of tejj to keep me until supper?"

Yohannes smiled, "of course," and called for Asfaw who was proud to produce his best gourd, which he thought particularly mellow. Ghannatu tried to hide his eagerness as the handsome young man poured a draught. Asfaw turned his square face to Yohannes, the light tan skin framed by close-shorn hair. "Yohannes, with the tejj we will no doubt consume this evening I will be overdue for a trip to the market for more honey to make the next batch," he said. "There is plenty of time this afternoon to take a horse and go; might I make the trip?"

"Go on, we have enough hands to prepare the food here," replied Yohannes, and Asfaw's excitement at rushing off on his errand nearly matched Ghannatu's at bringing the liquor to his lips.

## Chapter Four

Napier did not plan to shoot at anything until the king of beasts itself, the mighty bagh, came leaping from the brushy growth. He himself sat safe atop a swaying elephant, the platform on its broad back teetering when the pachyderm shifted its trunk-like feet. He wore an anachronistic hat that was something the rajahs wore in their days of hunting tiger, a white turban-like contraption with a red glass bead and a feather sticking up to mark him as the big man, who was to be given first shot at whatever burst into the field of view.

Hardly thrilling, thought Napier, as he waited for the trophy chance to be served to him on a silver platter, while all he need do was chase away flies. The waiting hunters had listened to the rise and fall of the drums and shouts of the beaters on the ground, imagining they were growing closer and feeling the tension rise in their throats, and then dismissing it as a trick of the ears. Now, though, Napier detected that the regular sounds were definitely in disarray, and his pupils involuntarily widened. He took in a sharp breath, and was careful to breathe out slowly, without sound.

Five elephants had been lined up beyond the woody knoll, two on either side of Napier's stomping, living chariot. Sabzi-sardar, the leader of the hunt, sat beside Napier and screamed into action. Before Napier knew what was going on, all five elephants barreled over the knoll and tangled with Jeevan's troop of beaters. More screaming, Sabzi understanding, instructions carried down the line and the elephants were off again while men scrambled to reestablish order and a new direction.

Sabzi turned to Napier and grinned, seeming oblivious to the rocking gait of the elephant that moved surprisingly quickly. "We have seen the tiger," he yelled, no longer faced with the prospect of the whole morning being a wild-goose chase.

Napier's blood was now beginning to rise, the action much preferable to the waiting. He had originally been sure he wouldn't fancy being on the ground with a ten-foot predator, but perhaps chasing it down on a horse – he could picture himself as Saint Michael slaying the beast, and had asked the sardar if he could conduct the hunt from such a mount. Trying not to insult his bravery, Sabzi had told him he would never find the tiger with a horse in this terrain, and his mount would spook if it smelled the cat. Napier was convinced of Sabzi's wisdom by the power of his current steed, as it bulldozed through underbrush and gave him an unparalleled view over the heads of beaters below. He found himself clutching his rifle more tightly as his mahout whooped with excitement.

Now the line of beaters to his right surged forward with renewed energy, and the pincer had closed from the left. Either they had been quick enough and had the tiger in their tightening arc, collapsing on the elephants who slowed as their mahouts reined them in with hooks and poles, or the redeployment of the left side had been too late. Sabzi was wild-eyed as the shouts intended to keep the tiger moving increased in frenzy. A piercing call penetrated his roving senses. The tiger was treed!

Without translating for Napier the elephants hustled at Sabzi's direction to the tree, while men on the ground backed off from its trunk. Napier needed no words, as the pointing and stares led his eyes to the strong branch where the tiger crouched. He caught a glimpse of its powerful frame before it leaped to another perch, and his view was blocked as it elongated its body towards the ground. Napier's heart was gripped as in a vise; could the beast jump on the back of his elephant from a tree? The beater's shouts turned to screams with an edge of panic as the tiger was among them, circling on the ground with no way out from the net of bristling clubs.

Somehow Sabzi choreographed an opening for Napier's elephant as the tiger searched in vain for a point of attack, conscious of even greater beasts bearing down with trumpeted warning. As it came into view again for Napier, its eyes locked with the man who would kill it, and it coiled itself as if to spring mightily to the height where the rifle was swinging into position.

Bang! The shot rang out, nicking the tiger on its right shoulder as it pounced for the broadside elephant. Napier cursed as he knew he had pulled too soon, letting his nerves get the better of him. The bullet's force had deflected the tiger into the dirt, but now chaos reigned as men fell back from the wounded animal and Sabzi bellowed that none should take the prize from another elephant.

Sabzi saw Napier fumbling with the effort of reloading and called, "Napier-sahib!" before tossing his own rifle to the white hunter. With the tiger backing and growling Napier was cold killer this time, dispatching it with deadly accuracy, another bang and a puff of smoke.

A curious silence followed the second shot, as there was no need for hullabaloo once the cat had perished. The surrounding men let their clubs hang by their sides and formed a regular semicircle, the elephants still breathing hard enough to hear, but nobody speaking. Napier felt his insides relax, his focus still on the prey that looked so much smaller and tamer lying in the dirt. His elephant shuffled and he asked to be let down to the ground; the next mahout over tapping to signal instructions, and he hitched a ride smoothly down on his neighbor's trunk. The men all were smiling and some clapping broke out, with isolated cheers, in turn raising the corners of Napier's mouth into a grin. "Ha," he exclaimed, "ha!"

Jeevan stepped forward to prod the prone tiger with his club just to make sure it was not playing dead, and Napier knelt next to its head to view the fearsome teeth up close. Sabzi spoke down from his elephant, "a pukka shot, Napier-sahib, you hit him smack in the heart with the second bullet." The ripples of conversation now started in the circle of men as they shared their own comments on the climactic moments, holding an arm here, slapping a shoulder there in happy relief at the day's success. "Will you take the meat? Some say it gives uncommon strength."

Napier twisted his upper lip at the thought of bush meat. "No, no, just the pelt. I don't want it stuffed, I want a rug." He walked around to see the damage the first bullet had done to the fur. It was too bad; he might have to make do with a limbless rug, but the head was in perfect, glassy-eyed shape. Sabzi gave some orders and the sharpest machete was brought out to flay the animal in the field. The elephants did not like taking a dead animal on their backs and though the men had long poles to sling it from, they were too tired to carry the tiger whole. Even the skin itself weighed a good amount, draped over the same poles as it was best to keep it spread out until it was fully dried. By the time Jeevan was unlucky enough to be given one end of a pole, the elephants were on their way back to the hunting lodge to drop off their passengers before a welcome bath in the river, where the mahouts would play in the water and give them a good scrubbing.

## Chapter Five

At the market on his patterned shawl spread out to show his wares, with his usual scowl sat the middleman for some local craftsmen. He also happened to be the purveyor of the tastiest honey. He had moved to this village a few miles from the prince's cave quite some time ago, and established a small business selling sundries. One year in, the monk Asfaw had become his regular customer, and he had felt sure that it was only a matter of time before he could glean in casual conversation some information about the prince in the mountain fortress nearby. Now it was a year later, and his patience had been reaching a breaking point, as all he had of use was confirmation of the cave's location and that the prince never left it. He could not risk direct questions and Asfaw had never spoken of the security measures or the sleeping arrangements.

Last week, he had expected Asfaw at the market at the usual time, in the morning before the crowds arrived. He had thought, now would be my chance to ask him if he sleeps on the floor, and offer to sell him a headrest I have carved. "It's good enough for a prince!" he would say, and they would have a talk about how the prince sleeps. He would offer him beer first to loosen the monk's tongue.

But Asfaw had not shown up for several days. He turned to the girl who sold onions next to him, and noticed she wasn't there either. An odd afternoon.

He felt nature's call and asked the coffee seller to his other side to watch his wares while he went to the field behind the market. There was a good place behind the trees yonder, and old man Mogus who owned the land never went back there. He heard a rustle as he stepped behind the screen of branches and his eye caught the corner of a monk's robe. A shout rose in his throat, but caught there before escaping, as a better idea came to him. "Shh!" he whispered. "Come out of there and I won't let on."

He tugged the robe and saw the girl behind Asfaw as he emerged from the brush, more terrified than sheepish. A broad grin spread across the merchant's face. Now he had some leverage. "Come with me, Asfaw. I have some special honey back at home that will make a wicked tejj – I want to show it to you," he said, not letting go of the monk's robe. To the oblivious girl, "you, stupid, get back to your onions or I'll tell your father! And watch my wares until I come back. I can't trust that coffee seller to pay attention."

The monk still hadn't spoken when they entered his dwelling. "Sit down and listen very carefully," said the merchant, shifting uncomfortably as he had still not yet had a chance to relieve himself. "I know you monks, you've taken a vow of celibacy, haven't you?"

Asfaw nodded, and gritted his teeth, then exploded to break his silence. "If the others find out I'll be thrown out of the order!" he looked at the floor, moaning, "It is a just punishment." Everyone is a sinner, thought the merchant, but I need this monk to be a real Judas.

Asfaw's face turned to the ceiling and he raised his hands, clutching his forehead, "what was I thinking!"

"What if they never find out?" the merchant asked gently. "That girl wants to keep it a secret as much as you do, and that leaves only me who knows."

"You think I will hide from confession?" Asfaw angrily stood up.

"Nobody needs to find out – I stopped you before anything happened, right?" By the monk's look the merchant knew this wasn't the first time something had happened, and knew that he had his guilty Judas. "Ah, I see," he smiled softly. "But your confession is private, and there is a difference between leaving quietly and leaving with public shame." The merchant's voice took a hard tone. "What you do to seek forgiveness is up to you, but it is up to me whether the whole world looks with disgust at you."

Asfaw sat back down. "What are you trying to say?"

Make it easy for him, thought the merchant. A wide and smooth road. "If you can keep my secret, I can keep yours. Deal?"

Asfaw made the deal, feeling dirty and exposed as he overpaid for some honey to bring back to the cave, and slunk out to where he had tied his horse. Asfaw did not want to know what foul cogitations were going on in the merchant's mind now that he knew where each monk slept, and how the cave's daily rituals were kept. He could not be on his way soon enough.

The merchant watched him go, and resolved that on the first foggy night that would cover his climb, he would have to make his attempt on the cave. Asfaw's guilt might soon overcome the monk and if he told his brothers of the breach of confidence, all would be lost. The merchant cracked his fingers and felt his scowl dissipate for the first time in months. His mission had been more than two years in the undertaking, but his family stood to benefit for fifty years from his promised payment.

The merchant had spent his days developing the skill he would need to get into that cave. Perhaps he could even teach his sons when he returned home; maybe use his reward to start a school for this new sport. At first he struggled to grip the boulders he practiced on, coming away with scratches and bruises after traversing no more than three feet off the ground. As his confidence grew, he found that he could bring his foot to match a handhold and move up with ease, or jam his whole fist into a crack and twist it for purchase where the holds were lacking. It was all about using the legs to save strength in his arms.

Now he was the only man in the whole village who could easily reach the wild beehives high up on the cliffs; though Asfaw still preferred the stuff from the kept bees. The villagers thought he was crazy, but he still slung a rope for his work – there was a difference between taking risks and being stupid. That monk Asfaw, now he was young and stupid.

Asfaw alternated between spurring the horse on to distract him from what lay behind, and slowing it to a crawl in fear of what lay ahead. They will surely see my guilt and shame written on my face, he thought;

but then again, had he not felt just as guilty after the first time with the girl, and the second? Nobody seemed to suspect anything then, so why would they now?

There was the cave, down came the rope ladder, and up went Asfaw to join the monks for supper. The air was moist and cool as he climbed, and he felt a fog would come on with the evening.

## Chapter Six

Tewodros felt as if the eyes of every monk were on him as he accepted the food he had not contributed to preparing. His stomach turned as he poked at the injera, but he was able to force down a bite or two as the conversation slowly came to life. Yohannes was sitting next to Ghannatu gave him a nudge.

"Tewodros," began the messenger, "did I tell you that I knew the king in the village when we were just boys?"

Food forgotten, Tewodros perked up. "Tell me, please."

"We are the same age – his tukul was four or five down the path from mine. My first memory of him was going to the well to draw water, side by side. The young ones always fetch water in the morning," and Tewodros felt glad that he also fetched water in the cave, just like his father.

"Some children live miles from the well, but your father and I could be there and back again before the day was too warm. In fact, we never walked, we always raced. Your father was so competitive, but his spirit would light a fire in those around him as well."

"Who won the race?" asked Tewodros, smiling, with teeth.

"Kassa was faster than everyone," chuckled Ghannatu, "with his legs and with his mind. It served him well when he rose through the ranks of Ras Hailu's army."

"Did you serve with him in the wars of the princes?" Tewodros knew the history well, but monks were not warriors and none could speak of the great battles first hand.

"I am not a fighter," Ghannatu responded. "But after Ras Hailu was killed and your father took command of his army, he happened to pass back through our village where I still lived. He remembered everyone from his youth and invited us to sup in his tent."

"Yes, to dine on the meat and bread your farmers had 'contributed' to his army," came caustically from a monk whose home had seen too many soldiers billeted.

"We need soldiers just as we need farmers, teachers and monks," Gebrewolde intervened.

Ghannatu continued. "I remember he said to me, 'Ghannatu, what do you like of village life?' and I said my life was a blessed one. 'Ghannatu,' he said, 'I have need of a trustworthy man. I have known you since your curly head was only so far off the ground,' and he held up his hand, 'and I think I can trust nobody more than you.' I always wanted to prove him right from that day," Ghannatu wagged a finger, "and I became his messenger."

"I cannot wait to meet him!" burst out from Tewodros, who instantly felt embarrassed until Yohannes smoothly said, "yes, it is high time that you meet. Ghannatu, tell us how Ras Kassa became king."

Ghannatu seemed to look inward, and smiled to remember that time long ago when he and Kassa felt invincible. "It was the message I carried that ended the wars, and made your father king," he said, with no braggadocio but in a way that showed his pride. "Ras Kassa always told me the messenger was the most important man in the army, as he relied on me to coordinate the military movements and to treat with his foes."

"He certainly knew how to inspire you," Yohannes observed.

"Tell me how you ended the wars," Tewodros thirsted to hear more.

"It all had to do with Ras Mulugeta, who still serves your father today. At that time, he was the most powerful of those wrestling for greater land and tribute. Your father knew that he could win a fight against any of the princes, except Mulugeta. He also knew that if he fought the other princes, they would weaken him and leave him exposed. Mulugeta was waiting in the north, ready to sweep down from Tigray when the dust settled among the southern warlords, who were too egotistical to band together against him."

Tewodros always had a healthy respect for Mulugeta when he heard the history. "Didn't Ras Mulugeta control access to the flow of guns into the Horn, and had two muskets for every one in the south?"

"Yes!" replied Ghannatu. "So what did we do? We went north to fight him! Haha!

"You see, your father was so shrewd," Ghannatu pointed to his temple, "he knew that Mulugeta feared the same thing as Kassa – to bleed each other until the other Rases flew in like vultures to pick apart their weakened armies. Mulugeta would never risk throwing all his forces at Kassa, and your father knew a bargain could be struck. So all we had to do was convince Mulugeta that we were coming for him with every man, musket, spear and stick we could muster, to defeat him and win the allegiance of the south by showing our strength. A brilliant strategy."

"But what if he decided to fight back?" asked Tewodros, worried for his father in this risky endeavor, though he already knew the ending.

Ghannatu paused. "God only knows what would have happened. Outside the trusted circle of advisors, the soldiers of course were not told of the bluff, so I suppose battle would have been joined we would likely have been defeated. But that is your father's gift, to convince men to believe in themselves and in him, so we all thought the plan would work," Ghannatu grinned, as Tewodros stayed rapt.

"I tell you, I still felt queasy when our troops drew up in the field in sight of Mulugeta's army. They were waiting for us on the way north, twenty thousand men with guns and spears. 'At least he stands up to fight like a man,' your father said."

The monks had all gradually, perceptibly leaned closer as Ghannatu continued. "Then, to my horror, your father turned to me and said, 'Ghannatu, you are my messenger, is it not?' I slowly nodded, knowing what was coming next. 'It falls to you, then, to take the message to Ras Mulugeta. All I need is a meeting and I will do the rest. Do not fail, my friend – we are all depending on you.'"

Tewodros gulped. "I rode out alone in front of the ranks, with the messenger's scarlet flag. Even my horse was jumpy under me, and it was agonizing to close the gap with Mulugeta so slowly. Any moment, I expected a stray arrow to pierce me, but I hope they mistook my frozen terror for calm and bravery!"

"I told Mulugeta's herald that Ras Kassa desired a meeting. I told him Ras Kassa was ready to fight, but he considered the northerners his brothers and wished to avoid bloodshed if a parley could be struck. I stuck to the words I was given to say, trusting they would work. I stood facing down that army for an entire hour while the herald delivered the message and Mulugeta considered his response."

"Why didn't you go back to our side to wait?" came another question from Tewodros.

"We had heard that Mulugeta was a gentleman, but I still felt too afraid to turn my back on all those soldiers. Now that I think about it, if he had decided to fight us he might have shot me dead right there! but at last the herald came, and I galloped back to Kassa. The Rases went inside a small tent, alone. Nobody knows how he pulled the bloody thing off but next thing that happened was Mulugeta and his many muskets were in the service of your father."

"When I meet him I will ask what he said to Mulugeta – perhaps he will tell me," said Tewodros.

"Perhaps, and you can tell the rest of us!" said Ghannatu. "Well, I suppose that's the end of the story. As you know, the southern warlords all capitulated to the combined might of Kassa and Mulugeta, and the golden peace began."

"My father must have told Mulugeta that the southerners would never accept a Tigrayan as their ruler," said Tewodros. "Mulugeta had to choose among a powerful role in a unified Ethiopia, remaining isolated in his stronghold in the north, or being weakened by perpetual war if he fought the south on his own."

"The young prince is very astute," remarked Ghannatu. "Your father kept his promise to Mulugeta and made him the Qenazmatch, the commander of the right; your father's right hand. And Mulugeta is also a man of his word, as he has served faithfully in that position ever since."

A silence fell on the group, and Tewodros finally broke it. "Do you think old Mulugeta is still waiting for his chance to rule the empire?"

Gebrewolde responded. "You know, Tewodros, I believe your father's plan in passing the empire to your care is to do so while he still has his health and strength. That way he can watch over you until you figure out how to handle those scheming generals for yourself."

Ghannatu stepped in. "Ras Kassa has been playing those politics for a long time now. He knows that Mulugeta is one of those he must keep close to the throne. But I am sure he is really looking forward to taking some rest at the hot springs – and to meeting you, Tewodros." He looked around at the monks. "Do you think we can be ready to leave in the morning? What reason is there for Tewodros to stay here longer?" Their response was to look at the prince, for him to make the decision.

Tewodros returned their gazes all the way around the circle of monks. He regarded his friends, and the only community he had ever known, with a sadness he had not felt to this point in his life; a sadness that would never be lessened with an extra day, or even a year of waiting to leave the cave. "I will be ready in the morning, Ghannatu," he said. In the next moment the sadness was overcome by the current of excitement. He had listened to stories his whole life, but now he would live his own stories.

He turned to his neighbor as the group began to break up for the evening. "Asfaw, when your turn comes for sentry duty on the second watch, check my place to see if I am sleeping. I feel I will be restless tonight, and if I am awake I will take your turn and you can sleep the extra hours."

## Chapter Seven

The rain lightened and then ceased, clearing the London smog so the mail clerk for the Foreign Office could look out on the sunset city through the grimy windows of Whitehall. Back into the corridors for the last run of the day, and then a pint at the Grey Heron would be the welcome reward. "Let's see," the clerk mumbled, trying to decipher the red scrawl that had shunted this rough-looking letter off from the palace to the attention of, "looks like a G, maybe an S...Slendon, that doesn't make sense. Glendon, that's it. Glendon," he looked up, and found the pigeonhole for the Africa desk.

An hour later the pigeonhole was empty as Glendon settled in for more work amidst the exodus of clock-punching functionaries. He had treated himself to a pig's trotter along with his boiled potatoes for tea, consumed in slow, irregular mouthfuls as he turned to his correspondence. Now here was something interesting. Glendon pushed his other papers to the side to create space for the letter from the king of kings, opening it slowly, yet earnestly. He imagined he could still smell a faint whiff of Ethiopia as the letter unfolded.

He briefly wondered why there had been no message from the envoys since the report of their arrival in Magdala, and why he was the first to read a document addressed to Her Majesty Queen Victoria, but the letter's contents quickly focused his mind. The revelation that his exclusive treaty had been rejected came like a punch to the gut, but soon the rationalizations flooded into his mind that it only spoke of the sophistication of the Ethiopians beyond what he had expected, and made a treaty with them all the more worth having as they might truly understand its ramifications. He wished he could have more trust in the men on the ground, and began feverishly compiling a list of the authorizations and approvals he would need to commence the negotiation process. Surely a formal trade relationship would be beneficial, even if it fell short of his grand schemes for Ethiopia. There were other ways to gain influence. By the time Glendon left that evening, there were several pigeonholes augmented with his meeting requests – even the Foreign Secretary's.

The next morning Glendon bustled in as usual, only to sit at his desk nervously tapping his new fountain pen, and getting up every fifteen minutes to check his pigeonhole. Nobody had accepted his meeting by midday. Three days later, after he had sent a reminder with a note reminding his colleagues of the British envoys languishing in Ethiopia while a response to their regent was formulated, the Assistant Secretary responded with a curt memorandum that the issue should be added to the agenda for their monthly meeting the following Wednesday.

By the following Wednesday, Glendon had lost nearly half a stone in frustration and arrived irascible and early at the meeting with Matthews. He was then made to wait until five minutes past the appointed time. He sat outside Matthews' office wiggling his foot and being ignored by Matthews' assistant, whose severe countenance with its permanent furrows still could not hide the fact that she had once been very pretty. At last, he passed the heavy oak doors with briefing papers in hand, but only his pet project on his mind.

Matthews looked haggard – China was also in his portfolio and ever since the opium wars, the lobbying from private merchants for government intervention in every perceived aggrievance to their treaty rights was ceaseless. "Glendon, have a seat. Give me the rundown then."

Glendon was now patient to go through the usual briefing on the colonies: the governor in Freetown importuning for more loans; the minor disturbance on the fringes of the Cape Colony; followed by personnel reports, before raising the burning question. "We have this matter of a request for a treaty with Ethiopia."

Matthews cut in. "There isn't any significant interest in that part of the Horn. If we're the first to sign a nonexclusive treaty won't that just cause the French and Germans and who knows who else to notice, and come in to undercut whatever terms we invent for a trade that doesn't exist?"

"We can request most-favored nations treatment. I think there is real value to being the first to establish official contacts with Ethiopia – a natural extension of our sphere of influence down the Nile and across the Red Sea from Aden. The French will establish a presence in the Horn any day now and the time is ripe to be the friendly hand that the Ethiopians take to counter their influence," Glendon laid out.

Matthews did not even seem to be listening.

"Sir?" asked Glendon.

"Yes, yes," said Matthews, his eyes re-focusing as he stood up and paused, before pacing a bit. "Glendon, do you know what makes this country beautiful?"

"No, sir."

"It's that the whole bloody island is well-kept, like a manicured garden. It's all those centuries of hard labor taming the land that make it beautiful. Do you have a garden?"

"No, sir."

"I have a small garden. You let things go for a few weeks and it's like you never paid attention to it at all. The weeds come, the animals, insects, it dries out. Constant care is what it needs." He sat down again. "What am I trying to say, Glendon?"

"We must tend our garden, sir."

"Exactly. Don't be drawn to that other type of beauty, that rugged wilderness. It's just not British." The last four words came out definitively, as Matthews' face looked as heavy and imposing as the oak doors to his office.

"Where would our empire be, sir, if it wasn't British to tame new lands?"

Matthews pursed his lips. "We're spread quite thin, Mark, to be honest. Ethiopia has the Nile, yes, but we have enough problems keeping the Pasha in Cairo warm without worrying about these far-flung frontiers. There's really nothing in the interior of Africa that we want and we can't justify any new infrastructure – can't we do something in Sudan first, and then progress south from there at the appropriate time? No, no, don't even answer that," Matthews raised a hand, "we are done discussing this."

Glendon opened his mouth, but there was a knock at the door before he could collect another argument to fill it. Why couldn't anyone else see the promise of Africa's riches as he did? He turned in his chair to see the mail clerk totter uncomfortably into the room, clutching a dispatch of urgency.

"Sir, from Aden – they have marked it with the utmost importance," said the clerk, depositing the dispatch on Matthews' desk and sidling towards the door in the hope he would overhear what it said. Matthews was still opening the envelope as the door shut with a thud, but Glendon remained in the room. Matthews skimmed the two lines and tossed the paper to Glendon. "Read it."

"British envoys appear to have been kidnapped under armed guard in Ethiopia. Distress communication received through French envoy left Magdala three weeks ago," read Glendon.

"Balls," said Matthews. "That's what I thought it said," and creases seemed to appear on his face like the bark of a tree.

A hot glow crept through Glendon's body and for a moment his stomach tensed. They would all have to pay attention to Ethiopia now. They would have to pay attention to Mark Glendon.

Matthews pinched the bridge of his nose and squeezed his eyes shut. "We'll need to convene the cabinet for this if it's true. British citizens taken against their will. How do we substantiate the report?"

"Why, the Ethiopians have written directly to the Queen on two occasions," said Glendon excitedly. "We need only send an official inquiry and for sure he will answer."

"Do it. Do it now. Nobody knows about this until we have more detail." Matthews glanced at his desk calendar. "We have a regular cabinet meeting in six weeks. This will be on the agenda pending further information, and I pray we receive a response in time – God forbid we should have to roust those buggers out of their routines for an extraordinary session."

## *Chapter Eight*

Tewodros sensed Asfaw stooping down in the cave's blackness to shake him, as his eyes fluttered open. He left his place on the floor to take his turn at sentry in Asfaw's place, as they had agreed after supper. He almost regretted the offer, now he had to rouse himself from rest. He felt the usual ache in his hip where the stone pressed overnight, and the tingle in his arm as the cobwebs cleared his brain.

I must sit with Yohannes, he thought, and it would feel good to take the fresh air. His mentor was the other sentry on duty and the reason Tewodros had chosen this watch. He stepped carefully around his sleeping brothers in the dim glow from the fire that was kept through the night, and added a log on his way to his post. The sparks sputtered as he stoked the embers – the second watch always felt the darkest.

There were two sentries, one at the eastern, and one at the western side of the cave's mouth. It was easier to talk if Tewodros left the western post to sit next to Yohannes, who was mildly surprised to see him, but glad. The Abyssinian night settled around them, like a comforting cloak over the shoulders. They began to speak in hushed tones, but there was no need to rush the conversation.

"These quiet hours can make a man feel small," said Yohannes, hard to make out with his dark skin shrouded by his habit and the black sky.

"You must feel the smallness more than most, Yohannes, as you have seen such a big part of the world. I wish I could travel like you have done and see those far places. Perhaps as king I will make visits of state to all the nations."

"You have passed quickly from being nervous about this monumental change, to having big dreams about it, o prince."

"Yes, you are right," Tewodros admitted. "But my stomach still churns, because I cannot wait for tomorrow, and the next day, and beyond – is that a good thing?"

"It is a very good thing, if it means you look forward to what is to come. Some say one can be happier not knowing what is out there in the world that they are missing, but you will see and do much, Tewodros. I hope that you will use your new freedom to experience as much as possible."

"In the Bible, King Solomon says it is all dust before the wind."

"Yes, but he still did all those things – the king has that privilege."

"Solomon was wise, but I will choose the more wisely with your advice, Yohannes."

"Then I advise we go abroad, and I will look forward to doing that as well. It might make me feel young again. My second piece of advice – never grow old."

Yohannes' words were marked by a tumbling stone, and the two men snapped to scan the approach to the cave. There was a three-quarters moon, but a creeping fog obscured much of the cliff beyond their immediate surroundings. A movement caught Yohannes' eye and he pointed Tewodros to a klipspringer, staring back at them from a rocky outcropping to the east below the cave. The noise dismissed, the sentries fell back into silence.

Further down the cliff face to the west, where the angle of the cliff made it harder to see the mouth of the cave, the merchant had frozen. He silently cursed the monk's robes he wore, as the loose sleeves hampered his movements. He strained to hear as he flattened his body against the cold rock, and soon the murmurs of the monks' voices above began again.

His movements had to be efficient, or he knew his muscles would not last the climb. For now, his fingers felt like steel hooks that could hang from the tiniest protrusion, but he stuck to his practice of using his legs to push him up the cliff. He was seeing partly with his hands, blind less from the dark and fog, but from never having climbed this particular cliff. He prayed the holds he needed would present themselves on the way up, and as he brushed his hand across the rock face he exulted in feeling a lip that he could curl his whole palm over. It had been some time since he faced such a challenge, as he was used to all his routes on the honey cliffs and could execute those moves almost automatically. The merchant was surprised at how much energy was sapped by simply holding still on the cliff while he calculated his next maneuver.

He cursed as he wiped a sweaty palm against his robe. Sweat was the enemy, and a clammy hand could slip no matter how strong his grip. He found a long crack leading up into the night where the strains of time had cloven the rock; one of his favorite features. He leaned back with both hands in the crack and his feet braced against the natural unevenness of the cliff. He made at least ten feet by inching up this way, the crack narrower and pressing against his fingers as we went, before finding a blessed ledge he could grab with both hands. He felt the strength in his back as he curled his body to hook both feet on the ledge, and brought his whole body up with one pull, standing for a while to rest and steady his breathing.

With exhilaration the merchant realized the cave mouth was already to his left, wreathed in fog. It was time to begin the traverse, and he had to trust that the sentries described by Asfaw were looking for intruders to come only from below and not sideways. He had to maintain the element of surprise at all costs, and he had a good chance since it seemed they had not seen him yet. He would have to kill the western sentry as quietly as possible and dash into the cave if he were to have any chance of success.

He dared not relax his focus as his forearms began to burn, but so close to his goal he knew he could get there. He still did not see the sentry – had that traitorous monk lied to him? He pulled out his knife to clench it between his teeth for the last few moves, careful not to knock another stone loose. The metal tasted awful, and he could sense the doubt hovering over his mind, ready to creep in when no more climbing moves were left to distract him. If there were guards waiting further in, he would have to give up on getting out alive but he might still make a run at the prince. He still could not see a sentry on the western side of the cave mouth, and if Asfaw had lied about the sentries, nothing else he had said could be trusted.

Tewodros and Yohannes chuckled softly and enjoyed their conversation as the assassin slinked inside the cave, expecting a challenge at any time. He went over the mental map again; there would be three rows of sleeping monks in the chamber that opened off to the left after thirty-odd paces. The prince slept against the inner wall, third man from the left. He would be young, fine-featured and with braids covering his head. The assassin clung to the dark edges of the main chamber and shielded his eyes as he passed a dying fire, to protect his night vision.

He entered the sleeping room and stepped ever so carefully between the two rows of snoring, tossing men, passing six of them on each side and nearly stubbing his toe on a gebet'a board. The glow cast by the fire just made its way into the side chamber, and the assassin could tell there was a gap between two monks against the inner wall. Clearly, there was an empty sleeping place where the prince should have been. The assassin shrank beneath his cowl and kept his blade behind his sleeve. Had Asfaw warned the prince? In the darkness he could just make out the sleeping forms around him, but he would only have one chance to feel the features of a man in any other sleeping place before driving his blade home, and the risk of making a noise was high. He carefully lay down in Tewodros' spot to consider his options, his knuckles tight around the knife hilt and pulse throbbing in his head.

The second watch was almost over and Tewodros put a hand on his friend's shoulder. "Thank you for talking, Yohannes. Do you think the others will relieve us on time? I am finally feeling like sleep." He looked around behind him and yawned mightily.

"I'll wait here if you want to go wake them," said Yohannes.

Tewodros walked in to the cave and turned left into the sleeping chamber. Asfaw must have taken his spot because it was flatter and more comfortable, the cheeky fellow – after Tewodros had saved him from sentry duty. Where was it that Asfaw usually slept? Someone was in that place too. Tewodros leaned down and could just make out that it was Asfaw, in his proper place. He looked at the man in his bed, and walked over to shake him awake.

The assassin reasoned that the longer he waited, the greater the chance of discovery. Had he miscounted? It had been too long for the missing sleeper to have gone to the bathroom. His patience expired – he chose the man to his left, and ran his hand over the man's head. There were no braids, but the monk had awoken. "What...what is it?"

"Tewodros. Where is Tewodros? He is not here," the assassin hissed.

"Here I am," came a quizzical voice from above him. The assassin smiled. He had to act quickly before the suspicion built further.

The assassin leapt to his feet, whirled and drew the dagger from his sleeve in one fluid motion, aiming to finish the stroke with a slash across the prince's face. The blade bit into Tewodros' cheek and the prince recoiled, his hand flying up to his face to feel the moist blood. The assassin's arm could now stab down to the throat for a killing blow as he lunged forward.

The monk he had awoken took the hem of the intruder's robe and tugged as hard as he could. It was enough to disrupt his balance and the assassin stumbled and fell.

Tewodros dropped his knee to the forearm of the knife hand while the monk who saved his life scrambled on top of the intruder and repeatedly punched his head into the cave floor. Strangely, none had yet uttered a sound, but now the intruder cried out in pain. Several monks sprang up and restrained him as Yohannes rushed in with a torch.

A circle formed around the intruder and Yohannes as the senior monk began to speak. "Who are you?"

"He tried to kill Tewodros!" cried an accuser of the obvious. The other monks shushed him.

"Who are you?" repeated Yohannes. "Why have you done this?"

"My name is no business of yours," said the assassin, flicking a glance at Asfaw who had joined the circle, looking ashen.

Tewodros grasped the hand of the monk next to him, "you saved my life. Thank you, my brother." Turning to the assassin and stepping forward he challenged the man, "what have you against me? Have I harmed you in some way?"

"You have done nothing to me, Ras Tewodros," said the man.

"How in God's name did he get into the cave?" interjected another questioner, as this was decidedly not obvious.

"He was in my sleeping place," added Tewodros.

Yohannes admitted, "we saw nobody enter the cave. But we did not cover the western side – we were talking together." At this Tewodros looked down, embarrassed.

"Still, did you so neglect your duties that you left the ladder hanging out all night?" from the questioner.

The assassin interrupted. "I climbed the rock face. Your fortress is not so impregnable as you thought, foolish ones. Still, I have failed," he said more to himself. Then, to Tewodros, "you had best beware, Ras Tewodros. There may be others. They will come for you, and your father," he mocked.

"My father? What is this? Who sent you? Speak!"

The assassin simply smiled a bloody smile and shook his head.

A babble arose among the monks. "Shall we kill him?"

"No, he hasn't given us any information."

"Are you saying we should torture him? What kind of barbarity would that be?"

"The prince's life is at stake – you heard this man. When you become an assassin you should expect no quarter when you are caught."

"He is likely a Mussulman from the southwest. Don't you know they invented this foul species of man, the assassin?"

"Our morals apply to him nonetheless – we can't torture him. Besides, there are assassins in every culture. That is not the way to speak of another descendant of Abraham."

"Always holier than me, aren't you? We can have the villagers hold him until the next magistrate's session."

"Undoubtedly his sentence will be death. It is treason! and attempted murder alone is enough for the death sentence."

"Then shall we just kill him?"

"Let him live," Asfaw's voice rang out clearly, and the assassin looked at him in surprise.

"Asfaw is right," joined Yohannes definitively. "In any case, we cannot make hasty decisions in the middle of the night. Bind his hands and let the sentries look after him while the rest of us try to snatch what sleep is left to us. We'll double up the guard duty for the last two watches."

The sentries dutifully tied the assassin's hands tightly with a cord and led him to sit between them at the mouth of the cave. The instant their hands left him, the man stood up and leapt to his death.

## Chapter Nine

The scheduled cabinet session loomed as the administrative peons of the well-oiled British government scurried to complete their papers for those deities of a different order, the Ministers who were more than mortal men, to cursorily skim. There had been no response from Magdala, but the Ethiopia matter remained a minor agenda item – nobody had made the effort required to amend and recirculate the agenda to remove it. Old curmudgeons took their places in a musty room and business as usual began, with Matthews in the second row of seats and distracted by the matters he was scheduled to report on at ten thirty.

At ten twenty-nine the doors opened. A messenger entered and whispered in the ear of the Prime Minister, Smith-Stanley, the Earl of Derby. Derby raised his hand to the rest of the room to wait, as the other Lord Stanley, the Foreign Secretary and in fact the Prime Minister's son, leaned in to discuss something. They both had the same hooked nose, but the father's sideburns looked unruly next to his son's neatly clipped and darker locks. Whispers made their way down the row to Matthews. It was a rumor that the Queen was coming. Matthews was discomfited – he did not like changes to a schedule that had been set well in advance. But he did like the Queen.

At ten thirty-three the doors opened again, and Victoria made her entrance. The lace on her head, the billow of her skirts, the imperturbable look of a mother to many; there was no end to the things that set this woman apart. A space was cleared for her at the head of the table, facing down its length to the Prime Minister. She delicately dropped a letter on the table. It had been addressed to the Queen, "FOR PERSONAL DELIVERY ONLY." The Queen spoke. "It appears that for my correspondence to reach me, one must specifically instruct the palace not to divert a letter to some Whitehall denizen or other. Am I not to be involved in the weighty affairs of state, of which I am the head?"

"Your majesty, if every letter addressed to you..." began the Prime Minister, his usual steely glare replaced by the worried look of a mouse in a corner.

"Never mind that," said Victoria. "You will consult me on this matter, as I have been already drawn in – it is too late to take the letter from me now. Have you discussed Ethiopia yet this morning?"

The Queen's question drew blank stares from the ministers, and she stared back furiously at the Stanleys. Matthews stumbled out of his seat and hurried to the younger Lord Stanley's shoulder, muttering something about the minor agenda item tabled for the afternoon. "This afternoon, Your Majesty," said the Foreign Secretary.

"Is the matter of a British mission taken hostage not one to be taken as a priority, then?" The room was thrown into hubbub. "And this is my government," sighed Victoria. She no longer felt the uncertainty of her younger days, and was quite sure when old and august men were simply being incompetent.

The government soon calmed down and it was established that the Prime Minister would look to his son, who would look to Matthews to bring the cabinet up to speed on the matter that nobody knew anything about. Matthews sent immediately for Glendon. "My under-secretary will be here very shortly to provide additional detail; he was unfortunately scheduled to be here at four in the afternoon. I can let you know that we received a troubling report from a French diplomat following our mission to attend the coronation of Ethiopia's new emperor. We responded immediately with a communique to clarify the situation, and it appears that the response from Ethiopia has come directly to Her Majesty." Matthews then stalled by requesting that he read the letter aloud. The letter was passed down and Matthews began, the words spilling out far more quickly than was his custom. His blood was up – Matthews did not like being on the spot.

"To Her Majesty Queen Victoria. We find it regretful that the responses to our previous communications have come from your administration and not from the Queen directly, as we find this to be a matter between heads of state. Despite our kind invitation to the coronation of His Majesty the Emperor, the King of Kings, the envoys sent on behalf of Great Britain were found to be exceedingly rude, to denigrate His Majesty and to demand an exclusive treaty with no authority to negotiate this treaty. When we attempted to contact you to negotiate this treaty in a respectful manner we were instead asked to declare our intentions with regard to the persons of said envoys. Hereby we do declare that we have no intention of releasing your envoys without an official apology for their behavior and a treaty negotiation attended by fully authorized representatives. Rest assured your envoys will be treated well with every courtesy as the Emperor's personal guests." Matthews looked up.

Glendon heard the last half as he was ushered in, out of breath from the dash over. He found the Queen of England staring directly at him. "Well?" she said.

"Your Majesty," Glendon stuttered, affecting a strange curtsey and glancing sidelong at Matthews. This was his moment. The Queen, the Prime Minister, good God they were all listening. Don't cock it up. "We had written to the Ethiopians to confirm the situation as we did not have enough information to yet raise such a delicate matter more broadly."

"This Emperor – King of Kings – whatever he is, this monarch does not sound like a savage. Is this a savage country? What did these envoys do to turn a routine visit into an international incident?" The Queen was now looking at the Foreign Secretary, who was looking at his father, who was no help whatsoever. Victoria let him squirm for a few more seconds, mouth flapping like a fish out of water. "If we see a treaty with Ethiopia as something to be desired, go and get a treaty. If I were treated as it seems this potentate has been treated, I would be offended too – perhaps you had better make it up to him before you have an international incident to clean up. I want to know how you propose to fix this by the end of tomorrow." She turned to the Prime Minister. "Derby, I expect you will come and see me yourself." She moved as if to go and looked back wryly, "I supposed it has not escaped your attention that if we control Massawa, those on the Continent will quickly run out of places to establish their own presence on the Red Sea." The Queen left the room as Glendon shivered in the moment.

Matthews was quite sure his head would not roll, at least while the rest of the government had little idea where Ethiopia was and needed his input to keep the Queen satisfied. If he could clean this up it might all blow over and his career could continue. "Matthews, you will have a full report on this with recommendations for further action by tomorrow morning at nine o'clock," said the Foreign Secretary. "We will need to convene an extraordinary session of the cabinet." A collective groan went around the room, and the agenda resumed, already behind schedule.

Glendon was amazed at how quickly the excitement dissipated, and the cabinet returned to the monotonous drone of its necessary business. His welcome overstayed, he was ushered out, feeling sick with triumph and overwhelming stress all at once. His step on the way back to his office was almost as quick as the running to the cabinet room had been, and he would not remember to take lunch. There was a mission to plan, and he needed to get to his desk to draw out the considerations on paper to properly think them through. He relished the thought of working all night. Already it was in the back of his mind that he might go himself to Ethiopia and lead the expedition to solve this problem in which the Queen had taken a personal interest. Mark Glendon, on Her Majesty's service. Would he need an armed escort or would that send the wrong message? Perhaps he could stop in Cairo on the way back and make progress on Sudan – the higher-ups would like that, the efficiency of a single trip. This was all going in his report. Matthews would get out of the cabinet meeting and want supper, and then the real action would begin.

## Chapter Ten

"The assassin mentioned my father," said Tewodros with his first sip of coffee the next morning. "We must go at once to warn him."

"Tewodros, you've been through quite an experience," said Gebrewolde. The red line on the prince's cheek indeed promised a rugged scar for the future. "We should take time to consider our actions and make sure you are okay."

"What is there to consider? I was supposed to leave this morning anyway. I am ready. Yohannes is ready. Ghannatu is ready," he gestured at those who would come with him.

"We may need to send more people with you for protection – in fact we might need to wait for an armed escort," said Gebrewolde.

"There is no need to be rash, Tewodros," Yohannes remonstrated. "Your father can protect himself."

"We have only a few horses, and it will take many days before a large escort can be organized. And who says I am safer here where there has already been one attempt on my life? You have kept me in the cave all these years; let it not be against my will from now on."

The words stung the monks who heard, and Gebrewolde spoke for them all: "Tewodros, we are your brothers and it is only the will of the king that would keep you here."

"Then I speak for the king," said Ghannatu. "I am to bring the prince to Sodere. Lend us one scout to ride ahead for security, and I am sure we can travel safely – when I left the king, two of his armies were nearby in the region and they should keep the peace."

Yohannes agreed. "Tewodros, make your rounds while we prepare the gear and send Asfaw for the horses. He will be the scout as well." Secretly Yohannes felt it would be better not to drag out the goodbyes.

One hour later the ladder was dropped and Tewodros stepped rung by rung to the bottom of the cliff, eyes watching his feet. At the end he looked up to see the monks congregated above him, many with their arms raised in farewell. In his heart he knew he would not return, but in his mind he convinced himself that he would spend good times with all of his friends again. The sun dazzled his eyes and he dropped his gaze to the rock in front of him, giving thanks for his home that was no more. His breath stuck in his throat and he turned quickly before it could lead to tears.

Tewodros' facility with the rope ladder was in stark contrast to his handling of the horse, as he had only ridden three times in his life. Ghannatu's pudgy hands helped to sling him into the saddle, and Tewodros marveled at how the messenger's bulk swung onto his own horse so daintily before he set off at a precocious trot. Tewodros bounced uncomfortably, his ribs rattling and his brain boggling around inside his head, but he refused to complain as he tried to keep up with

Ghannatu. He barely noticed the new scenery unfolding around him, enduring for half an hour until the horses stopped for water at a small stream. "Is it always so painful to ride a horse?" he asked.

Ghannatu laughed. "You have to move with his motion, up and down. It gets easier when you go faster, but it takes some skill to ride at speed."

"Faster?" asked Tewodros. "You mean we can go faster?"

Ghannatu sighed and looked to Yohannes for approval. "Let's try a slow canter. We should reach the hot springs today, so the horses can take the exertion." He showed Tewodros how to goad the horse forward and made it look easy with his jaunty lean in the saddle. A flat stretch of land beckoned and Tewodros dug into his steed, finding that the jolting went away when the horse shifted into a smooth lope. The wind blew in his face and he smiled for joy, kicking the horse harder and clutching the reins tighter as he broke into a full-scale gallop. Yohannes made to shout a warning, but the prince was off like a bolt of lightning.

"Whoo-eee!" he cried, shifting slightly in his seat. The movement threw his balance off and he jerked the reins, unsure now of his control. The horse juked right and in a moment of terror Tewodros was flung free from the saddle, floating in space, coasting into the earth with a thud and rolling to a stop. He was in blackness as Ghannatu and Yohannes thundered up. Asfaw heard the shouts and doubled back to catch the prince's horse.

Tewodros' eyes rolled back into focus to see the concerned faces over him, and he tried to speak but had no wind. Only a gasp came out. "Anything broken?" asked Yohannes, hands on his knees as he peered at Tewodros. "He looks alright," to Ghannatu, "just some bruises I think – and not only to his pride."

Tewodros sat up and held a hand to his solar plexus. "Just...the breath...knocked out." He grimaced and flexed his limbs to be sure. "Ride slower...Get there in one piece." He managed to force a weak smile.

"Look at that," Ghannatu approved, "he gets right back on the horse." Asfaw was off again, glad to be the scout rider on his own as the other three settled into a steady pace, riding in single file with the prince in the middle. The going was easy on the flat ground, though to the north like jagged saw teeth rose fantastic green peaks in row after row fading into the hazy distance, and in front the plateau rolled on to meet the gradual descent to the hot springs.

"Is all the world this beautiful?" Tewodros asked.

"There are many amazing places to see, and all of nature has its charms," said Yohannes, "but I do like the mountains. "Some parts of the lowlands are a bit dull, but you have yet to see the oceans, the great rivers and the deserts, and the lush forests near Lake Tana. Each will take your breath away."

Tewodros inhaled deeply and looked to the sun over the endless ranges that before had seemed like walls closing him in, but now the mountains beckoned as the door to his empire, and beyond to lands of Arab falconers and Greek fishermen, to the Holy City where pilgrims took their humble steps, and to mighty palaces where pale men had received the splendid missions sent by Ethiopian kings long past. What had been the horizon of his whole world was now just the horizon of today.

He thought of how his father would look, tall and strong, proud and noble as he greeted the son he had awaited for so long. His father would approve of the learning and training and enthusiasm that Tewodros could not wait to show off. Watching Ghannatu's horse in front of him, Tewodros fell into periods where his own horse matched the leader's gait exactly. When they were going at the same speed it was as if the riders were constant, fixed in place, and the whole world was moving under and all around them like a scroll.

Each man lost in his thoughts, three hours passed with no conversation to break the monotony of the ride. Tewodros began to feel some frustration as their shadows lengthened. "A better rider would have reached the springs already by now," he chastised himself. At last they came down to a defile and had to lead the horses through on foot. "Ghannatu, how much farther?"

"Don't worry; you will start to smell the springs very soon." There in the distance Tewodros could already see blasts of sulfurous steam issuing from the living earth, and curling up lazily to join their cousins in the cloudy sky. The riders came to the first pool in the series of volcanic springs, where the elements from below had turned the water the color of ochre, with a bright yellow rim. "I must say this devil's playground is quite a sight against all the world," remarked Yohannes.

"Where shall we go first when I am king?" asked Tewodros, tugging the reins to coax his horse well away from the boiling water. "I should like to see the Yemen. I will meet an old Sabaean in his native land." The next pool came into view, but this one was dyed a dizzy green. "Feugh! Something smells horrendous."

"It is the smell of sulfur," said Ghannatu, his horse backing and snorting as Asfaw suddenly appeared in the misty, rotten air.

"Come quickly! They are all dead!"

The horses jumped forward as Asfaw wheeled to lead them. Tewodros felt the wound on his cheek burning, his composure shattered as it was when the assassin's knife bit him. He saw seven bodies sprawled in awkward repose at the place where people came to bathe. There, in a bubbling pool turned red, was another. The men dismounted and Ghannatu waded into the hot spring, the others looking anxiously about in case the murderers could yet leap from behind the tumbled boulders.

The king's messenger staggered up from the steaming water, pouring with sweat and tears and bearing a body. "I am cold," said Ghannatu, dropping to his knees and looking in anguish at man he cradled. From the posture of the old messenger, and from the tearing pain stealing into his heart, Tewodros knew it was his father.

Tewodros took the corpse in his arms, feeling the chill that Ghannatu had spoken of despite the warmth of the water that soaked his clothes. The body was much smaller and more frail than he had imagined, but the face was still strong, and handsome, and its features recalled the prince's own. Tewodros traced a finger along the cheek that looked so familiar; he passed his hand across the noble brow and closed the eyes that held nothing but the specter of death. He looked up at his rock, his mentor, Yohannes. "I never knew this man." He blinked, and wondered why he could not produce a single tear. "And now I will never have a father."

"You can still miss your father, Tewodros. If not the man, then miss the time you wish you spent – that you should have spent with him. That is a true aching, for which I can offer you no salve, but your Father in heaven, who will never pass away." Yohannes felt as if his halting words were silly.

Tewodros looked back at his loss for a pause. "It is like when I left my brothers this morning, only a thousand times worse." He lifted his head, plaintively, "but what do I do now?" and cradled the king's body as a man carries his sleeping child to bed.

## Chapter Eleven

Unable to schedule the same conference room used for yesterday's general meeting, the cabinet was crammed into a discommodious atrocity in the basement. Glendon had managed to accompany Matthews and was in the room, eyes still burning bright from last night's marathon planning session. He rehearsed in his head the excruciating detail behind Matthews' plan of a diplomatic mission to iron out the situation. Today Glendon had more time to take in the people in the room, and to him the ministers all had the balding heads of vultures, and he could scarce tell one buzzard from the other.

Only the sound of shuffling papers was heard as they waited for the less punctual bureaucrats. As he scanned the faces in the room the glint in almost every man's eye seemed calculating, ready to pounce on the weak, and not particularly happy. Am I going to end up like them? thought Glendon. Am I already like that? There was one man that looked different from the others, not just from his darker complexion, black bushy goatee and eyebrows, but because his angular face oozed supreme confidence, as if this meeting was just wasting his important time. Glendon had never seen Benjamin Disraeli in person before.

Stanley-Smith began the meeting at nine o'clock sharp by slamming the morning's edition of the Telegraph onto the table. "We have a leak," he declared.

Grumpy heads swiveled back and forth, leering at their co-ministers and looking for a guilty red face. The headline of the liberal rag screamed what the penny sellers had shouted, "British subjects captured!" and the garish caricatures of a thick-lipped, animal-adorned foreign potentate would grow even more cartoonish as the other newspapers picked up on the scoop. Glendon sat stunned and empty-headed; he might as well burn his night's work of the papers that rested on his lap.

"For now I don't care who spoke to the press," continued the Prime Minister. "Every conservative in a closely contested seat, and every one of us will be out of a job if we don't handle this correctly. The general election is six months away and the opposition will use anything at their disposal to unseat our party."

"The public will have their way with us if we cannot at the height of our empire's hegemony deal decisively with a mere African despot," mused the Foreign Secretary, running a finger along his second chin. "We cannot brook this sort of insult to our emissaries."

"When I beat Gladstone for the Oxford seat," began Hardy, the Home Secretary who always felt the need to legitimize his comments by referring to his defeat of the liberal lion, "I felt that as a conservative I was most well served by stoking the patriotic fires, so to speak." He peered over round spectacles and ran the tip of his tongue over his thin lips. "Some sort of rescue would be necessary, seems to me at least, and better to make it a dramatic one, a national mission, so to speak."

Disraeli broke in stridently, unable to hold his patience further. "The power and glory of Britain is at stake here," he declared.

There he goes again with his favorite topic, thought Matthews and many around the table, though they all knew Disraeli was far cleverer than them, especially when it came to foreign affairs.

"This cannot be some simple rescue mission," continued the Chancellor of the Exchequer. He looked around the table. "This has to be a War." He paused again to let his statement sink in, the thought of war rising up before him as a perfect political playground. Greatness was made in war, he truly believed.

"Think about it. There is no risk from an African foe, and Britain needs a war we can win. I tell you none will come to the aid of Ethiopia, and we will have a victory that shows two things. First, we are not afraid to wage war when anybody lays even a finger on a representative of the crown. Second, when the Eastern question comes to be of importance, as it surely will, the Ottomans will know we are not to be trifled with."

"Winning a war is always a sure horse to ride to victory in the polls," observed the Home Secretary, his voice reedy after Disraeli's thunder.

"You say there is no risk. What happens if ten thousand savages descend upon our rescue mission and destroy it?" supposed the Foreign Secretary, with no real force behind his supposition.

Disraeli grinned from ear to ear, a rare display of his rather good teeth. This was the exact reaction he wanted. "We must be swift, decisive, no question about the outcome. The Ethiopians must be so overawed by our military machine, must be so shocked by the sight of imperial regiments descending upon their shores, that they capitulate immediately without thought of resistance. I intend that no British lives should be lost in this endeavor."

"Can you imagine how much that will cost?" boggled Stanley-Smith the elder.

"I am the Exchequer," replied Disraeli, a touch smug. "I will find whatever it takes in the budget."

"Will you deal with the Queen as well?" asked the younger Stanley-Smith. "Somehow I think you may be more welcomed, and more persuasive, than the rest of us." They all knew Disraeli was the monarch's darling, more than any since Lord Melbourne in her early days, and all were quietly jealous.

"I will," replied Disraeli. "Do we have agreement?"

Mumbled assent was proffered, and that was good enough. Glendon was in awe at the decisiveness that was possible in government at its highest levels, untrammeled by the rubber stamp routines he faced day in and day out. If only he had the power to act with such speed. "Our little expedition has spiraled beyond reason," breathed Matthews into his ear.

"Matthews!" rapped out the Foreign Secretary. "You will brief the Secretary of State for War. See to it that this stratagem is adequately carried out." Matthews winced as the responsibility for things going badly had just landed squarely on him. The War Office was notorious for fouling up the best laid plans of the civilian government.

The meeting broke up and the dance began of important men leaving in order of their prestige. Disraeli could not be bothered with the choreography, and sidled over to sit by Glendon, who found the Chancellor leaning over to address him. "We're alike, you and I."

Glendon almost wanted to blurt out, "but I'm not Jewish." Fortunately he was too shocked to do anything but hold his tongue.

"We're not like these noble men," Disraeli continued, the word "noble" dripping with disdain. "Us commoners have to earn our place with grit and determination," giving Glendon a brotherly smile, no teeth this time. "We have to be better than the others even to sit at the table."

"Yes, sir," was all Glendon managed, while his heart burned to feel a kindred spirit after all these years. On the other side of him Matthews did his best to eavesdrop without appearing to be interested.

"Do you know, they say the Queen will offer to ennoble me very soon?"

"You certainly deserve it!"

"I shall turn it down," Disraeli snapped, and softened his voice again to a confidential tone. "When I am Prime Minister let it be said that I am still a man of the people. Any rate," and his hooded black eyes bored into Glendon's, "I read with profit what you think of the Suez Canal. Very interesting," he tugged at his goatee, "very interesting. You're on to something with Africa."

Abruptly he stood up and left. Glendon watched his slightly hunched shoulders as Disraeli walked out and felt as if he would do anything to serve that man. Then it was Glendon's turn to retreat with Matthews to the office behind the heavy oak doors.

## Chapter Twelve

"What shall I do, Yohannes?" the prince asked again, but Asfaw interrupted curtly, backing up to the prince and shielding him with outstretched limbs.

"Look, who comes there?" Several hooded figures showed their silhouettes as they approached over the boulders, revealing long staves in their hands. "Hi! Who is it?" Asfaw challenged them as his companions drew up in a tight group around the king's body. "Do they carry spears?" he whispered. "They will have to come through me."

The leader in a gray burnous stepped forward, yet his men kept their distance as if they were just as nervous as the prince's party. "Those are just the staffs of herdsmen," said Ghannatu, pointing to the long wooden shafts that split into two prongs at the tip for prodding cattle; "this must be the local villagers, and their headman."

"And who is to say these villagers did not murder all these men?" whispered Tewodros.

"We would be dead by now if that was the case," rejoined Ghannatu, and went to greet the headman. "What happened here, good man? We have simply come to bathe."

The headman's hood fell back to show a solemn countenance. "That is the king Kassa. They must have been mercenaries who left as quickly as they came. Only a young boy on his way to help the bathing attendants saw a group of about twenty men running that way," he pointed, "but we do not know who they were. Did you see anybody on the way here? I tell you we had no part in this and revealed the king's presence to nobody!"

"Soft, my good man. We accuse you of nothing," Ghannatu put out a hand with his palm facing the headman. "Where are the king's men? Surely he travels with more than these."

"I hope that is them," Asfaw pointed. "Those are definitely spears this time." A detachment of soldiers came over a rise and moved deliberately down to the bathing pools.

"It is them, Alula. I see the Fitaurari Tekle-giorgis." The Fitaurari was the commander of the vanguard in the king's army, his height, powerful shoulders and erect posture unmistakable. Ghannatu balled up his fists and strode towards the soldiers, who kept their disciplined composure throughout his harangue. "How could you fail to protect your liege?" Ghannatu screamed.

"The king insisted that he could move more quickly without the full camp," explained the Fitaurari, face impassive and voice deep and sonorous, but its edges betraying his distress. "It was entirely against my advice, but our scouts reported that the king's soldiers were the only armed parties in the region. Ras Kassa was impatient to reach Sodere. Ghannatu..." He was not a man given to words, and now he snapped back to his men and gave sharp orders for bearing the bodies away.

"Who is this Tekle-giorgis?" Tewodros was still unsure of where to direct his anger and blame.

"This is a faultless man," Yohannes said to Tewodros. "I knew him many years ago and he would have done his utmost to save your father." Yohannes stepped in front of the still-steaming Ghannatu. "Tekle-giorgis!" he called.

The Fitaurari turned, unsure of who in this rabble could be addressing the king's general so familiarly. "Yohannes! How have you walked, my brother?" he gushed.

"Solely in the byways of the Lord," came the reply. "If only our meeting again could be under better circumstances." The men clasped hands.

"My tent should be ready now," gestured Fitaurari Tekle-giorgis, inviting the men to a better place while they all struggled to absorb the shock of what they had seen. "Please bring your fellow monks with you." As they walked he turned back to Ghannatu, asking in an undertone, "weren't you supposed to go and fetch the prince? It's a good thing he wasn't here when this happened." Ghannatu inclined his head and Tekle-giorgis' mouth dropped open as he struck his own brow. "I suppose it is a good thing his presence is not obvious. I still don't trust the villagers," he continued. "Let us speak more in the tent."

Tewodros followed the polite invitation and the broad back to the Fitaurari's tent, in awe at this man's charisma and how easily the general took the lead.

When they were seated and water had been brought, and gratefully sipped, Tekle-giorgis broke the stream of each man's thoughts. "Ras Tewodros, my most sincere apologies for failing to greet you earlier. I am the most devoted servant of your late father, the great king, and none of his servants mourn his passing more than I."

"You have addressed the monk Asfaw. Tewodros is on the other side of Yohannes," Ghannatu confided to the Fitaurari.

Tewodros was gracious in reply, his etiquette too deeply ingrained to forget, even under these circumstances. "I have from my teacher Yohannes the highest recommendation of you, Fitaurari Tekle-giorgis. I look forward to your acquaintance but there is a pressing matter at hand. Who is this murderer? It has been made clear by all the people remaining in Sodere that the crime was not their fault," he ended on a caustic note, which he at once regretted.

"Ras Tewodros, I take all the blame for what has happened," spoke Tekle-giorgis. "I assure you that now my allegiance lies with you, and my army of ten thousand men camping here is yours. Though I will never succeed in expiating my guilt, let my service be the least I can do for the memory of your father."

Ghannatu was quick to join the sentiment, pledging his support for Tewodros, and it was Yohannes' turn to speak. "Tewodros, I agreed to come with you as you took your new mantle. Now it seems the way is much harder – it was never going to be easy, but no man will fault you if you do not want this struggle, now that…" Yohannes cast about for a way to say it. "Now that – "

Tewodros cut him off. "Yohannes, you taught me of suffering and I always thought I might have my share. But you also taught me never to shrink from my duty, whatever it might be. I dare not presume that a king's duty is harder than a monk's, or a shepherd's, but no matter how hard it might be, there is nothing I shall do but strive to be king, and the best king I can be."

Tekle-giorgis marveled at the maturity of this young man, as Yohannes placed a hand with dark and wrinkled palm on Tewodros' shoulder.

"Then, now that you face great responsibility, what little I can offer is perhaps even more valuable. I am fully committed to the path you choose, as your servant but foremost as your friend."

Tewodros looked warmly at Yohannes and Ghannatu, and even Tekle-giorgis whom his instinct told him to trust. "I know you will all be an invaluable support in this new life outside my old cave, and I doubt any would make better counselors than you."

"Then listen to my counsel. 'Mine is the vengeance, I shall repay, saith the Lord,'" quoted Yohannes with strong eyes. "I do not want your heart to be guided only by thoughts of what violence has been done to your family today. It is a great tragedy and we all feel for your loss and mourn alongside you, and with you we wish to preserve the legacy of your father as one of a unified and peaceful Ethiopia – not an endless cycle of blood feud, as the nomads in their wildness still live out every day. For your sake too, Tewodros, it is not good that a man withdraw into the company of only his dreadful thoughts, but it is a powerful help to plunge yourself into the work you have been called to do. The king is dead; long live the king, and his name is Tewodros." Yohannes knew that if Tewodros quailed now, there was no hope. But the boy's face held true, and it was a man's face.

Tekle-giorgis joined in softly. "We all share your passion, Yohannes and thank you for your words. I must hold your last thought, however, as the succession is not clear cut."

"What do you mean?" said Yohannes.

"It is not a given that the other Rases will stand aside and let the hereditary prince take the throne."

"Also let us not forget your own would-be assassin, Tewodros. This may be linked," added Ghannatu. "I will tell you of this later, Tekle-giorgis." The Fitaurari nodded, but his face showed concern.

Ghannatu continued, "there are three princes that have the potential to direct the future of the empire. Old Mulugeta is the first – we all know he has chafed since the beginning that he could not achieve dominion over the south. He rose to be your father's right hand, the Qenazmatch. But was that enough for him?"

Tewodros remembered Ghannatu's story of how strong Mulugeta's army had been.

"Then there is Ras Makonnen, the Grazmatch, commander of the left wing. He will move quickly or not at all; a rash and impulsive man." Ghannatu looked around at the circle of men in the tent. "He has no fear, that man."

"I have seen him in battle – this much is true," Tekle-giorgis agreed.

"Finally, Dedjazmatch Balcha, the Keeper of the Door. He has become accustomed to his high rank and would be loath to lose any of his power and privilege."

"So these were my father's other generals," said Tewodros. "If these men, with their power granted by the king were to seek the crown it would make a callous betrayal of my father's memory indeed. Is there any other man in the realm with the wherewithal to challenge me?"

"The power in this empire comes only from the king of kings," said Tekle-giorgis. "Nobody else could hope to trifle with the king, or even go against any of the four men whom your father allowed to command armies. And of course, you are the only child, Tewodros."

Tewodros cracked a strange smile. "I did not know that I had no brothers and sisters; just that my mother had perished in childbirth. It seems I am a man without a family." He quickly went on. "But no mind, it is clear to me that the first mover here will have the advantage. The others will think twice before challenging the player that shows a bold strength from the beginning."

97

Tekle-giorgis agreed, "a good thought, Tewodros."

"Our prince is not the only one who will have this insight," Yohannes countered. "Tewodros, I think you must speak to each of these generals and assure them of their continued power if they support you as the negusa negast."

Tewodros was one step ahead. "Yes, I know I cannot override them all. But they will never support me if they see that I have no strength. How can I demonstrate this, is my question?"

There was a shout outside the tent and the village headman was hustled in. "We just saw my nephew, who returns from the market two days' walk from here," he said in between sharp breaths. "There are reports of another army moving nearby. They say it is Balcha." The men in the tent looked at each other with this new surmise.

"You see, he moves quickly – Yohannes was right," said Tekle-giorgis.

"Perhaps he simply comes to join the king. He cannot know the king is dead," responded Yohannes.

Tewodros' own breath was now rushing in and out as he spoke, barely hearing the words of his council. "If Balcha comes as the aggressor, we cannot risk being unprepared. We must rattle our spears, and if he has come in peace he will stand down. If he comes for a fight, this is my chance to prove my strength."

Yohannes held his tongue as he knew the prince had nothing to lose – if he could not defeat Balcha now, the kingdom would never be his. And if the thought of losing the battle had occurred to the prince, it could not overcome the giant heart of one so young.

Tewodros leapt to his feet. "To arms! To arms!" he cried. The command seemed strange, coming as it did from the young upstart to the veteran Tekle-giorgis, but it spread through the general's ranks like wildfire.

## *Chapter Thirteen*

Glendon waited a few minutes as Matthews cleared some space on his desk and sat with his head bowed in thought. Both men were tired. Matthews lifted his head. "Mark," he began, "you hold my career in your hands."

"I – I'm not sure I follow."

"I have never received the level of resources and political backing for a free hand in affairs of state, as we have now. That means," Matthews pointed a finger at himself, "they will blame me if anything goes wrong." His finger swiveled to point at Glendon. "And I will blame you."

Old, slow Matthews never took a risk, thought Glendon, and he would never rise any higher. "Sir, this is the opportunity of a lifetime," he said in earnest. "We can give them the budget we need and they will find us the money. We can carry out my- our plan without half the usual headaches. When we win this war, we can force the Africans to give us anything we want!"

"But what do we want, man? I'm damned if I even remember the reason we were poking our nose into this in the first place."

"The scramble for Africa will come, sir. Ethiopia is in a perfect location, and anything we can do to get our foot in the door will benefit us in the long run."

"So now we propose to spend thousands, millions of pounds for a treaty with an economic backwater," scoffed Matthews.

"Why stop at a treaty?" Glendon leaned forward in his chair, the ambition growing like a firestorm in his very being even as he continued speaking. "You said it yourself. Why waste unlimited financial and military resources on some treaty? The rules of diplomacy have not yet crystallized with the other European powers. There is no custom we would break by going beyond a simple treaty." The fire was showing in Glendon's eyes. "If we annex the territory – a new colony – we have the source of the Nile! We have the Sudan and Egypt at our mercy!"

Matthews smiled at the vinegar in the young man. "There are no rules, Mark, but there are rules. We have political backing for a rescue mission, rescue war, what have you, not for empire-building."

Glendon sat back in thought, absently chewing a thumbnail. After a moment he returned to the edge of his chair. "I have it, sir."

"What is it?"

"Do you remember the Sindh rebellion a few years back? General Napier?"

"Yes, yes, I do. Percy Napier. The rascal, instead of putting down the rebellion he conquered the whole bloody province. Brutal chap, I heard."

"Precisely. But you see, he asked forgiveness ex post, instead of permission to exceed his mandate. And his reward? Knighthood, the public loves him. I believe he's been sent back to India in case they need him to put down the next insurgency."

Matthews looked Glendon dead in the eyes. "So you're saying we have an expedition with one aim, and come away 'accidentally' with quite another outcome. Nudge nudge wink wink."

"I'm saying Percival Napier is the man for our job."

Matthews puffed out his cheeks and exhaled noisily, turning to the ceiling. "I'm the one that will get the axe if anything goes wrong with this infernal affair. On the other hand, I'm out anyway if the conservatives can't keep their majority." He looked back at Glendon, as if sizing him up. "You are still low enough down that you will survive a change in administration – but not if you're linked to a hare-brained military action that has no liberal support."

Glendon was not sure if he was being called on to respond to Matthews' ramblings, but his superior continued. "I have come to like you, Mark. Let me give you some advice. If you want to keep playing this game, you need to play both sides. If the liberals win the general election, it will be William Gladstone who is Prime Minister and he will decide whether you take over my job. Go to him informally – I can't – and get his blessing before you put your name to this debacle. That way he will be hard pressed to get rid of you if he wins."

"We don't need the liberals to get this through Parliament now," Glendon protested. I want to be Disraeli's man, he didn't say.

Young fool, Matthews didn't say. "Perhaps you think you don't need a safety net," he sighed. "Let's say the mission goes well. I've seen my share of wars in far places, and they always take much longer, and cost much more than you think. You will still need the liberals to see it through."

"And if the liberals stay the minority party?" Glendon argued.

"Then I will still be your master, and I will be quite upset that you ignored my direction to go and see Gladstone." He added coyly, "If Disraeli found out he would more like than not admire you for it."

"I will do it," Gladstone acquiesced. The old man didn't take risks, but he was damn cunning about it.

"Good. And get me your detailed plan with Napier leading the mission while you're at it – if you can't convince Gladstone we're doomed to pursue this folly anyway. At least the cabinet will take care of the press, we won't have to deal with those vipers." Matthews turned his chair and the meeting was over.

This time the story spun to the press was carefully managed, that the empire depends on trade and it must therefore protect trade emissaries at all cost. Glendon began purchasing every evening paper he could lay his hands on between the office and the usual cafeteria where he took his supper, avidly reading the scraps from this or that piquant pundit lauding the jingoistic strategy, or questioning whether the expedition was simply the military's way of ensuring their budget remained sufficiently bloated. Never had his work been so in the public eye, and he was consumed by the feeling of importance it gave him. Shame, he thought, after all my hard work, it'll be some man named Napier who will finish my story for me. The bastard will have all the fun, but I won't let him take all the glory. Glendon poked at his dry beef with relish. They will know my name. Everyone will know my name, and I will have respect.

*Chapter Fourteen*

The dawn was a busy one, as Tekle-giorgis' soldiers staked out positions of strength lest Balcha's intentions were sour. Asfaw, good man that he was, had volunteered to ride out with the scouts to track the approaching general's movements, even though Tewodros had given him leave to return to the cave, to the life the young monk had chosen. The prince was pleased with the activity, but Yohannes' whiny attitude was a constant downer at his side.

"If you act like you're getting ready for a fight, you might get what you ask for," he grumped. Yohannes hated war, hated violence and could not reason his way past his principles. At least this activity kept Tewodros occupied when other, darker thoughts might take sway, he consoled himself.

"I must force the Dedjazmatch to make his intentions clear," said Tewodros.

"Does he even know you are here? Does he even know the king is dead?"

"The village headman saw the Fitaurari obey my word," said Tewodros. "He knows all – and you know that such gossip will not stay long in Sodere."

"So what if he knows. What sort of response can he possibly make to the question of an army facing him, except to fight?" replied Yohannes. "You have not been long out of the cave, and already you are jumping to war."

"Fine, Yohannes, fine," Tewodros was exasperated. "You are right, we should give Balcha a chance to talk before fighting."

Yohannes was satisfied. "We even have the king's messenger on our side. Why not use Ghannatu?"

"A good idea," Tewodros smiled involuntarily at Ghannatu as he came, and wanted to call the man Uncle. "My friend, will you carry one more message for us?" Ghannatu left with a swift horse and a simple question. With the king dead, and without revealing the whereabouts of Tewodros, would Balcha submit to the hereditary ruler as Tekle-giorgis had done?

Tewodros wasted no time calling next for his seasoned commander. "Forgive me, Fitaurari, if I am too blunt. Will we win if it comes to a scrap?"

"Our vanguard keeps the crack troops," replied Tekle-giorgis. "However, Balcha outnumbers us."

"That is not an answer," said Tewodros. "Call in the village headman – if we lack numbers perhaps we can recruit some men from the area. They did bring us the news of Balcha's movements after all."

Tewodros could not keep still while they waited, his coffee-brown eyes looking at the ground as he paced with arms clasped behind his simple white cotton garments – no more monk's robes for the prince. "My father's body," he murmured as Yohannes was seized with concern for how he might counsel Tewodros in matters for which there could be no proper words. "I will wait until we can return to

Magdala and give my father the state funeral he deserves." He looked up. "We cannot bury him here."

Yohannes and Tekle-giorgis nodded as the headman was brought, still nervous, to speak with Tewodros.

"I am Ras Tewodros, son of Kassa, and I have come down from the mountain to take the crown." Tewodros felt rather silly saying these words as soon as they had come out. Did a king speak this way? "You have given us useful information, but will you pledge your allegiance to me and join us in the king's army?" It was not easy to give an older man orders. Perhaps I will get used to it, he thought.

To add to his discomfiture, the headman stuttered and began to sweat profusely. "W-w-we had heard stories that the king had a son whom no one had ever seen," he stalled. "It is my honor to meet you."

Tewodros looked at his advisors, unsure what to do now that his command did not bring an immediate result. Tekle-giorgis stepped in perfectly. "I can understand that you do not want to make a pledge of your loyalty, when there is no guarantee of who will be Ethiopia's master in the days to come," he said. "For the same reason, I am not worried that you will go to the other side," he chided the headman. "Take some time to think, and be assured there will be no conscription from my quarter. I only take men into the king's army who fight because they desire to follow me, and serve the king. That is why," and here he looked square at Tewodros, "we can surely defeat Balcha. Come with me now, Ras Tewodros, and view the deployments to judge for yourself how we can acquit ourselves in a 'scrap.'"

Tewodros was only too happy to ride out and see the lines, as the day was fair and the air was far better than the stuffy tent. What energy rose to meet him from the straight-backed soldiers; what shouts rang out to coordinate potential fields of fire! The troops had staked out high ground on the two low hills ranged across the half-mile between a ravine, and a rocky slope leading up to the plateau that swung around behind the hot springs, and from which Tewodros had arrived. In the opposite direction, the hills commanded the gentler southern approach to Sodere, and this was the direction whence Tekle-giorgis expected Balcha to appear, bounded on one side by the ravine and the other by the plateau. It would take Balcha some effort to traverse the plateau and come down from behind the pools, through the fields of boulders, and in that case Tewodros' men would have time to redeploy and face him on the ground in between the two hills and the pools. In either case there was a clear advantage to the men of Tewodros, and the Dedjazmatch would have to think twice before joining an attack.

Tekle-giorgis had decided to place his picked men on the right side of the line, facing south. They would wait on the second hill, away from the ravine and in position to roll up Balcha's forces with a counter-attack. To see these men as the first part of his review of the troops inspired great confidence in Tewodros, as their discipline was second to none and their ranks were perfect. Thrust towards the sky were the obsidian-tipped spears that marked these as the best soldiers in the army; most of them had proved themselves with kills and victory. The black, volcanic rock could be sharpencd to cruelty, an edge more deadly than metal, and a black death came to the mind of any man who saw the bristling forest of those spears.

From this hill Tewodros could see to his left the dull hot springs, steaming at the base of the plateau he had ridden across just the day before, though so much had happened since. He tore his eyes away from where he had met his father, to the plain below the hill to his right, then to the small valley that was between the two hills he commanded, and that formed a gateway to the hot springs. On the other hill the rest of the Fitaruari's troops looked like swarming ants, that could any moment cascade down into the ravine on the far side that was too deep for men to cross.

The prince rode down from the brow of the hill, to where Tekle-giorgis had reinforced the depth of the center. With so many brothers around them, the soldiers felt strong and well and despite the thought of battle a smile could be seen on many of their hardened faces. The captains continued to drill the riflemen on firing as one to maximize the effect of each volley, how not to waste two bullets on one man. They used a system of flags to signal each corps along the line, so there was never a time when the units were all reloading at once and the enemy could take heart.

To Tewodros, who had only learned things in his cave of a classroom, the open land and the practice of tactics was almost too much to enjoy, and he tried to keep a grin from his face. At the same time, he felt as if he were not enjoying it enough, as the ride went too quickly and he could scarcely pause to exult in the moment while these new and exciting phenomena flew all around him.

Over the second hill, and the left side of the line had just broken for lunch; the men squatting battle-ready with a weapon in one hand and bread in the other. So far the prince had been taking it all in but had not spoken to the soldiers, and now he addressed a few of them. "How is the food?"

Tekle-giorgis laughed. "They don't speak your language, my prince."

"How can you tell? What do they speak?"

"These men speak a Surmic language," replied Tekle-giorgis. "See the scars across their chests?" Tewodros could track the lines of raised scar tissue from a crude knife that decorated these warriors, a mark of killing men which would never fade from their bodies, even if their minds could block the memory. "They are from the Omo valley, close to their compatriots, the Hamer men with the mud braids," and here the dull brown-colored, short dreadlocks that framed those other faces were indicated. "I know how to recognize their tribes from when I spent some time in the southwest. At home the Surma and the Hamer sometimes have differences over grazing, but in the king's army they fight together. Look, here comes their captain who can converse with you." There, striding to the group with a salute was another Surma – he had the most scars.

The sun came out from behind a cloud and the Surma captain looked up. "Going to be a hot day today," he said in a curious accent.

"Perhaps in more ways than one," smiled Tewodros, and the Fitaurari introduced him, triggering a gracious bow from the captain. "Please, join your men for lunch," said Tewodros. "I thank you for your valiant service. We will bring this Balcha to heel!"

The leaders rode on, and it was just when they reached the end of the line, looking down the long low cut of the ravine, when the men at the top of the hill sighted Ghannatu's horse. "The messenger has returned!" spoke Tewodros as their mounts wheeled. He was improving as a rider with every fall of the hoof. It was not until they had reached the brow of the hill that they saw the returning rider weirdly lolling to one side.

Again down the hill they rushed, and already the infantry had taken the horse's bridle and led it behind the lines, much hullabaloo in their wake. The man leading Ghannatu's horse shouted up with his left hand gesturing, "he has killed him!" There was a note stuffed into the ropes that lashed Ghannatu to the horse, saying that Balcha bows to none but Kassa, and Kassa is dead. All the joy of the day was sucked out of the air, and Tewodros with grim face gave a short command: "We will bury him in Magdala with my father."

Back in the general's tent, it was impossible to get the prince to hold his peace. "We cannot stand for this.

It is our comrade. It is an insult. Only a man with no justice would do nothing in the face of a crime like this. What kind of thug is this Balcha? We must teach him a lesson at once. Fitaurari, when can you marshal our troops to the attack? I want to march tonight."

Yohannes took advantage of the prince's pause for breath to caution, "You are playing exactly Balcha's game, Tewodros. He wants to draw you out in haste to improve his chances of defeating you."

"Why take the risk? Let him come when he comes," urged Tekle-giorgis. "Our position here is strong, and you know that Balcha has more men." As he finished speaking, a scout was ushered in and whispered in the Fitaurari's ear.

Tewodros clenched his jaw in frustration, but Tekle-giorgis' eyes widened as he relayed the scout's message to the group. "Tewodros, you will not have the decision to make. He comes now to the attack."

Tewodros exhaled as the adrenaline rushed through him, and immediately felt at a loss for what to do. Yohannes would certainly be no help now. His general, however, knew exactly how to take charge. "Bring my battle dress!" barked Tekle-giorgis, and in the chaos a soldier who happened to be nearby was pressed into service, a dour Amhara man named Eshetu. He was a lean, wiry man with darker skin than usual, accentuated by prematurely graying hair at the temples, and he hustled to return with a fine obsidian spear, leather tunic and shield. With this unsurprising gear, however, the soldier carried a headdress unlike any Tewodros had ever seen: a golden mass of flowing hair to surround one's face.

Fitaurari Tekle-giorgis donned the lion's mane, looking back with hard face and confident eyes to acknowledge Tewodros. "This soldier Eshetu can see to your attire as well. I go to gather the captains." With this he sallied forth.

Tewodros was taken and fitted for his own tunic, then given a spear and a shield, while voices rang out around the tent. The prince paused in expectation, his mouth seeming to form a question as the soldier sought to usher him out. "Yes, sir?" offered Eshetu.

"Is this all?" asked Tewodros. "There is no..." Tewodros indicated his head, but Eshetu did not understand. "I saw the Fitaurari had a headdress."

"Ah," the soldier smiled, and explained. "The Fitaurari faced down and killed that lion with his own hands, to win the mane he wears. It is a mark of one whose nobility and bravery are revered, and proven, that he can wear this to go to war." Tewodros instantly wanted this respect for himself, and burned with sheepishness as he followed Eshetu outside, without the power of the mane.

Tekle-giorgis had found a gathering point in the lee of the hill, where its shoulders formed a natural amphitheater. Here, the voices of the scouts would carry to brief the captains of what they had seen. The first scout gave an estimate of the number - Balcha's column was more than the Fitaurari's men by half. "How do they march?" asked Tekle-giorgis.

113

"A narrow column, very long," was the response.

"They know they will have trouble taking the high ground from us – Balcha moves as a spearhead to try to break right through the middle of our lines, in the valley," mused Tekle-giorgis. "It will present a smaller cross-section for rifle fire. Very clever."

"Balcha's camp has not been struck," spoke another scout who had ventured even further on his patrol.

"This means that Balcha expects a quick and decisive encounter," Tekle-giorgis told Tewodros. The scouts continued the briefing as the ratio of rifles to spears was wildly guessed at, and the colors of the cavalry's caparisons postulated as evidence of this or that troop or company being present, with their attendant reputation. The horses did not lead the infantry, suggesting either their reserve for a flanking maneuver that would be hard pressed to go uphill against Tekle-giorgis' right or left, or their employ as a backstop to goad an unwilling soldiery forward and chase down fleeing deserters. Either interpretation was a basis for confidence, but the flurry of information left Tewodros struggling to keep up.

When the scouts were done, the Fitaurari took over to confirm the plan of action. Tewodros listened intently as the orders were clinically given, and could see that the captains were similarly focused as they trusted their commander. There was none better to execute the military profession than my Fitaurari, he thought, and was surprised when Tekle-giorgis turned to him and asked if there was anything the general had missed. Tweodros' mind went blank for a moment, then his dreams from back in the cave flooded in and he felt it was his duty to address his troops; to inspire them with high words like those he had practiced over and over in his head for a moment like this. "Should I speak to the men?" he said in a low tone.

"This is a good idea," smiled Tekle-giorgis. "After all, they fight for you."

Tewodros replied, "No, they fight for each other and for Ethiopia," and turned to the captains lined up in front of him, pausing to take breath and meet their eyes, calling on the Holy Ghost to aid his declarations. "We fight for our empire, the worldly nation that makes us brothers, we who take up arms as brothers. Look now on the faces of your fellows. In days to come the hoar of age will steal the bloom of youth, and all of them shall die. But you knew them now, in this fine moment, at the peak of their glory, resplendent on their faces and their arms." Tewodros spoke in a rush, as those who had not yet learned the cadence of speaking to crowds. "And for some who die today their glory will remain undimmed in the memory of those who live to tell. And for those of us who live, the memory of our brothers shall be a strength in the failing of old age. For this time, this moment now, exists in all eternity. So let us now win eternal glory – Forward, men!" And his spear was thrust to heaven to lead them towards the battle line.

The captains broke into a run as they scattered to their units, some ululating, and the men in the lines responding, as they went. All of a sudden Yohannes was there at the prince's side, clapping him on the shoulder and congratulating him on the speech. "That was a good job, Tewodros. Now the men know that you are the true leader – and that they fight not just for the sake of fighting."

"I didn't know how those words would sound when I said them aloud, Yohannes," admitted the prince. They moved up the hill near the hot springs to join the banner of Tekle-giorgis, and his picked men. Now all eyes were on the column that could be clearly seen approaching, undulating like a snake through the rolling terrain. "He will not even attempt to parley," mused Yohannes. "See, the soldiers do not slow – they attack!"

"What cheek," remarked Tekle-giorgis, even as a great shout began to roll up from the advancing column. Tewodros was anxious, but offered his view, "we must fire before any charge gains momentum. If we break their confidence they will not fight as well."

"There will be no chance to treat if we shoot first," warned Yohannes.

"You yourself said he has not come to parley!" said Tewodros.

Teklegiorgis paused for the prince to change his mind, but Tewodros did not. "Then we will shoot," and as soon as Balcha's line was barely within range, he coldly gave the order. "Fire!" and the signal flags went up, and down the line started the crackle of the first volley and the puffs of white smoke blowing, repeated in a beautiful pattern with perfect timing.

Down in the center of the line, Eshetu had been assigned to the second volley. Though he saw the crumpling at the front of Balcha's column when the first bullets hit home, the enemy still came on relentlessly, and it was fear that caused him to sail his shot over the heads of the oncoming soldiers that now unslung their own rifles for return fire. From the back of Balcha's column the sound of the shouts surging from the enemy officers then reached Eshetu, as the order was given to press the charge.

Eshetu clumsily reloaded, almost dropping his rifle as he sensed a man fall to his right and a round pass somewhere to the left. The repeat of the alternate volley was reassuring as he rammed home his bullet, and the shouts from Balcha's column turned to screams for a moment. He aimed feverishly, this time picking out a man whose features he could not quite see and squeezing the trigger purposefully. The dark figure stumbled, but kept coming and Eshetu did not know if his shot had succeeded. There was no time to wonder or to think of the possibility that the same man would shoot back at him; Eshetu knew that the only way to get through the hell of combat was to focus on the one thing he could control, and the one job he had to do – reload, and fire. If every man around him had the same discipline, they had a good chance to prevail.

Though he stood out of harm's way, Tewodros felt the challenge presented by Balcha as aimed at him directly, and he must respond. Now was not the time for meekness. "However this is over, it must be over quickly," he said to his general. "We must do more than fire first. We must seize the initiative before he breaks through the line – let us send our best strike now to smash the side of his column – we will chop him in half, or drive him into the ravine. Then we fall back to the center to hold the valley, while those troops redeploy up this hill." The prince looked for a reaction from Tekle-giorgis – was his inexperience patent to the seasoned commander?

"You are right – if he breaks our line it will be too late to counter. Little did Balcha suspect you are more brazen than he!" grinned Tekle-giorgis.

Encouraged, Tewodros took an even bolder tack now. "Let me lead the charge down the hill! I want the men to see I am not afraid."

Tekle-giorgis just chuckled and shook his head. "There are other ways to inspire your subjects," was all he said, tapping his skull. "I will lead this charge myself," and he marshaled his picked men.

Tewodros chafed inwardly that he could not taste the action in person; that his boyhood dreams could not be tested against the real sound and fury of battle; but his mind calmed his heart as he knew the king must stay unharmed. Looking at the men who now followed his command, he felt a part of the action yet, and imagined that these soldiers here were his right arm, and those his left, and he clenched his hands to feel his muscles tense.

The obsidian spears clicked into place as one, the thousand points glinting in the sun. How could Balcha's soldiers see this and not tremble? The cadence was called and Tewodros watched, as the black-tipped death began its rush down the hill, even as the enemy column was closing to within fifty yards of the prince's center. The horses streamed down alongside, to distract Balcha's men and tempt them to take low-percentage pot-shots at the riders, while protecting Tekle-giorgis' flank from any of Balcha's cavalry that might detach from his rear. Now the engagement! Tewodros could feel its fury as the first spears were driven home.

The forward progress of Balcha's column slowed as Tekle-giorgis' men, as one fist, punched into its side. Almost like a black fluid, Tewodros watched his counter-attack trickle through Balcha's ranks, who in their confusion knew not whether to continue to press forward, or turn and face the new threat. Several hundred men ran towards the only open space they saw, and soon met the ravine while the troops on the second hill took heart and sent a force to cut them down. Tewodros' heart leapt as he heard the cries of that impromptu charge, what brave men they were.

Now the counter-attack was through the column and some thousand of Balcha's men were surrounded; trapped between the line they were charging, whose rifles were silenced to eliminate a stray round striking one of Tewodros' own men, but whose bayonets bristled; and the line of black spears now at their back. Tewodros saw them almost as one drop their weapons and raise their palms skyward, and a detachment from the center of his troops issued forth to take their surrender. Tekle-giorgis led the rest of the center up to reinforce the hill the prince still occupied, broad smiles on their faces to a man, of relief and of triumph.

"We have struck a blow! Do we finish them?" cried Tewodros.

Tekle-giorgis, seeing the surrender of the cut-off head, had already ordered the line of black spears to engage the rest of Balcha's column and reverse their charge. "See, they break and run," he said, as the swift turning of the tide had turned the hearts of Balcha's troops. "We have won for sure!" and almost as he said this, a white flag appeared amongst the officers at the rear of the foe.

The prince had not expected the battle to be over so quickly and felt the tremendous current of adrenaline drop out of him, leaving his hands shaking though he had been kept well back from the action. He hid them behind his back as the Fitaurari suggested he walk back to headquarters, while the captains carried out the instruction to secure prisoners, to wait for Balcha to come under his flag of truce and confirm the terms of surrender. There might yet be a ruse up Balcha's sleeve, though the victory had seemed decisive enough.

Tewodros waited for the Dedjazmatch in the commander's pavilion with mixed feelings. His rage and horror at seeing so much murder was focused on Ghannatu's killer, but Yohannes had spent a long harangue convincing the prince that to execute a defeated nobleman would forever leave the other rases with no choice but to fight to the death. "Remember what I said about vengeance – this time you must listen to me," his tutor had pushed, so Balcha would have to become his bedfellow. If he made the alliance,

Tewodros would be that much stronger to stand against Ras Makonnen and Ras Mulugeta.

Balcha stepped into the tent, and an afterglow of victory and the excitement to take the surrender of a vanquished foe coursed through Tewodros. The Rases took their time to size each other up. Balcha's gaze was shifty above his hunched shoulders, his eyes seeming to skim across Tewodros' face without ever stopping to meet the prince's fixed stare. The Dedjazmatch was not an imposing man, but had the air of someone who would slit your throat in a dark wood if you crossed him. His crime against Ghannatu added to the aura of fear and underneath it a sense of disgust, both of which the prince had to work mentally to cast aside. It was Tewodros' place to break the silence.

"Now will you bow to the throne's heir?" Tewodros' question rang out in a clear voice. Balcha genuflected, with his eyes cast to one side, and gave his assent. "I will support your claim to the kingdom, Ras Tewodros."

The next part made Tewodros feel somewhat queasy, but he had agreed the course with his council. "And will you further accept my patronage and serve me, as you served my father, as the Keeper of the Door?"

"Yes, most certainly I will continue as Dedjazmatch," replied Balcha, now facing Tewodros straight on but still, somehow, seeming to look from the corners of his eyes. "And, if it please my liege, now that we are joined together perhaps I can recruit some replacements from the men of this region for the troops I lost."

"There will be no replacement for the faithful Ghannatu," Tewodros could not resist saying. "In my army we will not abide such treatment of messengers," and this was all the castigation he could give to Balcha without letting his emotions master him. "For now, I see no need to swell our ranks, but let us go together to take a pledge from your men. I must insist on them giving their word to me directly, for each man should live by his own honor."

"Without honor, who can truly live?" agreed Balcha, the words somehow slimy in his speech.

After the pledge, with its shouting and firing of rounds in the air, the party began. "We do not feast because of any battles, but we will feast together to celebrate this new unity for the cause of a continuing and unified Ethiopia, under the son of King Kassa," proclaimed Tewodros. The men fired shots in the air, and the winners were able to join the losers to eat and drink and make merry for the night, and leave the questions of tomorrow for tomorrow. Raw beef was consumed in great quantities, and Tewodros saw men slip away one by one as they met the eyes of this woman from the camp followers, or danced energetically with that other one first. Though he felt the stirrings of some curiosity to join the others in search of gentler company, it was still a great unknown. He felt too bashful to strike up a conversation with any but his familiar fellowship of men, and preferred to relax. There had been enough that was new in his life.

# PART TWO:
# NAPIER'S ELEPHANTS

## Chapter One

*"The blood-dimmed tide is loosed..."*
*- YEATS*

Glendon waited nervously in the foyer of the opposition leader's London club. These exclusive temples of luxury and ease usually evoked a reaction of disgust in him, but that feeling was overcome by the prospect of a meeting with the fiery Gladstone, where there would be no Matthews to hide behind. The nerves were not helped by Gladstone's piercing stare when the two men were settled in overstuffed armchairs next to, but tilted towards each other. Gladstone did not drink and did not offer any refreshment to Glendon, his leonine head hanging heavy on a thick neck, the wild whiskers betraying a sense of the energy that lay beneath the surface. Another one who looks different than the vultures, Glendon thought. He looks like he has ideals.

"So, this cheeky African chap has called our bluff, I hear," Gladstone began, referencing the latest reports of the Ethiopians' defiance in the face of British threats of military intervention.

"It is no bluff, sir. The plan for the expedition is fully cooked. My superior arranged this meeting so I might have a chance to convince you of its merits."

"Yes, you want my support in Parliament for a cockamamie plan concocted by the master chefs of our esteemed conservative cabinet." Glendon's nerves frayed even more – this was not going well. "Are you a conservative?"

The question hung for a moment. "I prefer to remain unbiased to do my job in the best interest of the nation."

"I was Exchequer once, you know. I will enjoy seeing Mr. Disraeli's acrobatics to try and match my budget-balancing act with this slug of military expenses on his account. That's almost enough reason for me to support it." Gladstone grinned. "But tell me, why we are spending so much money on this particular expedition?"

Glendon had done his research, and knew Gladstone had a reputation as pro-free trade. "I think the more treaties we have the more commerce can flow freely, and increase the wealth of the many."

"Don't just tell me what the newspapers are saying – everyone knows I am for free trade. But I am also for emancipating the Irish, a better kind of freedom. To impose trade freedoms by the coercion of a gun, held to the head of another people? That would be a strange partnership of philosophies indeed."

"We are not the aggressor here. A foreign potentate has kidnapped Her Majesty's subjects!" Glendon pleaded.

"So you are protecting life and limb, not this bollocks about trade. And is there no diplomacy that can free these men? Can we not offer the Africans a lesser sum to let the hostages go, without risk to our soldiers?"

Glendon opened his mouth to explain that the conservatives wanted war for political gain, and quickly shut it again. He had promised Matthews not to share anything he knew from being present in the cabinet sessions. "I was given direction by my superiors and this is the strategy. I only seek to carry it out as best I can."

"But you are here, to put it bluntly, because you want to be in my government if I become Prime Minister."

Glendon did not bother denying it; Gladstone saw through him so well. He felt himself drawn to the figure that even in an armchair projected strength, perhaps as much as he was under Disraeli's spell in that cabinet meeting.

"I suppose that means you think the liberals have a chance of winning. That's good, at least," Gladstone continued. "So tell me, what is it you hope to get from this expedition?"

Now Glendon could work from the notes he had memorized. Perhaps Gladstone was done toying with him. "To be honest, I think we have a chance to expand our presence in Africa. I think the continent will grow in importance and we will be ahead of the rest of Europe if we plant a foothold in Ethiopia. The sheer scale of necessary supplies and armaments calls for construction of a port facility and rail line to the interior. This will not only facilitate our troop movements in the near term, but our resource extraction in the future." Gladstone seemed to be nodding along and Glendon took a deep breath. Might as well go for broke. "In the end, the expedition may well lead to colonization. I believe that is a strong possibility."

"Did you not hear what I said about the Irish? About taking people's freedom?"

Glendon was taken aback at the look on Gladstone's face, almost of disgust, and sank back into his chair. "As a colony, we would bring progress to Ethiopia," he protested. "We would make institutional improvements to their government. They aren't like us – like the Irish – we have seen already how despotic this King of Kings can be."

"Our burden to bring them progress, is it?" sneered Gladstone. "I struggle with this notion even in the colonies we have in Asia, and elsewhere in Africa. But Ethiopia is a Christian kingdom, white skin or not! When we attempt this sort of imposition on believers, we get America – we get Ireland. God cannot be on our side when we seek to be masters of our Christian brethren."

"They are not of the same faith our Queen defends," objected Glendon, his voice reedier and querulous. "If we open the country to our mutual commercial benefit, surely we will also open them to the spiritual benefit of the missionaries that are sure to follow."

"Are they not Coptic Christians like those in Egypt? I am against the oppression of the Catholics in Ireland; how much more should I advocate for these Copts who stand together with us against the arrogance of the papists!" Gladstone did not move from his chair, but his eyes flashed and it seemed he was haranguing Glendon from a pulpit standing six feet above. "The Alexandrian See is as old as Rome, and their legitimacy only benefits the Church of England. Our faith is better served by ecumenical relations with the Coptic bishops, than the bleating of any ragged missionary that might travel to Ethiopia." He settled back down, and looked into the fireplace as a befuddled Glendon had nothing to say.

"My apologies – you have awoken a passion of mine and I am sure our discussion has taken a turn you did not expect."

"I am only discouraged that this expedition does not have your support," said Glendon. "I only hope that you continue to consider its merits." With this he took his leave, Gladstone's detachment a signal the interview was over, Glendon unsure if he had shot himself in the foot if should the liberals soon lead the government. Bloody Matthews and his brilliant suggestions.

## Chapter Two

In Ethiopia, the morning after the Balcha victory was the first day of court for Tewodros, and with his blood raised by that first battle, he had only thoughts of brazen war against Ras Mulugeta, and victorious charges of horse. His mind ached with the dullness of the property disputes to which he was expected to pay attention, as the font of justice. The camp remained in Sodere but would have to move soon, before the weight of so many soldiers exhausted the peasants' resources.

Tewodros felt his head nod just as the testimony of a cloudy-eyed ancient man as to the memory of a boundary line was interrupted for a lunch recess. "I must stretch and walk," the prince declared, and brought Yohannes with him.

As they strolled among the lanes of the camp's impromptu marketplace, the smells and flies of butcher's stalls about them, Tewodros pushed again for the steps that had already been voted down by his council. "But don't you think, Yohannes, that a quick and decisive attack against Mulugeta would turn him to our side just as Balcha saw the reasonable course?"

"Remember, it was Balcha who attacked you," sighed Yohannes, "and his brashness failed. You cannot rule this whole great empire by force alone, even if you are so lucky in all your battles."

The prince was silent, his mouth working a bit as he struggled to think of a new argument. He had none as they returned to take their mid-day bread. Back to court again as the meal was cleared away, Tewodros groaned inwardly to see the old man on his walking stick feel his way back to the witness stand through his cataracts.

"I don't care if the banana tree was replanted in a different place!" he felt like shouting, when actual shouts began to rise from outside the tent. Tewodros sat straight up when the village headman forced his way in with a bleeding man.

"Bind his wound, now, call the surgeon," cried Tekle-giorgis quickly. "What has happened?"

"We entreat you, before there is another attack, let Ras Tewodros consider using his rifles to aid us," said the headman with head tilted and hands clasped in supplication. "This is the second man savaged by the same lioness. She has been taking our cattle too, one here, one there for six months now."

The bleeding man spoke shrilly as the surgeon arrived to dress the dripping gash on his arm. "I saw her in the field right before she pounced, a big lioness. I looked at her right in the eyes, a killer's eyes, but she left me there just as if I were a fly brushed out of the way. I must have been blocking where she wanted to go, but I don't know, I don't know. The lioness went to the south, back up to the higher land."

"We will send a hunting party," said Tewodros. "Do not worry, you will be rid of this pest." The brief excitement was shuffled out and the court proceedings resumed, with Tewodros even less able to pay attention now. Finally, he determined that the banana tree was an inferior marker of the property line to the boulder, and it was deemed too late to begin another case that day.

"I suppose being king is more of this court-sitting than the riding and the traveling," he remarked to Yohannes as the two sat with Tekle-giorgis for some tejj at the downing of the sun. The social ease was not there yet with Balcha, and Tewodros preferred to save the necessary effort of engaging with the other noblemen for another day.

"If you rule with justice, the people will love you," replied Yohannes. "That is better than having fun, I think."

A pause followed, as Tewodros thought of the fun of other youths that he would never share, but did not voice his reflection. "Listen, Yohannes, I want to do something, and it will be good for me to get away from all of this duty upon duty for a while – I need some space to breathe and think."

Yohannes smiled inwardly – one session of administrative work and the young prince was ready for a vacation; but Tewodros had been through much in the past few days. "That I think would be wise. A man needs to meditate from time to time," agreed Yohannes.

"I want to go and kill this lion," said Tewodros.

"Um," said Yohannes.

"Look, the men in this army only know me as my father's son. You've seen how they follow the Fitaurari when he wears the lion's mane! I need to prove myself to them."

"Killing an animal to win glory is less than noble," protested Yohannes.

"Better than killing men to earn respect," was the retort.

Tekle-giorgis entered the fray to mediate. "I think Tewodros is right. The prince needs some time to clear his head, and the hunting party will head south to try and find this lioness. Let Tewodros slip out of the camp on his own tonight, with none but this group knowing it, and he can perchance meet the lioness first and judge for himself if he likes his odds with rifle and spear against the beast." Yohannes looked like he wanted to tear the Fitaurari's head off.

"One of my aides, Daniel, is an expert tracker; he will go with Tewodros and be able to advise on a safe course of action in the event."

"Done!" cried the delighted Tewodros, with a grin that could not be resisted. "I will leave as soon as the stars come out, and make sure that nobody sees me go. Give me four days for the trip, and make excuses that I am ill and wish to see nobody but you two."

And so it was that Tewodros and Daniel were beyond the sentries, having walked through the wee hours until they were together alone on the plateau while a chill hung in the air and the fingers of dawn had yet to uncurl. This was the first time in his life that only one other human being was within earshot, and when they sat down to rest, the silence boomed across the hills.

When the sun came up the men trudged with heads down looking for the spoor of a lioness, as Daniel had instructed Tewodros. The prince had to work hard to keep up with his guide, a hardened man of the back country with a sunburned yet honest face, and muscles like springy cords, not so big but tough as a piece of dried meat, and never seeming to tire.

Several times what Tewodros supposed to be lion-bent grasses or interesting droppings were confirmed in curt tones by Daniel to be the work of deer or mule, and any spark of excitement quenched. Other than those interactions, there was only quiet and thought. At first Tewodros found his mind consumed by the past, of who sent the assassin to the cave; how his brother monks were faring; how stupid he looked falling off the horse; and who had killed his father. Is this what life has to give? Must I wait for the hereafter to find what I seek, though I know not what that is?

These thoughts came, but they bounced off the indomitable vigor of youth, and the prince answered himself. No, I will make good things from my lot, and I will seek to be a great king. He began to turn over more and more the questions of the future, of how many men were in Makonnen's army; how he could delegate certain judicial functions; and where they would move next after Sodere. When he became conscious that he had moved on in this way, the prince deemed it a good thing.

Eventually all his musings were dulled by the midday sun, even as it brightened the unyielding terrain they ceaselessly criss-crossed. Perhaps by now the hunting party had already found and killed the blasted lioness.

Perhaps not. "Sir!" called Daniel and waved Tewodros over to where he was looking down intently, and then squatted. "There were two lions here – they lay together. They are not long gone – I can still smell the musk." Tewodros could smell nothing. Daniel looked up at him. "The smaller one has gone that way, in the direction of the hunting party," he pointed. "I think they may catch it."

"Then let us follow the bigger lion," said Tewodros, and all the rest of the day as Daniel flitted from paw-print to the latest shrub that had been marked as territory, he could think of nothing but heroic encounters where he, the prince, defeated the animal with feats of strength and derring-do.

"He is moving fast," said Daniel. Good, Daniel calls it a male, thought Tewodros, and it will have a mane. The tracker continued, "we will not catch him tonight, but I see a herd of gazelle over there. Perhaps we can eat meat when we rest. If we are even lucky, they gather because of a watering hole."

Tewodros strained his eyes and saw the black dots grazing where Daniel pointed. "Those biscuits we packed do leave something to be desired," agreed the prince. In their limited conversation, Tewodros had found out Daniel was his Christian name, taken at his adult baptism. The guide was from Borana in the far south, where a youth of following cattle and finding water had inculcated his skills.

"It is good I brought my bow," said Daniel. "If the lion hears our rifle he may not stop to sleep in this range. When he lies down and sleeps, it may be for many hours and that is our chance to catch him." Tewodros followed the guide as he spoke and soon was keeping low and swinging around to upwind of the herd. The men crept closer to the animals slowly and with bated breath; two hours seeming to pass in an instant as their focus and excitement never waned. At last Daniel drew the bow, then relaxed the string and offered Tewodros the shot.

The prince's hand hesitated – he did not want to be responsible for missing dinner. Nonetheless he grabbed the bow, sighted on a near gazelle and slowed his breathing. In an instant the gazelle raised its head, horns outlined against the sky, knowing something was watching it. The entire herd tensed as Tewodros loosed the whistling arrow, punching into the hindquarters of his mark.

In a flash the gazelles were off, darting and zagging away with the limping victim left pitifully behind. The men whooped and hollered, taking mere seconds to run down their prey, circling its last defiant stand before Daniel rushed in with his blade.

Once the blood was drained from the neck, and Daniel drank some where Tewodros refrained, the guide draped their supper over his shoulders like a classic shepherd and the men made for the lee of an outcropping where they might have their camp.

"Will a fire not reveal our position?" asked Tewodros as Daniel began to gather brush.

"To whom?" laughed Daniel. "There are no shifta in this area." The bandits that stalked more well-traveled routes would find poor business in such highlands.

"You are right," Tewodros grinned. "Let me help dig the pit." Soon the flint was struck and the dry wood crackling, and the only thing missing in all the world was a thimble of tejj. As the gazelle cooked on its spit, the little fat that dripped made hissing noises in the fire, and they talked of what else but lion. "How many have you hunted, Daniel? What was the best kill that you saw?" asked Tewodros.

Daniel replied, "I have not kept count, and every kill shows bravery and strength in its own way. I cannot take the clean shot from fifty meters over the struggle at close quarters with a spear. But there was one man I knew who lived outside the walls of a village in the south and could speak with lions – that was the most impressive."

"A lion tamer?" asked Tewodros. "You saw this?"

"With my own eyes," continued Daniel. "Sometimes he would put on his little circus for a group of travelers – with his whip he could make the lion sit down, or stand up and jump over a large barrel. He had two animals he would call and they would come if they were nearby; solitary males who had made their territory in the area."

Tewodros was imagining the spectacle with wide eyes, the flicker of the cooking fire dancing in his pupils. "A lion tamer."

Daniel carried on, "Of course he fed the lion treats if it performed the trick – just like training any animal. And he always gave them food at the beginning so they would not be hungry for the spectators. I asked him afterwards and he told me, even he could not tame a lion who had tasted humans, because once a lion is a maneater it will eat more and must simply be killed."

"This I have heard," said Tewodros. "Did this man have some special power – you say he could speak with the animals?"

"That I am not sure," said Daniel. "He told me it was very easy to tame the lone males, as long as they were not in a pride and had no others to protect, and as long as you fed them well, for they are lazy beasts if they can be. In fact he said all it takes is confidence, and if you hit the lion when you first meet him, he will know you are the boss," chuckled Daniel. "I don't know, he sounded like he could speak with them when he made the noises like a lion, but maybe that was just for show. I don't know if they have their own language."

"Just act like the boss and they will think you are the boss! I like it," said Tewodros. He glanced back at the meal over the fire. "Look, I think the meat has cooked."

"Yes, it is good now. Not too overdone," Daniel moved the spit and took his knife once the meat had cooled enough to cut, the aroma tempting him the while.

"I have never tried gazelle before," remarked Tewodros as he tore off his first bite of tough, dry meat. His jaw soon ached but at least the charred gristle was delicious, and filling. Tewodros could not remember the exact moment when his happiness was subsumed by blissful sleep on the hard earth.

When he awoke, Daniel had devised an ingenious pouch from the gazelle's hide, to carry some dressed meat with them. There was practically no camp to strike; only muscles to stretch before setting off while the morning star was still visible, picking up an easy stride to rejoin the lion's track where they had left off for yesterday's gazelle hunt. In the cave he was responsible for chores and lessons, and as crown prince for so much more, but for this trek he was completely free and he relished every moment.

They were back into the rhythm of Daniel's tracking, and Tewodros' mind was blank when he looked up from his feet succeeding one after the other, and saw that the morning light touched the tops of the far mountains. A peace transcending his understanding came upon the prince. His thoughts of yesterday became conversations with God today, giving thanks for the biscuits in his belly; asking wisdom for the choices he faced; praising how the Lord gaveth his victory in battle but took away Ghannatu.

"A fresh one," commented Daniel in lower tones than usual as they came upon a pile of scat. They paused for a moment and contemplated the rise to their left, some boulders to the right and what seemed to be the tops of some trees over the rise. "It could be that he was sleeping here and has gone to the woods now that the sun makes it too hot," whispered Daniel. "We are downwind, thank goodness."

They crawled on their bellies slowly to the top of the rise, Tewodros on tenterhooks and ready at any second to leap up and run, or shoot, or both. The view from the top was through some tufts of dry grass, down towards the wood.

There he stood, facing away from the men, tail twitching away some flies, perchance lazily watching a movement of some tree-dweller. He was magnificent. Nearly ten feet long, his tawny coat was healthy, but showed the taut musculature underneath. The most striking feature of this king of the beasts was his black mane.

Tewodros was mesmerized by the power of this animal. His absorption was only interrupted when Daniel prodded a rib, to hand him a cocked rifle with a curt nod. Tewodros looked at the instrument of death in his hand and then, as if still in a dream, he turned to Daniel. "Does not this lion look full to you?" he said beneath his breath, indicating the distended belly of the beast.

Daniel nodded. "I want to try and tame it," said Tewodros, and looking back towards the animal, almost to himself, he continued, "if God is truly with me in this course, he will show it by protecting me. I still want you to cover me, of course," Tewodros managed a grin, and handed the rifle back to Daniel.

Daniel looked at him in shock with extended arm to take back the rifle, and the lion looked around, then lifted its paws one by one to turn around and face the two men, lifting its head with a slight snarl. Tewodros took his spear and his hunk of gazelle meat and moved slowly down towards the lion, never breaking contact with the cat's eyes, and praying, "I know I should not test you Lord, but I need a sign from you." Daniel's hands behind him trembled, aiming the rifle between those same eyes. Tewodros breathed slowly, deliberately. Any time a seed of doubt crept into his thoughts, Tewodros banished it by whispering, "I have faith. I have faith." He paused three paces from the lion, which had not budged, and stood still, speaking to it in measured tones.

"You are too noble to shoot in cold blood. I am Tewodros, heir to the empire of Ethiopia, and I will have kings serve me. I will have you serve me, my black-maned lion, and they will know I am master of beasts and men." His heart pounded so hard he thought his ears would burst, but he kept his breathing deep and slow. Tewodros reached out with the haunch of gazelle and dropped it in front of the lion. "Eat! I will feed you from now on and you will not need to hunt, or go hungry. Or eat me!"

The lion looked down at the meat, looked up at Tewodros, and took a step in the prince's direction, raising a giant paw. Daniel's finger fluttered on the trigger but Tewodros immediately smacked the lion across the nose with the haft of the spear. The beast stepped back, lowered its head and gobbled up the gazelle. The prince's eyes were so wide he might never blink again, but Tewodros once more reached out, albeit slowly, to bury his hand in the fluffy mane, and relief flooded in with a smile when the lion glanced up and kept eating. "Daniel, he is not hungry for humans," he called out. "Bring me rope." Daniel approached cautiously, his rifle in one hand and rope in the other, and the lion took two small steps back, growling while watching him. "He is a friend," said Tewodros, placing a tense hand on Daniel's arm. He took the rope from Daniel, who went back to training his rifle, and approached the lion.

The beast bared its teeth, but at once Tewodros gestured with the spear as if to smack it again and the lion stood down. "No!" he wagged his finger. "Daniel is a friend, but we must keep you on the leash for our journey." The lion was cowed and sat meekly as Tewodros tied the rope around its neck. "Good boy," he continued. "Let's see – I will call you Judah!" He fed his lion Daniel's portion of the leftover meat, as Judah could never be too full. Tewodros looked back at Daniel and laughed, "it is just a matter of confidence, my friend!"

"He is a lion-tamer," said Daniel in awe. "It is no wonder this will be the king." Yet he still insisted on walking behind with rifle unslung as the men and lion began their walk back to Sodere. With some coaxing from Tewodros and tugs at the rope, the lion would walk beside the prince and keep pace; a constant companion and concern.

The monk and the general back at camp were not expecting the prince to return until the next day, especially as the hunting party had already come in with the dead vermin to please the villagers, having found the man-eating lioness not too far away. Yohannes had told Tekle-giorgis, "it is good that the prince has this time away," and Tekle-giorgis replied, "yes, although a shame he could not be here to receive the villagers' thanks for ridding them of this pest." Yohannes was relieved that his young master had not been the one to run into the lioness and taken it on. There were still a host of other disasters that could befall Tewodros, and the next day could not come too soon to ease Yohannes' worry.

But it was that same evening, in the gloaming when the dark was chasing the west, that Tewodros appeared. He and Daniel were not alone.

"And what rough beast is this?" whispered Yohannes, as the villagers and soldiers fell back, nay sprang back to make way for the prince. The men all around could scarce believe the power that Tewodros seemed to have over this fearsome animal, and if any had doubted the unproven prince as too young to lead, they now had a measure of respect and a sense of deference that was greater than any that Tewodros could have earned by participating in the battles that any man could be a part of. He was now a man apart, as a king should be.

## Chapter Three

Gladstone felt Glendon depart and checked his watch, a heavy disk on a stout chain that always slipped down into the pocket of his waistcoat instead of hanging smartly like silver bunting. It was nearly time if he wanted to catch the next train to spend the weekend at Fasque, his father's estate, and he did want to get there for supper. He looked up to see a man in a bowler hat, quickly doffed.

"Might I have a word, Mr. Gladstone," the man spoke.

Gladstone thought he had seen the man around the clubs before, usually talking to one member of parliament or another. "I have a train to catch."

"I represent the Suez Shipping House – one might accurately say a subsidiary of the East India Company. I understand you may take an interest in this Ethiopia matter that has been in the papers, and I am hoping to have the opportunity to impress upon you the importance to Britain's commercial interests of gaining access to Ethiopia's resources; even of controlling its position on the Red Sea."

"How did you get in here?" demanded Gladstone, marching past him and out the door. He did not think of the man again until he was settled on the train, riding the railway he had helped to champion into existence; the wheels trundling comfortably underneath his compartment, and the yellow of the rapeseed flowers interrupting the otherwise dreary passing fields on the way to the West Country. Most of the lobbyists he encountered were much less brazen, and now that he held such a high position, those who approached him had become considerably more servile.

"Blast," he muttered to the window. These conservative fools had started an initiative that would be extremely difficult to derail. Gladstone fully expected the liberals to take the majority in the election, and now it seemed the actual folly of this expedition would play out on his watch. The private interests would never let go of an opportunity to have extractive infrastructure built in Africa entirely at the expense of the public purse. Much as he would rather get a treaty quickly in place and support the Ethiopians in a strategic manner, politically he could not be seen as open to negotiations with a head of state who was accused of kidnapping British diplomats, and lampooned as a savage. That Glendon fellow had made a decent argument, and Gladstone felt a twinge that perhaps he had given the young man too rough a go of it.

His thoughts churning as the train fled the approaching dusk, Gladstone could not take his typical nap on the journey and arrived at the station more irritable than usual. As he approached the gate of his father's house a carriage issued forth and passed him in the twilight, two men in bowler hats staring dispassionately at him through its windows.

He was at least in time for supper, fresh venison this evening from the estate, and a warm candle-lit glow at the family table. "Would you pass the claret," asked his sister Helen, as Gladstone was peering through the decanter at its clarity.

Gladstone obliged. "How is business, father?"

"Good for now – the price of sugar is rising just as my latest cargo arrives from the West Indies. I shall have to consider how long the captain should lay offshore before coming in to Liverpool."

"Beware you not end up a speculator."

"What I am wary of is your kind and their inclination to remove the tariffs that protect our planters in Barbados."

Gladstone was well aware that his father's mercantile success had put him in the funds and position to launch his political career, and was grateful. But he always made the same point: "You know that my loyalty must lie with the public interest in matters of trade policy."

"The public is a base bedfellow," was the retort. "We will simply have to diversify away from the sugar trade."

"Father had visitors today," said Helen, always on hand to help her father steer the conversation in the right direction, and returned to sipping her claret.

"Yes, who were those men? I saw them leaving as I arrived."

"Suez Shipping House," said the senior Gladstone.

"Curious. They tried to see me today as well. What did they want from you?"

"They want to see if I would enter the East Indian trade, as a partner in a new mercantile venture. It's a bet on whether the Suez canal becomes the primary trading route. The opportunity would be worth millions."

"Did they make mention of the Red Sea at all? Of the countries around it?"

"No, no. But I'm not surprised they came to see you. These are your new constituents, William. These corporations are not going away, and the more you embrace their rise, the more you will be at the forefront of Parliament for years to come."

"Why even have a Parliament, then? Let the shareholders of the trading companies rule England!"

"Now, William, Father is only making a point," said Helen. "I know you are some sort of liberal, but the aristocracy has ruled England for centuries and we have done just fine. They are the wiser guide of the people, after all, and they are disappearing. Perhaps the power of the trading companies can be a replacement."

Gladstone pushed his plate away. Sometimes the compulsions of filial piety were too much to bear, especially when his father made a good point. Idealism could only carry one so far. At least here, he thought as he drained his glass, he could act in the name of free trade, and this Ethiopian nonsense might yet honor his father's interests at the same time.

In Buckingham Palace, Victoria was soon after to note that the expedition had sailed through

Parliament. Those men do love to play at war, she thought.

In India, the Viceroy sat in his splendid sanctuary, shielded that day from the heat by a fanning servant, and from the horrors of petty decision-making by his myriad clerks. Even they could not keep this particular communiqué from arriving on his desk, and he was forced to summon his military liaison. James Firth took himself far too seriously, from the impeccably pressed khakis to his belief that the civil service he performed was akin to the work of an archangel. The Viceroy was displeased at Firth's easy manner, as if he belonged in a room with the most powerful man on the subcontinent, and spoke of the expedition in tones as clipped as a telegram to get rid of Firth as soon as possible. "We need Napier. Arrange a meeting soonest."

"I believe he's off shooting tiger, sir," was the aggravating response.

"Well bloody well go and get him, then!"

## Chapter Four

Tewodros strolled all the way to the king's pavilion and beamed proudly as he ruffled the black mane of the lion he was leading. As if on cue, Judah yawned, revealing epic canines, and followed up with a rumbling purr in the hush. "I've had to feed him all my meat to make sure he wasn't too hungry to meet you!" said Tewodros, laughing. "Let's find him a cage to sleep in, and then I'm famished."

The meal devolved into a council when the food was done, as decisions had to be made. "It's settled," said Balcha, "we move next to the northeast, in the direction of the capital but with several places to stop and spend some time along the way. I say we cannot enter Magdala until the succession is resolved."

"Yes, that is the question, isn't it," said Tewodros. "What is our next move in this regard?"

Tekle-giorgis was the first to speak. "I see we have come to politics. Here I cannot help you," he declared, sat back and crossed his arms across his chest. No more was heard from that general.

"Our first step must be to invite Makonnen and Mulugeta to submit to you," said Yohannes. "Perhaps they do not have such an appetite to risk division of the empire," and here Yohannes did not look in Balcha's direction.

"We must still have a plan for what to do if they do not submit," Balcha pointed out. "You speak of division as a bad thing, yet would Tewodros be content with ruling the western marches and leaving the north to Mulugeta, and the nomad's marches to Makonnen?" and here he looked at Tewodros.

"For my part," spoke the prince, "I have no problem with engaging the other rases in battle so that the winner can have Ethiopia as the prize. I will not let the empire simply fall apart that we have shed blood to build. I agree with Yohannes that the first step is to seek a peaceful submission. It is better to master these powerful men as I mastered my new lion. However, I fear I cannot take the same approach – if I simply ask them to submit to me, they will surely say no."

"As a recipient of that same question, I agree that saying yes was not even a thought that crossed my mind," said Balcha.

"So I will ask them to submit to something greater than me," continued Tewodros.

Yohannes had been feeling somewhat marginalized when his advice was contradicted by Balcha, but now began to see something new stirring in the prince. His pupil had graduated beyond his tutelage, and the old tutor had a feeling that he would be proud of what Tewodros did next.

"Is it not true that when my father became the king of kings, he sent for the head of the church to obtain his blessing?" asked Tewodros.

"Yes, it is true," replied Balcha. "The Abuna sent his blessing to your father. He felt that asking the head of the church to endorse his reign would add legitimacy in the eyes of the people and the other nobles, as well as show his faith and devotion to God. But remember, he did not claim a divine right to rule over Ethiopia from the beginning – it was his defeat of the other rases by showing force that gave him the right to rule. The Abuna was just...decoration," Balcha concluded.

"I will not seek to use force against the rases," said Tewodros. "Neither will I claim that God has given me a right to rule, as I am no better than other men. Instead I will submit myself to a higher power – call it justice, or law, or call it the power of God. I will ask the Abuna, the bishop of the Orthodox Church, to decide the succession for Ethiopia. This will be an institution I create, divinely inspired but an impartial way to ensure that I do not force Ethiopia to accept my rule, but I accept the commission to be Ethiopia's servant if her religious leaders ask it of me. And if the Abuna's blessing is upon me, Makonnen and Mulugeta dare not risk going against the Church. They will have no legitimacy in the eyes of the people if they do so."

"And what if the Abuna is against you?" asked Yohannes.

"Who is wiser than Christ's vicar on earth to judge whether I should rule?" was Tewodros' response. And Yohannes was proud of him.

There was one hiccup, or depending on how it was viewed, a fortunate circumstance. The old Abuna, the same that had blessed Kassa, had passed away the previous year and the replacement had not yet come from Alexandria, the seat of the Coptic church. Each

Abuna was appointed for a life term, but when one passed away it sometimes took months for word to reach Egypt, then more time for the Alexandrian see to identify and confirm a successor, and the return voyage of the next Abuna might bring him to Ethiopia after a full year of interregnum.

"The last I heard when I left Magdala, the new Abuna was not yet en route," Balcha said.

"This solves one problem, which is that any claim of the Abuna being in anybody's pocket will be much more difficult," Yohannes pointed out. "Nobody could have bribed him before he even arrives."

Tewodros was quick to seize on this. "Indeed, if the Abuna is to be viewed as impartial, how much more would his imprimatur on the succession be acceptable if he signs and seals the decision before he leaves Cairo? Let us send directly to Alexandria for a decision on who should be king."

Although Tekle-giorgis could see that the prince's plan of action was already irreversible, he had a word of caution to add. "Even though going by land is a better route than the Red Sea, it is easily some weeks' journey just to reach the first cataract. After that I think the Nile is navigable, but do we expect the others to sit and wait for months?"

"The quicker the better," said Tewodros. "But you are right. You must find me a place to easily defend myself while we await the Abuna, and hope that Makonnen and Mulugeta will be content to wait as well." A message went swiftly in three directions, the first carefully phrased to ask Alexandria to send the new Abuna forthwith with a bull to bless the succession of Kassa's son, or an alternative regent to the throne of Ethiopia, and the next two to ask each of Makonnen and Mulugeta to accept the process for defusing the power struggle. It would be expected that Makonnen and Mulugeta would send their own arguments to the Egyptian Copts, but Tewodros took heart that an Egyptian might be counted on best to select the most stable outcome for Ethiopia in order to minimize interference with the Nile. For the Egyptians, the politics of Ethiopia needed to be as predictable as possible, so they could be trusted to manage the river that brought life to the deserts of Egypt, and nothing was more predictable than a strong, stable emperor that the Abuna could keep an eye on. In light of this the prince had no second thoughts whether the Abuna's decision would be right for his people. Whether the plan would work against his rivals was another question.

The first answer to that question came quite quickly. Displaying the same lack of desire for a violent engagement as he had shown when Kassa marched on the north, Mulugeta seemed thoroughly tamed by Tewodros' insistence on the Abuna's blessing. A message came back from him in which he made it clear that he viewed Tewodros' action as a significant concession and a guarantee that the prince would not act with impunity if he became the emperor. "If Ras Tewodros is under God and law," it was written in the old man's own spidery hand, "I will feel at ease being under Ras Tewodros." Mulugeta, not entirely lacking in guile, also informed Tewodros that he had sent his own messenger to Egypt to clarify his conditions for endorsement of the succession process, and verify the message from Tewodros that the Alexandrian See had been asked to decide.

"Congratulations!" Yohannes told Tewodros. "Your first maneuver has brought the Qenazmatch Mulugeta to your side. But I am afraid Ras Makonnen is now in a corner."

"How so?" asked Tewodros.

"If he ever wants a chance to rule, he has to act now to change the game. You will have to watch him most carefully."

"But Yohannes, this is good training," said Tewodros. "I know I have to come to terms with looking over my shoulder for the rest of my life."

Yohannes wasn't quite sure how Tewodros had managed to look on the bright side and sound so cynical at the same time. He was glad nonetheless that the waiting of the next few months would give Tewodros plenty of opportunity to prepare mentally for many of the new challenges they might face. Things had been happening far too quickly up to this point.

## *Chapter Five*

It was time for milking, and Haymanot took the gourd her grandmother had washed, kissing the old woman on the cheek as she passed through the door on her way to the corral where her father would have penned in the plump cow, their pride and joy and most valuable possession. She sang as she walked, a lilting tune that skipped in perfect thirds up and down as the mountains ran in every direction around her. The ground was rough but she glided nonetheless, approving of the fresh green grass that showed the drought had spared them this year.

There was Papa, perhaps getting a little bit shorter with age but his back straight as ever, opening the gate to let her in before he moved on to turn the soil in the field over there. "You are too good, too pretty and too intelligent to be sitting here milking the cow," he nagged Haymanot as he did every other day. "When we save enough money," but he always stopped there as he did not know what Haymanot could do with the means to leave the village, only that something better must exist beyond his ken.

"You know I am happy here, Papa," she scolded him back. "What more do I need in life than a home, a hot meal every night and honest work for my family?"

"As long as you are happy," he seemed convinced and wandered off as the bees hummed and there was no hurry to the day.

Haymanot pulled the udder rhythmically, her hands incredibly strong but still womanly with long

157

fingers and shapely nails that belied her hard work. "You are peaceful today, Moonie," she called the cow, on account of its She had never lied to her father, and though she wondered sometimes what there was in the wide world, it was true that she would be content becoming her grandmother. A practical woman is a good woman. She thought she had read that in the book of Proverbs once. In fact it said wife, but she had yet to find a boy in the village that measured up to her – some were tall enough, but none were clever enough.

The last of the milk hissed into the gourd and Haymanot licked a warm drop where it had splashed on her hand. She could almost taste the lush grass, and knew from the flavor of the milk if Moonie was well fed. She gave the cow a slap and hoisted the gourd up and on to the cloth on her head. "You never had to marry, Moonie, and you're no less of a woman. Who needs a husband anyway?"

She didn't need to sing on the walk home as the bright sun made the whole of nature into a symphony around her.

*Chapter Six*

Tewodros' camp had settled down into a large valley with ample lines of supply that could sustain them until a messenger, or the Abuna himself, was expected from Egypt. The days blurred into a long agony of waiting, until distraction from the prince's quiet stalemate came in the form of Ras Makonnen's maneuvers.

The hills to the north were a pleasant backdrop to the weekly meetings that Tewodros now liked to take outdoors, with his senior advisors. Tewodros settled onto his three-legged stool; simply, roughly carved in one piece from a local bole and the preferred seat of the prince for its lack of pretense. "What news have we this week?" he intoned, watching the shadows scud across the hills as the clouds blew along in the fair sky.

A scout was brought who had come down from those same hills to give his report. "It appears that Makonnen has mobilized most, if not all of the forces available to him," he said calmly. "They are making a beeline for the other side of that ridge," the scout pointed. "At their current pace they could arrive in three days." Agitation ensued.

"This is how the Grazmatch responds to your message, Tewodros! Can you stand by and watch him?" goaded Balcha.

Yohannes tried to counter, "perhaps he is just taking insurance. If the Abuna rejects your succession, he will be ready to defend himself from the possibility of your resorting to force."

"Yes, but if the Abuna accepts Tewodros, he will also have taken a good position to launch his own aggression!" cried Tekle-giorgis. "We must prepare our own contingencies before Makonnen gains the advantage."

Tewodros looked around, at Balcha almost smirking; and Tekle-giorgis' frustration showing on his face to the same extent Yohannes' showed worry. "If the Abuna rejects my succession I will gladly hand the throne to Makonnen," he said clearly. "If I cannot abide by the rules of succession I claim to have committed to, I will have no honor, and you know what I have said to my men about honor."

He continued despite Balcha's spluttering. "We must make no sign that Makonnen can interpret as hostile. We keep the same staggered pickets we have been running around the camp, but we instruct the men that there will be no skirmishes – they are only to fall back to warn us of an attack. There will be no offensive, but we shall be ready to raise a well-ordered defense. Tekle-giorgis, I want you to make the camp impregnable."

"We will be digging trenches come tomorrow," replied the Fitaurari. "But Makonnen will see it," he warned.

"Let him see it and think twice before he tries anything," said Tewodros. "Anyway, nobody could view a trench as anything but defensive." The prince retired for the night at his customary time, but it was some hours before he slept.

In the morning Dawit, the lieutenant in charge of duty assignments for the northwest camp quadrant, a slight and brainy fellow with little penchant for violence, was going down the row of sleeping tents. He stopped at the fourteenth tent, third row, and called the corresponding name from his list. "Eshetu!"

Eshetu rolled over on his sleeping mat. What foul devil of his dreams was this that now called to him so gratingly? "Eshetu!" Ah, there he was, poking his head in the tent as Eshetu blinked his eyes open. "Sentry duty, post number twenty, you are to relieve a certain Alemu in thirty minutes' time for an eight hour shift." The apparition was gone so Eshetu stretched for a bit before realizing he had to scramble to make it out to the post in time.

With a boiled egg in his belly, and with lunch rations, rifle and waterskin in hand he was soon on the way, not bothering to try and tame his frightful hair that stuck out in all directions. Only his fellow sentry would have to look at him, and he hoped this time he would be paired with a good conversationalist. Eight hours could be a very long, boring stretch otherwise.

He passed a work crew taking shovels to a makeshift moat on the way out of camp, and reflected that the boredom of the watch was infinitely preferable to blistered hands and an aching back. His usual way to post number twenty continued up a gentle, grassy slope to a zig-zag, steep footpath cut into the hill, where the grass petered out and the red earth was seen. He broke into a jog, puffing his way up the hill with his thin but knotted, muscular calves. If Alemu complained of a late replacement, the last thing Eshetu needed was a black mark against his name – then it was shovel duty for sure. Over the rise and along to the post, which overlooked a defile between further hills through which any number of men might pass, unobserved by any but the sentries of post twenty. The Amharic word for twenty, haiya, had always sounded more aggressive to Eshetu than the other numbers; to him it was the sound a man might make as he struck a blow. "Haiya," he said to himself, chopping his hand through the air.

Even up here Eshetu could faintly hear the distant watch bells from the camp – he had arrived just in time, as he called out to Alemu. Both sentries looked up at the approaching man. "You're both Alemu?" he joked. The sentries were relieved one at a time on a staggered basis, so there would always be a fresher man on each part of the picket line.

"Yes," replied the first Alemu, "but it is I who have been on watch for eight hours." With nothing else to add he picked up his things and strode off towards the camp.

Neither did the second Alemu have anything to add, as the two men sat in brooding silence for a time. Eshetu ate another boiled egg, and thought a corpulent cloud looked like an elephant.

"Who are those men over there?" said Alemu Number Two sharply, snapping Eshetu out of his daydream. Eshetu shook his head to clear it; and he was supposed to be the fresher sentry!

Indeed there was some sort of patrol of six men coming up the defile, and they turned just within rifle range to strut in front of the sentries as they looked mockingly over. From down the picket line Eshetu could hear a scattering of shouts as challenges were raised by other sentries; perhaps there were other patrols testing and finding the watchmen all along that way.

"Let's fire a warning shot!" was Eshetu's grand idea, brandishing his rifle and waving it quite boisterously.

"No, you fool," was Alemu's response, "our orders are no aggression!" He reached out and grabbed the barrel of Eshetu's rifle to push it towards the ground.

"Hey, get off!" yelled Eshetu, and he tightened his grip on the rifle to pull it away from Alemu. Of course, as he squeezed his hand, he squeezed his trigger finger too in the process, and the rifle went off with a loud bang.

Both men turned their heads and froze to stare at where the bullet went. The fourth man in the patrol had crumpled. The other five men started running up towards the sentries as Alemu fired his rifle over their heads.

Soon Makonnen's patrols from other parts of the picket line were converging on the incident, and as Alemu and Eshetu legged it back to the camp screaming that they were under attack, a skirmishing party rushed past them on the zig-zag path. There would be a stand-off but Eshetu heard no further shots fired as he returned to the camp. Some dim specter of court-martial and other nasty punishment hung around him, but Eshetu had no idea what his mistake would cost him. Now he prayed, please, let me have shovel duty and that be the end of it. Soon enough he and Alemu found Dawit to make their report, and almost immediately Eshetu was summoned all the way to the command tent for a further explanation.

There was another scout waiting to his left, who leaned over to see if Eshetu had heard the latest news. "Apparently one of Makonnen's patrolmen came over to join our side. It's all over the camp. Apparently he said that many of their soldiers are ready to serve Tewodros, but while Makonnen is alive they are too scared to defect."

Eshetu did not have time to scoff at the story before he was summoned into the pavilion. Walking in, he took a step back when he saw that Tewodros himself was sitting there. He could not tell if the prince recognized him.

"Why did you shoot?" the prince was livid, and Eshetu took two more steps back. "Don't you realize Makonnen wants us to come at him, so he can tell Mulugeta we are the aggressor? He has even sent spies to spread rumors about his men defecting if only we would kill him. Don't you know Mulugeta will turn to his side if we attack him, and they will have an alliance to put one of them on the throne no matter what the Abuna says?"

Eshetu thought the questions quite unjust, as a simple rank and file soldier like himself shouldn't be expected to go beyond his direct orders and see the big picture. Despite this, he understood the point clearly and felt even worse about his accident. "I'm sorry, your excellency. It was a mistake and I only meant to fire a warning shot." Eshetu did not know what else to say.

Balcha helped him out. "With the chance that we receive a reply from Egypt any day now, Makonnen needs to ratchet up the temptation for Tewodros to attack. What were these patrols but a provocation? This soldier," he gestured to Eshetu, "could not even know what we heard two days ago, that Mulugeta is also maneuvering into position south of the valley, and will camp there to be ready to act once the Abuna responds."

"I agree, Dedjazmatch," said Tewodros, and Eshetu could swear he saw the prince wink at him, as if to let him off the hook. "And now these rumors swirling around the camp about his army defecting if we kill Makonnen, I have no doubt the Grazmatch planted that seed. If he is so desperate to spark some rash action, perhaps he is predisposed to take such an action himself and we will have the high ground again – at least morally, or even politically speaking. Let us hold tight and see what this Makonnen will do." The prince glanced at Eshetu, continuing, "as for you, no more mistakes! You may have dressed me for battle before, but now you will have exemplary discipline –

and you will show it off with your shovel to the other men digging ditches. Dismissed."

When Eshetu had left the pavilion, Tekle-giorgis took over as Tewodros' lead tactician. "We must be ready if Makonnen attacks – under cover of darkness, let us move half the men into the valley in the south. If he breaches the defenses, we fall back through the valley and he will follow into an ambush that will annihilate him."

"And what if Mulugeta sees us mobilizing down towards him?" queried Yohannes.

"I am not worried," said Teklegiorgis. "If he sees the maneuver, we can send messengers to explain, and I know him, he will not take action unless he perceives that we directly threaten him. Let us focus on Makonnen."

And so it was Tewodros found himself standing in the dead of night with no moonlight in the valley, for the clouds had come to graciously mask his movement, wanting to supervise and straining to see as the soldiers filed quietly past to fill positions in the scrub on either side to the south. It would be an uncomfortable night for them, and Tewodros wished he could show his appreciation somehow, but even his breathing seemed too loud in the secret air.

## *Chapter Seven*

Napier's favorite time of day was just about to begin when he reached his quarters, and he somewhat hurried through his toilet so that his steps rang on the lodge's patio in good time for a gin and tonic before supper. He sat down in the cool shade still wearing his distinctive turban. The leaves of a banyan tree dominated as he looked up, and dappled the sitting area most pleasantly. None of his usual peers had joined him on this particular excursion, and having had the fun of it he could not imagine why they had declined his invitation. Instead he called his servant to sit with him as a sundowner was best enjoyed in company. Reluctant at first to sit with the boss, the servant was cajoled and took a garden chair but no drink.

Napier somewhat regretted his charity in the awkward silence that followed, but even the lament over a lack of conversation was overcome by the haze of sunset and the breaths of thickening air. He felt the gin slowly spreading to his fingertips and the evening became orange, pausing for a split second at the moment where time seemed to stretch out to infinity. The noise of bats leaving their roosts increased, and the motes of dust disappeared with the light.

The tramp of boots on the terrace was most unwelcome, but the dinner bell rang almost simultaneously and the spell was broken regardless. A messenger had arrived, and scanning the scene asked an attendant where he could find Percival Napier. The attendant pointed at the turbaned guest, and the messenger even more rudely burst out, "By God, man, where's your pith helmet?"

Napier knew this must be a chap from the civil service as he lacked the customary military deference, but was in too good a mood to put him down. "And who are you, sir?"

James Firth removed his comparatively unimpressive headgear and remembered some manners, introducing himself as the bearer of an urgent summons from Whitehall. Napier started, "must I return to England, then?" but when the answer was "no, no," he calmed down, felt his first post-excitement hunger pangs and invited Firth to join him for supper and explain his message over a nice curry.

"What's this, sir, nobody up these parts knows how to cook an English meal?" asked Firth.

"Quite, I had a spot of lamb yesterday that chewed like an old boot. We'll see how the cook does with his native cuisine, to make up for the first night's disaster."

"None of these natives seem to want to serve us a proper curry, I find," said Firth, allowing Napier to precede him into the dining room. "The first Englishman to taste the spice must have spat it clear across the table and ruined it for the rest of us who have acclimated palates."

"I told him to make it plenty spicy, like his mama used to cook," Napier reassured his compatriot. "Like your amma, eh?" he called out, spying the chef peering into the dining room from the kitchen doorway.

"Yes sir, very good sir," with a toothy smile, and the man disappeared to be replaced by a waiter bearing cold towels. Napier removed his turban, and the cool relief of the towel against his sticky brow was almost the best moment of his wonderful day. A fantastic vindaloo was soon steaming on the table and Napier purposely delayed Firth still further from the main topic while he tucked in, a good meal to end a good day.

Napier had just finished describing the tiger hunt, when the last spoonful of yoghurt was greedily slurped up to cool Firth's tongue. The men leant back for a welcome cheroot to calm the stomach, and Firth took the opportunity to speak lest Napier launch another dilatory maneuver.

"I am to bring you directly to Bombay tomorrow, orders of the governor-general himself." A cocky stream of smoke issued from his head, tilted back towards the rafters. This was the most important business he had conducted since he met his desk in the colony.

"Well," said Napier, responding with a lazy smoke ring that remained a quivering 'O' for a good two feet, "I have bagged my bagh, as it were, so I don't mind at all. But my dear man, what could possibly be the hurry?"

Napier was pleased to hear the waiter groan at his tiger pun, though Firth ignored it and proceeded to describe the expedition that Whitehall had cooked up. After the bits about the hostages, the outrage back home, the strategy of overwhelming force, and the port being built, he leant forward confidentially, though there was nobody to eavesdrop. "I believe, sir, that your Sindh action was what recommended you for this command." Firth placed extra emphasis on the word "Sindh," and leant back again for a pregnant pause.

"Yes, I should think so," said Napier, fully understanding but wanting to goad Firth into declaring outright that Napier was expected to do more than simply rescue hostages. "I rather showed my ability to keep within the mission's budget on that occasion." Looking sideways he could see the messenger squirm.

"I – I believe you might be briefed at greater length by the governor-general once in Bombay – he is making his own way there from Calcutta as we speak. This is a matter of great national importance, of course," declared Firth. Emphasis on the "great."

"Will you be joining me in the field, then, to ensure it goes as intended?" continued Napier, not done.

"Sir, I am simply the messenger," admitted Firth. "Allow me however to answer any questions you might have on the road to Bombay, as I have been present at all the planning meetings thus far. You will also have the opportunity to do a bit of background reading and I think you will find this volume quite useful," and here Firth produced and handed over a tome entitled "Travels to Discover the Source of the Nile."

Napier took the book and felt its cover. "James Bruce – the Scottish explorer. I can't read while I'm moving, it makes me quite ill." The men pondered this in silence for a moment.

"Right, then, in the morning sharpish?" said Napier, the cheroot smoked and the curry coma coming. He was not one to take tea after supper, and was looking forward to a rampant sleep after jolting around all day on an elephant's back.

The messenger had nothing more to offer, so the two men retired, Firth to find a room, and Napier to his quarters with a spring in his step. He knew not whether it came from the day's trophy, or the evening's revelation of a splendid expedition for the undertaking.

## Chapter Eight

Tewodros watched the honor guard approach, Ras Makonnen in its midst and the Grazmatch's colors flying. No doubt he wanted to make something of yesterday's skirmish before the confrontation cooled. Tewodros' team had scrambled to script a meeting, and had decided on two stools of equal height spaced ten feet apart in a clearing on the southern end of the camp, opening up to the valley beyond. As Tewodros had said, "only Makonnen, I and my lion will sit."

Eshetu rested on his shovel and looked up from the ditch as Makonnen entered the camp, shading his eyes to wonder at what this could mean. The Grazmatch was a tall man, willowy but with a head that was too big for his frame and teeth that were too big for his other features, which on their own would be handsome brown eyes and a fine, delicate nose. Eshetu heard one of Makonnen's men remark, "they must all be digging ditches – the tents over there seem mostly empty. They must be expecting us to charge them from all sides!"

Eshetu knew there were only ditches on the east side, but even he did not realize that there had been a troop movement in the night. The contingency plan did help Tewodros feel slightly less nervous as Makonnen entered the clearing, surrounded by his guards.

It helped even more that Makonnen could barely stop staring into Judah's great, yellow eyes long enough to greet the prince. Tewodros stroked the giant cat's mane and held back a smirk as he watched

Makonnen settle uncomfortably onto his stool – the lion's gaze was enough to make any man quail. The urge to smile faded as an aide whispered in his ear to remind him, "Makonnen's army is drawn up behind the eastern hills."

The Grazmatch spoke first, blurting out, "you, what makes you think you have the right to rule an empire? Your mother no more than an onion seller!"

Tewodros knew his mother had been poor and it did not bother him, though Makonnen's directness did take him aback. "Let the people say such things, and it may even make them feel closer to me as I came from one of their own. But not you, Ras Makonnen – it is not gentlemanly." Judah chose that opportune moment to bare his teeth and agree. The young man's chastening only fueled the anger in Makonnen to just below boiling.

An aide came running into the clearing but neither Tewodros nor Makonnen could remember whose staff the aide belonged to. "Mulugeta's army has been seen moving up from the south!" Tewodros looked agape at his advisors just as they looked agape at him.

Makonnen stood up, gesturing at his colors that flapped in the breeze. "You and the other Rases have struck a deal against me! If my banner is downed, my army has been instructed to attack," he warned.

"I am not in league with Mulugeta, I assure you!" said Tewodros, standing up to face the Grazmatch. Involuntarily, the retinue of each moved their hands to whatever weapon they carried. Tewodros' mind whirled without reaching any conclusions. His escape route was cut off and not enough men were left in the camp to protect him from Makonnen's army if they attacked. How did Mulugeta move so quickly?

Makonnen's banner dropped to the earth. Fitaurari Tekle-giorgis drew a sword. "This is crazy!" cried Yohannes.

Makonnen's army began to appear on the ridge, stark against the clouds, and swarm down as the cry went up in the camp to man the defenses.

"Makonnen, if we fight each other then Mulugeta will have both of us. What is the signal for your men to stand down?" urged Tewodros. "Tekle-giorgis, tell our men not to engage; fall back from the trenches!"

Then it was Balcha who interjected, "Tewodros, there is no time to dither – signal the ambush, they might still be able to cut off the approach from the south!"

"Ambush? What ambush!" Makonnen was close to hysteria now.

Tewodros wished Balcha had kept his mouth shut but had no time to focus on him now. "Much of my army is to the south, Ras Makonnen, and I have only taken defensive measures. It was to protect my retreat if this meeting showed me that I had to fear your aggression. But now it must be Mulugeta who has played a different hand – let your army stand to his fore and mine fill in to his rear once he passes the ambush, then he will be crushed in a vice if he tries anything at all."

"And we will be crushed with him," wailed Makonnen.

"If Mulugeta is here in force, we may all die before anybody's army can converge," yelled Balcha. "We need the element of surprise – we need the ambush, and then we can escape!"

"Signal the ambush to show themselves and challenge the Qenazmatch's force, but not to attack," ordered Tewodros. "Makonnen, tell your men to stand down."

But Makonnen was looking over Tewodros' shoulder to the south. "It is too late for the ambush," noted Tekle-giorgis. A company of soldiers had already appeared.

## Chapter Nine

Jeevan was miffed at receiving the honor of presenting Napier-sahib with the tiger's pelt, as it meant a red-eyed morning before the sun was up. He stood ready with two fellow beaters and Sabzi-sardar outside the lodge in case the British officer decided to make an early departure to avoid some heat. He was somewhat comforted by the discomfiture of Sabzi-sardar having to join him, as Sabzi had clearly been drinking copious amounts of gin last night.

Napier appeared after a languorous breakfast, collecting his pelt without looking at Jeevan, and acknowledging Sabzi with a curt nod. Jeevan rolled his eyes and poked the arm of his companion, mocking in a low tone, "are you there? We must be invisible – the Sahib cannot see us beaters."

Firth followed lazily out from the lodge to supervise the preparation of the horses that would take them to the railway station, and noticed Sabzi stepping forward and balancing on his tiptoes as Napier ignored him. "Hi, Napier, I think this chap wants to say something to you," he called out.

"What is it?" said Napier, turning.

"Please, Mr. Napier-sahib Sir, we are most pleased to make a gift to honor the visit of Mr. Napier-sahib to our lodge."

"Yes, I've got the tiger skin, thank you."

"No sir, it is another gift."

"Well, go on?"

"We would like to present to you sir the very elephant you have been using for the successful tiger-shooting, sir!" Sabzi beamed, and could not contain a smile as he spread his hands, and coming around the corner was the beast itself with a majestic, plodding gait.

"Criminy!" said Napier. "I'll call him Goliath."

"Look at the size of the thing," joined Firth. "How the hell are we supposed to bring that with us?"

"Is no problem sir, no problem," assured Sabzi. "Partway to Bombay we can send him downriver by raft – the Narmada is calm here, sir," Sabzi waggled his head. "Then to Bombay they take many elephants, no problem, in army barracks they can keep for you, Napier-sahib."

Napier smirked. "Not many officers will have their own elephant, eh?" and Sabzi was most pleased that Napier was pleased. His happiness was short-lived as the sardar had to look away from the elephant until Napier left. Goliath was rocking back and forth and last night's gin threatened to come up.

Later that day as the two British made their way by modern means to the metropolis on the coast, out of the mists of time was rising the mighty Narmada, in a slow intransigent flood to the same end. On its banks the trees bent with leeches extended like quivering fingertips from the leaves' ends, searching for a passing langur. Instead this strange day, if they could but see, they would have witnessed an elephant

177

floating by, on an ancient barge made of trees carried down from the hills by his ancestors.

## Chapter Ten

The knot of men in the camp's council stood slack-jawed, yet tense at the same time, watching the approaching soldiers as they came up the valley. The banners of the vanguard drooped as the waiting men drew up in their small ranks around Tewodros and Makonnen, hands flickering to weapons and minds flipping back and forth with nowhere to go. The men in Tewodros' trenches, and Makonnen's advancing troops, seemed to sense the moment and held in stasis waiting. Suddenly a gust of wind, and the banners unfurled across the ravine from right to left, bursting out in the orange colors of the Abuna!

"The Abuna has no army – this must be Mulugeta's men escorting him," remarked Tekle-giorgis.

"Perhaps he has chosen Mulugeta?" postulated Makonnen.

"There, I see Mulugeta, he is waving to us now!" pointed Tekle-giorgis.

Tewodros could see a big grin on the face of the man Tekle-giorgis pointed to, a face that looked more grandfatherly than anything with its surprisingly gentle brows and humor etched in the corners of the eyes, but the tension in Tewodros' jaw prevented him returning the smile. "God, give me the grace to accept if you have chosen Mulugeta to lead," he prayed inwardly. Even the prince stood back in deference as the Abuna entered the clearing in heavy robes, and Mulugeta a step behind.

179

Yohannes was swift to offer the Abuna one of the two stools, but the other remained empty as there was no way to differentiate among who might sit there. The Abuna turned to Yohannes, recognizing a fellow man of the cloth, and asked, "where is Ras Tewodros?"

Tewodros stepped forward, sorry that he now only had a humble stool to offer the bishop. "I am he."

The Abuna stood. "In the presence of these witnesses, I bring the decision that was made and sealed in the presence of the patriarch and reflecting the will of the Church. You have asked the succession to rightly be decided by a higher power, and in the name of God, I reveal the answer," and from his sleeve the Abuna drew a proclamation rolled up and sealed with the seal of Alexandria.

"So even Mulugeta does not yet know," whispered Makonnen, with a sidelong glance at his rival who had said nothing since the Abuna's arrival.

"Hope springs eternal for Makonnen," Tekle-giorgis observed drily, but in his mind were running the scenarios of what each man would do, and how violently, depending on what the Abuna said.

The Abuna broke the seal, bits of wax dropping to the earth as he spread his arms to unroll the papyrus. The Abuna mumbled through the obligatory prefacing language, with every ear around straining to hear. "Glory of God...mumble...peace and well-being of the people of Ethiopia;" then clearly was heard the part where this Abuna had been appointed as Abuna in accordance with the standing procedures by the patriarch and the council of bishops; then "said Abuna does declare his ruling...mumble...right of primogeniture...it is right and just that Prince Theodore son of Kassa shall be, with the blessing of God and the Church, the King of Kings of Ethiopia." The Abuna concluded and looked up at Tewodros, almost quizzically.

"Let us all bow to Tewodros!" cried Tekle-giorgis lustily.

Now a grin broke out on the young prince's face, but he was quickly overcome by the moment. The men around him, all older, all respected, were bending on one knee as shouts radiated through the surrounding soldiers: "Long live Tewodros the King!"

Tewodros looked at Yohannes' face to steady him in this storm of adulation. Even though he had been given the time to prepare, there was no way to be ready for this moment. With Yohannes gazing back warmly and the eyes of everyone upon him, the king felt it called for to make some remarks.

"Today," Tewodros began, and the shouting subsided, "an empire was saved." His gaze ranged now to Makonnen, Balcha and Mulugeta. "Let us work together to continue my father's good work, and create in his name who was taken from us too soon, a lasting legacy of peace. Let us use that peace as our platform to improve our lot, to build our traditions, and to treat with our neighbors as a strong and just Ethiopia. And let us see one another again soon in Magdala for a coronation feast, when I will have had time to prepare a better speech!" There was applause, and Tewodros lifted his arms. "Come, let us make today just as much a celebration of our new Abuna, with a feast in his honor, and in honor of his good news."

The king led his archbishop to the central tent personally, and now quite a retinue followed. Tekle-giorgis caused the galleys to scramble to prepare a banquet for the noblemen, but each of the Rases was more than happy to leave his soldiers standing at arms in case another tried anything. The trust would take some time.

Tewodros made sure to sit between the Abuna and Mulugeta during the meal, as the newest faces of what would be his inaugural inner circle. "How do you like our country so far?" he engaged the Abuna, for the head of Ethiopia's church was always an Egyptian. The Abuna's Amharic was not good, though his lessons on the trip from Alexandria had been many. "Very excellent," he nodded, as he tried to face down the raw meat served in heaps in front of him. He would need all the spiritual fruits from his long life as a cleric to adjust to this new life.

The Abuna looked like he wanted to say something, so Tewodros focused his attention on the bishop. "I am very impressed with how you have become king, Ras Tewodros." This particular interlocution it seemed the Abuna had rehearsed in advance, as the Amharic came out smoothly, yet accented strangely. "I understand you used no violence except when attacked, and it seems today that you have made a peaceful transition that will be well received by the people. It is a most noble accession to the throne," the Abuna inclined his head to the king.

"You do me too great an honor," replied Tewodros. "The Lord has made my paths straight."

The king was interrupted from the other side by a gursha from Ras Mulugeta, an absurdly large fistful of food that was shoved directly into Tewodros' mouth by the general as a sign of companionship, and a traditional gesture. As the king reciprocated he felt by some unspoken signal that the old saying about a gursha would be true in this case – Mulugeta would never now betray him.

"Now that you have promised us a coronation feast, don't keep me in suspense," said Mulugeta when the gurshas had been chewed and washed down. "I had enough of that when I found the Abuna wandering towards our camps a few days ago, and he wouldn't give up the secret until he could speak to us all together – and I too much of a gentleman to force him to tell me. I remember how grand your father's coronation was and I am looking forward to another one before I die! When will it be?"

"Ras Mulugeta, I am anxious to reach Magdala and bring this to pass," replied Tewodros. "But I want to do it most correctly. One of my chief desires, now that we continue to have a unified front to present to other nations, is to raise the standing of Ethiopia beyond our mountains and deserts."

"This would be good," acknowledged Mulugeta. "These days we see the Turks begin to threaten from the sea, and an alliance with others, strengthened through trade, would help to keep the Turks more interested in free commerce than raiding our ports, or worse."

"We must talk more about the Turkish ambitions," said Tewodros. "Later I plan to travel on visits of state, but my thought for my coronation is to invite as many leaders of nations as will attend, to demonstrate our culture and our openness to formal diplomatic relations."

"Yes, that is wise. I think some will come, from Sudan, Egypt and the major Somali clans at least. Perhaps the Europeans and Arabs, too," mused Mulugeta.

"What have you heard of the British?" Tewodros asked keenly.

"They have a woman in charge," was Mulugeta's response. "If you mean to invite her, let's get the message on the way to Aden and to Cairo right away! That will take some time and we want to have the coronation by next year, no?"

"Yes, I have heard at Cairo the British have a machine that can take a message by wires in an instant to another city," said Tewodros. "We will set the coronation for one year from today and that will give even this Queen a chance to attend. It is done!" and in the morning the first messages went.

## Chapter Eleven

Napier met Goliath at the barracks in Bombay, glad of a break from the monotony of inspecting the lines of men who were converging in companies to join his expedition. The day was typically hot and stifling as he entered the animal compound, the smell of manure practically slapping him in the face. He recognized his steed's prominent scar on the brow and notched left ear, so Goliath was easy to pick out among the masses of elephants kept at the barracks. "How many beasts are here?" he asked the mahout as he clapped his hand on Goliath's mighty trunk.

"Not sure Sahib, at least seventy, maybe eighty." The mahout saw Napier's eyes light up, as if a switch had been flipped in his brain.

"How many pounds can an elephant carry?"

The mahout blew a thin stream of air through his lips, and shrugged his thin shoulders as he responded, "maybe lifting five hundred with the trunk; maybe double on the back. That is why they carry the heavy guns in some regiments, sir."

"You don't say!" Napier cast about for a means to express himself physically and ended up pumping the mahout's hand, before awkwardly moving on to his two o'clock planning meeting where the smell of sweaty officers in a stuffy room was almost worse than the animals.

Napier held court with his subordinates, receiving updates of the equipment and men that had come in.

"The chaps in London have requested that we field-test the new Snider-Enfield rifles – first time they will be used in a campaign," said Colonel Smithers. "We've just received a thousand of them with a hundred cartridges each."

"Confound it, the Indians aren't trained to fight with breech-loaders," barked Napier. "Give them the ability to shoot multiple rounds that fast and they'll spend them all firing willy-nilly before the officers can get the commands to all sides of the square."

"Word has come through from London – it's a priority to get these new rifles rolled out across the army and they must be field-tested," apologized Smithers.

"I wonder who is in Enfield's pocket," Napier grumbled as he was thinking, and an idea came to him. "What happened with the Gurkhas I requested? How many have we got?" In his bedtime reading of Bruce's travel writings Napier had noted the descriptions of Ethiopia's high altitude and the shortness of breath it gave to men unused to living at such elevation. The more Gurkhas he could get the better, as the hardy soldiers conscripted from the Himalayas had not only distinguished themselves in battle for the British Raj, but were reputed to run up and down the slopes of high mountains with far greater ease than other men.

Colonel Smithers brightened. "We have a full battalion of Gurkhas returned to Bombay and ready to join the expedition, sir!"

"We will give them the new rifles and use them in this way," said Napier. "The Gurkhas will travel faster in the highlands than the trailing army, and will set ambushes as the opportunity arises, or generally make quick strikes before retreating to our main line. For this purpose they should benefit from a higher rate of fire, and the Gurkhas can be trusted to make good decisions with their ammunition as they operate independently on their forward missions."

"Bloody brilliant," murmured Smithers, mesmerized by his commander's military acumen.

Napier continued. "Now, to the next matter." He cast about for the most junior officer in the room – there, it was Lieutenant Burnside, of course wearing preposterous sideburns up and down the sides of his pimply face, that he thought made him quite distinguished in the officers' club. "You – Lieutenant. How much does a twelve-pound gun weigh?"

Burnside blinked twice, then again. "Twelve-pound gun, sir?"

"Yes, what's the weight? Are we not planning a massive expedition involving the transport of ludicrous amounts of equipment across vast distances?"

"Yes sir, ludicrous."

"And in order to properly arrange for that transport, do we not need to estimate the weight of the equipment so that we bring the appropriate number of pack animals?"

"I shall have to look that up sir."

"Lieutenant, the efficient administration of an army's logistics is the cornerstone of its ability to fight. These numbers should be at the forefront of your mind."

"Absolutely sir, I apologize."

"I have just learned that we have at our disposal a method of transportation that can move several hundredweight and has been proven in the Indian regiments, and we will not be at the mercy of the Ethiopian terrain when maneuvering the heavy guns. What do you think it is?"

"I wouldn't know, sir."

Napier looked around the room. "Elephants. Lieutenant, I want you to calculate how many elephants we will need to carry cannon and shot and adjust the provisioning accordingly. Understood?" Colonel Smithers was not so sure if this was brilliant, or simply eccentric.

Glendon was quite sure when reviewing the expedition's budget back in London, and trying not to panic at the number of digits in the total, that the line item for forty-four elephants was truly bizarre. Each line in the budget swirled in Glendon's brain to visions of the sleek rifles, dull puttees rolled up with spare kits, sweet Kendal mints for rations and other real, live things behind the dry numbers, but try as he might he could not picture the elephants. The focus of course would be on the cost of the chests full of silver Maria Theresa thalers from Austria, apparently the coin of the realm in Ethiopia, which Napier proposed to bring in abundance to try and achieve the mission's objectives through bloodless methods. At least a little bribery was more palatable and easily hushed up than the death of British soldiers.

Glendon made his notes for Matthews' review and sent the budget up with no small measure of dread – if Napier bungled things, both their careers were over. As or the dent he was putting in the national treasure, he felt not even a tinge of guilt.

## Chapter Twelve

Tewodros insisted that no time be wasted in packing up the camp, as he was anxious to begin his tour of the country he had never seen, but was to rule. "You can't try to visit every village in the empire!" the exasperated Tekle-giorgis had said, when trying to plan the route that would end in Magdala for the coronation.

"When will I have another chance, my Fitaurari?" was Tewodros' counter. "Besides, we are sending only Mulugeta ahead to prepare at Magdala, so with three armies to feed we cannot stay long in one place." Tewodros did not quite yet trust Dedjazmatch Balcha and Qenazmatch Makonnen to move off on their own, and a united, large force would make a grand impression on the country that it would be foolish to rebel.

"In that case, we will see the highlands and the lowlands, the lakes and the deserts, the fox in the mountain and the zebra in the plain," Tekle-giorgis was resigned. "In three days we start for the Bale mountains. Now you've learned to ride a horse, you can forget all that because only a donkey can climb those cliffs!"

The next few days in camp were a blur, with administrative details coming thick and fast. But in Bale, when they left the armies and retinue behind to climb the rough paths, it was easy to forget amid the din of the donkey chimes, lurching up the spine of the mountain to reach the village that lay nestled in the alps on the other side. No need to think through the shuffling of honorary titles to ensure that none of the preening noblemen purchased by patronage would think to slow their collection of tax for the royal treasury. No incessant decision-making pushed on the king by functionaries too cowardly to stand behind an order on their own. Here in the pure sweet air, Tewodros found, he could lose himself in the muted green and gray landscape, and no images of his father's unseeing eyes would come boiling to the surface – only pleasant recollections of the country they had passed through on the way here.

The contrast of vivid pink and white was hard to put far from his mind, when at the salt flats of Lake Abiyata last week they had scared up the flock of flamingos feeding at the water's edge, into rising as one cloud of whirring, beating beauty. Or just yesterday, when he had seen his first Simien fox, standing stock still with ears pointed straight up, poised and unafraid as it watched the entire convoy pass from its rocky vantage point. The only stress of this side trip was the difficulty of counting high enough to comprehend his blessings.

Down the other side of the pass to the village, where the crops were growing below and the cattle had been sent to the high pastures, a pleasing symphony of cowbells welcomed the royal entourage along their way. Freshly built huts still had a scent of juniper as Tewodros passed into the village square. Yohannes was with him, breathing in deeply and saying, "from here it will be a long circuit through many towns and villages to reach the capital where the full brunt of courtly duties will come to bear. Let us relax and enjoy while we can remain in this mountain fastness."

"Yohannes, we have work to do even here," replied Tewodros, "although it will not feel like work with these hints of paradise around us," and just as he said this he saw her. "We, ah, we will do well to test my court reforms here," as his eyes followed a young woman across the square, her posture perfect as she balanced a gourd atop her head, "starting small and then using the model for the bigger provinces."

Yohannes laughed, seeing where the prince was looking, "it is good you are eager to work. Let us see if we can meet some of the locals at a festive dinner and save the talk of judicial systems for the morrow." The men retired to where their tents had been pitched, to exorcise the aggravations of travel with their sandals cast off and a welcome stretch.

An hour later, Tewodros stepped out of his tent. Though the air was thin in the mountains, he felt he could truly breathe for the first time since Ghannatu's horse was seen in the distance. Ghannatu's loss still pained him, but the even deeper pang was the breaking of that tenuous connection to his father that came through Ghannatu's stories, that spoke of Kassa's life as an ordinary man before he was king, and would now be silent forever with the messenger in his grave. The past is the past, thought the prince, and the rising peaks all around him were emblems of the rising hope of his future, now that he had traded the trammels of his cave for the responsibilities of a monarch.

And now there she was, right in front of him, the girl who had floated in and out of his thoughts the past hour. "Your Lordship, I am sent to inquire if you need any refreshments before the feast this evening." Tewodros saw Yohannes looking his way from afar – the old dog had probably put the girl up to this. She had very nice manners, and Tewodros felt clumsy speaking to her in the way he spoke to the menfolk who had been his only real interlocutors all his life. "No, no, I have no need of anything," he responded.

"In that case, may I take you on a tour of our humble village?" she continued. To Tewodros, walking with a girl sounded worse than standing up to speak in front of Tekle-giorgis' men before they fought Balcha, but he knew the alternative was to lose her company and he battled through the shyness. "Yes, that would be excellent," he mumbled, and off they wandered. He made a mental note to ask her name – it turned out to be Haymanot.

Tewodros struggled to keep up with her long strides, desperately casting about for something interesting to say as he felt thick-headed in the presence of her easy manner. "Have you seen the flamingoes at Abiyata?" he blurted out – he couldn't very well talk about growing up in a cave, and if politics bored him they would surely bore Haymanot.

"I have not passed that ridge," she pointed to the north, and traced it down and around to the south with her long finger, "or that one," and then to the ridge on the other side, until she had traced a wide circle all around them and made a small laugh behind her other hand.

But Tewodros had stopped walking, and the look on his face was nothing like laughter. He was staring at a small group of village children, shrieking as they chased each other from house to house with gay abandon.

"What is it? Is something wrong?" she placed a hand softly on Tewodros' arm, and the touch shot through him like cold fire.

"Nothing – it's nothing," he said. "Only – I knew no other children growing up. You see," and he could scarce believe he was spilling these embarrassing facts to her, "I lived with the monks. My father, you know, he sent me to the cave. I felt like an old man since I can remember," he trailed off, thinking what he said was not even making sense.

Haymanot knew the practice of the Ethiopian monarchs, keeping their children apart. "I see," she said. "So you could not have a family even? I'm sorry, your Lordship," she looked down, "it is not my place to ask this, forgive me."

"No, it is quite alright. Just – I never talked about this with anyone. I never had a family!" Don't cry, thought Tewodros. You've already made a fool of yourself in front of her.

Haymanot brightened. "Never mind that! You are the king now, are you not? You can make your own family! When people get married they start a new family, don't they? It doesn't matter if you had one before, everyone can share that dream!"

Tewodros felt instantly better as they resumed walking, and wondered how he had lived without this person to talk to.

Yohannes watched them leaning slightly towards each other as they went, and chuckled to himself. Despite all the advisors in Tewodros' retinue, he knew none of them could do the essential work of a queen. The celibate monk had worked hard to shut out romantic notions long ago, but he also took pleasure in knowing that Tewodros would have the chance to experience love as a balance to his burdens so young. Now that had been set in motion, he turned to a quiet corner to spend some time with his rosary beads.

Tewodros was excited at supper, and not just from the blushing Haymanot who poured their wine from time to time. There was a free debate raging over how much of his authority he could delegate to courts that would sit in each province to break the crippling backlog of disputes that had built up. "The courts must be different in each region, adapted to the traditional structures of authority," he rejoined. "I will return on a rotating basis simply to review the procedures and correct injustice – the people cannot wait for the king to frequent their region simply to have a case heard."

Balcha played the conservative, "but this will change your father's ways, your Lordship. Yohannes has done a splendid job," he bowed towards the monk, "of opening your eyes to the scholarship of ruling as it might be in other places. But in Ethiopia, the king traditionally stays close to the people by hearing their disputes in person. What message will you be sending if you disengage from this practice?"

Yohannes offered drily, "I am not sure why we have scholars if their theories are not tested in practice. We have a long circuit through many towns and villages from here to Magdala – let us at least start small and see how this village, and others we choose along the way, receive the reforms of the king. If they improve the lives of people here and there, we will soon see them in all Ethiopia."

Tekle-giorgis, always reluctant to join in these debates, did have one observation that he could not help but contribute. "You speak of staying close to the people, but no matter how the king connects with his people by judging their circumstances, there will always be a gap with the commoners who have so little, and the nobles who live this different life."

"This may be so," responded Tewodros, "but I do not need to embrace this gap. I will overcome it instead, because when I work to improve their lives, it will send the message that I care for my people. Then I will be in their hearts." He was looking at Haymanot as he said this.

The king continued on his tour, winding ever closer to the day of his official coronation.

*Chapter Thirteen*

Napier wrapped up his planning meeting two minutes early and stepped sharply to the parade ground for the evening colors. He would have time to inspect just the first three lines, as he wanted to make some remarks to the men before the flag was lowered. The crunch of gravel under his boots and the straight backs of the men were satisfying, but he recognized Jeevan's face in the ranks as one of the fresh conscripts, and the inexperience of those he would command made him shudder. "I'd rather have a few crack regiments on penny rations than money to burn and all these Indians from the bush," he told himself, but then he thought of the flexibility he had to try the elephants as his new war machines, and was pleased.

Up to the podium now, and time to give the troops a bit of what ho. Napier flexed his vocal pipes over the stillness of the men at attention, and it sounded almost trumpet-like as he began. "We all know, the sun does not set, on the British Empire." He had a habit of looking left, center, right as he spoke, above the heads of the men, and pausing between sentences to swivel his neck back to the left.

"Likewise, there is nowhere on earth, a man may run and hide, from the might of the British Empire. You men, are the right hand of Empire; you are that might. And now, we in the Hindu Kush, we go to the ancient land of Cush." Napier thought that bit quite clever – he had come up with it last night.

"We go to teach a lesson to those that would trifle with our citizens. We go to make an example to others that none shall trifle with Britain, or they will pay the price! We have the best men," he glossed, "the best equipment, the best training and the best tactics of any army, I dare say, in the world. You are representing Britain at her peak, and you must rise to that challenge. Whether or not we face a disciplined army with gunners, or a rabble who carries only spears, you must be the best you can be – because the world must see that the British army is the best there is." Napier nodded to the honor guard and the shouts for colors punctuated the evening, the flag lazily flapping down and the men thankful for the brevity of their commander's remarks. It would be a real pleasure to unwind the tight puttees from their ankles, take off their boots and wiggle their toes in the cooling air.

Night fell, the men were at ease and Napier was restless. He issued from his quarters and passed through the orderly lines of the camp, hearing laughter from some, and singing from others. Here were the permanent barracks where the white men stayed, with the windows open to let the breeze through, and Napier paused underneath one that belied a particularly rowdy gathering. "Fancies himself the modern day Hannibal, does he? All those bleeding elephants. Is he off his rocker?" It sounded like that pimple of a Lieutenant, Burnside.

"Have another swig of this arrack, and it'll change your mind. You'll think he's a genius," replied Alfred, an army lifer and something of an elder statesman of the regiment, as the bottle of native liquor made another round of the group. This batch was made from rice and Alfred took to physically holding his nose as he downed his next shot.

Napier smiled and trotted up the steps into the barracks. "A little more respect for a Major General of the Empire is in order, I should think," he said in a low voice as the arrack bottle swiftly disappeared behind a bedpost. Alfred stood up, a tall, rangy man with a graying pate, and the rest of the men followed suit in a general scraping of chairs. "Sit down, sit down," said Napier, taking an empty chair, and thinking back to the days when it was easy to be one of the men. "I wouldn't mind a taste of whatever's been passed around the troops – can't be any worse than what they serve at the officers' club."

Alfred grinned and poured the general a generous draught of the arrack. "I do miss the old toddy we had in Crimea. I was partial to the sweetness, sir."

Napier made a face as he sipped, and studied the pourer who stood out from the other men for the age on his brows, the sunken cheeks and his lanky height. "You were at Sevastopol, then?" he said with respect.

"Aye, sir." Alfred did not like to talk about it.

"Remember the hills we had to climb? The elevation in Abyssinia is thousands of feet higher at the country's capital than at the port where we land. I think we may appreciate the elephants by the time we reach the top." The man to Alfred's left turned beet red

199

and Napier knew which one had called him Hannibal. He downed the rest of his arrack. "God, that's bloody awful. Well, I'm glad to see the men keeping their spirits up," and stepped out again with a curt "carry on," wondering if anyone had noticed his pun.

When the men were quite sure their commander's steps had faded beyond earshot, Burnside muttered much more quietly this time, "what a looney." In fact there was nearly a full moon that night.

"Now then," said Alfred, "it was good of him to have a drink with the men. I know some generals might feel it beneath them."

"Still, dampens the fun a bit, doesn't it," moped Burnside. "Though I'm sure he is a genius after all. We'll be glad to have a leader like him when we get into it, in the field."

"See there, you've changed your tune - now I know you've had too much arrack!" laughed Alfred.

The nights passed quickly as the army prepared for departure, their anticipation of fresh exploits growing while the crops ripened around them in the greening of the land. Before long Napier stood with Smithers at the docks in Bombay, surveying his fleet. They had decided to consolidate the elephants aboard four of the vessels, and Napier watched their mahouts cajoling them up the gangplanks, two by two as it must have struck Noah's vision in ancient times. Those four ships were already nearly fully loaded with sufficient fodder for the voyage on the high seas to feed the massive appetites of these beasts. Four ships just for his pets, thought Napier, cringing inwardly. When he had realized how copious their appetite was, it had been too late to back out and he had to be careful to hide his frustration or risk being a laughing-stock.

Napier instead shifted his focus to another bane of his expedition, thrust upon him by London with nary a raised eyebrow, and the expense of which dwarfed that of his mighty elephants. He turned to Smithers, "is there any update on the facilities at Massawa?" The port being built would aid the landing, but it risked falling behind schedule and announced his location unequivocally to the Ethiopians.

Smithers checked his notes, as he knew this issue was apt to set Napier off and he did not want to get it wrong. "It seems there is some difficulty with the railroad to the interior – the feasibility study was entirely discouraging. "

"Someday they will create an iron horse that is not trammeled by rails – that moves on its own treads, can carry men and even mounted guns. Until then, even more reason for my elephants!" laughed Napier, glad of another justification for those four ships.

"Nevertheless, sir," brightened Smithers, "the port facilities proceed apace. They should be prepared for our arrival and unloading at the expected time."

"No resistance has been met by the advance corps, then? And no disease – they haven't had the dengue?" Napier asked, wanting to be proven right that the planners in London were idiots.

"None, sir," reported Smithers.

"Well, I suppose there is no way they will scrap this idea now, then. It seems from Dickie Burton's reports that the further down the coast one goes, the less inspiring it becomes and the more we'd be setting off right in hostile country." Napier had been reading the accounts of more than one explorer after getting through the travelogue that Firth had given him. "I would have liked rather to emulate Bruce's journey – land at Suakin," Napier had dreamed of seeing the coral city, "find the Blue Nile at Khartoum and follow it back down into Abyssinia."

Smithers rolled his eyes – his commander may have been brilliant, but there was a touch of the romantic about him that Smithers saw no place for in the military setting. "I suppose since we are traveling all that long way, sir, it would be good to check on what the Pasha is up to down in Sudan, while we are in the region. We don't have good intelligence on the Egyptian activities that far south. But through Massawa we must go." Questioning London was out of the question for Smithers.

Down below on the dock, Jeevan followed a coolie past where the officers were talking, finding his way to the berth that would be his home for the days to come. Like almost all the Indian troops, he had never been to sea and the mounting excitement of the expedition could be felt as a palpable energy. He could almost hear it buzzing on top of the deep rumble of the steam engines when the fleet was finally leaving Bombay. Jeevan would see Aden, where they would replenish supplies before crossing the Red Sea to Massawa, and then he would be witness to even stranger lands. The troops were all crowded on deck to wave back at Bombay as the steamships gathered way, and the shores of India faded behind them into a dream.

Into the open ocean, and Jeevan stayed on deck as much as he could to take the salt air and try to calm his stomach. It was good when the breeze picked up and he could see God's breath on the water, the cat's paws stretching into the distance. The Britisher Alfred was on the railing close by and Jeevan ventured a comment to his superior in his broken English. "Even heaven's wind not enough for this great ship to go – needing earth, fire, water for the steam. All elements!"

Alfred smiled at the unexpected connection with the native, who might later serve at his side under circumstances where color ceased to matter. "All the elements are heaven's gift, no?" He looked behind him at the towering smokestack, and then at the great clouds sailing above to dwarf the puffs of steam from the ship. They were near the center of the fleet and the line of ships to either side seemed endless, and his feeling on looking at the armada on a bright sea was that nothing could stop their mighty progress.

Alfred's mind wandered to past times when Alexander's vast armies took months to travel across the Earth's geography, and the thought of being in Aden so quickly struck him as a great sign of the advancement of his modern time. Yet he knew to be true, and said to himself, "one day these will be the days of old."

## Chapter Fourteen

Many of the men who had already served Tewodros in the field were called up to participate in the coronation; some for their gallantry, some for their connections to the commanding officers, some for standing in the right place at the right time to receive the honor. Many had taken part in the old king Kassa's funeral procession a week earlier, a ceremony that Tewodros had insisted on despite the logistical burden of two massive parades in two weeks. Among the participants was one of the Alemus who had manned the sentry post in the hills where Tewodros had waited for the Abuna. Winding his way through the masses of men and women who would be part of the coronation procession, he spotted his old compatriot, Eshetu. "I didn't know you played the drums," said Alemu, in his finest dress uniform. The burnished silver of his shoulder clasp glinted in the sun and caused Eshetu to squint his eyes.

"I'm a music man," replied Eshetu, smoothing the soft hair on the goat hide of his drum. "But it doesn't pay so much as soldiering." He adjusted the strap of his instrument just as Alemu fidgeted with his rifle. Both men were proud of their costumery and wanted to look immaculate for the parade.

Eshetu felt important, and set apart from the crowd in his flowing white robe, new leather sandals that still rubbed his heel too much, and the truly special part of his outfit, the intricately embroidered woolen vest with green patterns curlicued in and out of a laddered lattice. His drum too was clothed in finery; a darker green and black spotted pattern on the fabric covering the barrel of the drum. He tapped the face of the drum experimentally with his crooked stick and was pleased with the resonance of the sharp raps that rang out. The tightness and pitch were just right.

"Well, it's time to take our places," he told Alemu. "The procession starts at noon."

"Yes, but by the time the horse guards get going and the flower girls are out of the way, we won't be moving until half past," grumbled Alemu, already too warm in the extra layers of his sash and jacket. He shifted his rifle to the right shoulder and wandered off to join his regiment.

Eshctu's group of drummers was already in a knot behind him, joking and playing little duets to warm up. There had been processions of state before, including the recent funeral, but this one felt different, bigger. A coronation parade was the biggest of them all.

Someone offered Eshetu a pipe. "No," he protested, waving it off to be passed to the next man who took an enormous toke. "How can you smoke so much?" Eshetu was incredulous. "You know the parade route is over a mile – we'll be dancing and drumming non-stop for at least an hour. How are you going to keep it up?"

The answer came out in a cloud of smoke directed purposefully at Eshetu's head. "Don't worry, youngster." The old man pointed to his neighbor, "he will drum and you will dance while I'm taking a breather!"

Behind Eshetu sounded a quick series of triplets and he turned to join in the rhythm, anxious to show what he could do. The old smoker looked approvingly at the speed of Eshetu's stick and nodded his head, smiling. "Don't tire yourself out now, young one," he jibed. Horns were beginning to sound and each act in the parade began to draw itself up in rough order, but to Eshetu it still looked like total chaos with the festoonery milling about him. He felt his hand gripping the stick too tightly. The horse guards had moved out!

Behind the horses, so well-trained they did not spook, followed Judah the lion, whom Eshetu could see as the parade began to string out. Daniel was leading him and the beast plodded off with remarkable calmness, but evoking just the impression of majesty on the crowds that Tewodros had intended by placing him at the head of the parade. A somber unit of elite soldiers in perfect step tramped past, those of the obsidian spears, to complete the introduction of awe. Then it was time to start the party, and next were the colorful scarves and fast-paced moves of a troupe of Gurage dancers, whose excitement would infect the crowd and start the first surge of cheers for the rest of the parade to maintain.

Eshetu was shuffled into place now, in between a more tempered dress regiment of Amhara troops ahead, and behind his drummers the cruder spears of a Borana detachment that could be counted on to brandish their weapons and cry out with infectious abandon. From now on it was about interacting with the crowd more than noticing the other acts, and enjoying his own music as the forward march began. Eshetu channeled his nervous energy into smoothing his hair, his uniform, and the skin on his drum. As they approached the first spectators lining the parade route, the drum leader turned with a gleaming smile that would stay fixed on his face for the whole performance, and lifted his stick to count in the first rhythm.

The drummers all struck in unison and the crisp sound carried them like a wave into the thick of the parade. Eshetu saw a young boy, no more than ten years old, whose mouth and eyes were wide with astonishment at the kaleidoscope before him. Eshetu swelled up with energy that made his movements grander and more dramatic as he played. He made eye contact with the boy's mother, who grinned and waved enthusiastically, sending Eshetu further into the parade route with joy. His movements slowly retracted to a measured level as his muscles began to complain and his breathing became more labored. He was almost to the halfway point and needed to save some fuel for the home stretch, but the forward progress had stalled while some traffic jam of performers unwound itself up ahead, and he found himself drawn into a duet with another young drummer, leaping back and forth while they played to keep the crowd whooping. There always seemed to be some reserve of strength to keep on going, and if Eshetu let out his own punctuating shout now and then, it seemed to invigorate his arms and legs. Now they were on the move again and could return to a more sedate rhythm and dance, as the crowd need only be interested in their act for the few seconds it took to pass them by.

The faces in the crowd began to blur together and the applause began to meld with the rhythm of the drum in Eshetu's head. The drummers progressed beyond the bulk of the commoners to approach the stands where the dignitaries were seated. Now in those stands, a group of three faces stood out starkly to Eshetu, and he almost forgot to play as he wondered at the flaxen hair framing bright blue eyes set in pale white skin. In return, the faces gawked back with undisguised, vulgar fascination at the drummers, dancers, soldiers, cavalry and other sundry pomp streaming in front of them.

In Magdala for the coronation, the British envoys struggled with their natural instinct to be diffident in the face of the magnificent spectacle they were observing. The city stood atop a plateau, commanding the juncture of three valleys – one a steep ravine leading to the north, one a gentler canyon away to the southeast, and the third a broad cul-de-sac extending west below the mountain that rose up from the city's northern bulwark, where peasants still tilled the land and a river came down to wend its way between the high plateaus. From where the valleys joined, a steep approach led up to the city, in the shadow of the king's palace, a two-story fortress of stone from which archers could cover the approach, and the ruler could see out over the rugged terrain that protected him. Behind the palace the city sprawled out with dusty streets past the quarters of noblemen who attended the court, to the more modest dwellings of merchants and craftsmen, then to the scattered huts of the poor before the table broke into a jumble of rocky outcroppings and the mountain ranges to the south. It was from the south that the parade approached, using the wider streets to make its way towards the king's crowning.

Across the parade route the Englishmen could see that Klaus something-or-other fellow, who seemed genuinely interested in the proceedings for some reason and chatted with Pierre from time to time. It did make the envoys feel somewhat more important to know that the Germans had decided to attend the event as well, but they were not quite sure if this was also a bad thing for the mission. As Eshetu passed them by, all heard the roar of the crowd crescendo from the rear of the parade, and knew that the king was coming.

"I say, how much gin was left in your case, Trafford?" said Boyle to his companion, turning away from the performances and speaking across their compatriot who sat between them. "Not that it matters without any ice to be had." It had been a long, excruciatingly uncomfortable road from London.

"More than a few drams, to be sure," Trafford replied. "Shall we have done with this infernal sun, and the interminable savages? We will see the king anyway at this private audience tomorrow – that's the point, isn't it?"

"It might be rude to leave early," ventured Johnson in the middle. "And we're blocked in by these noble types in their white dresses."

"Fine, fine," agreed Trafford, as the wave of anticipation washed even closer with the approach of Tewodros. Even these men could not help but feel a breathlessness as the heralds cried out, "the king is dead, long live the King!" in grander echoes of Yohannes' words in the tent at Sodere; and some in the crowd waved branches of palm and cheered in faint reminiscence of another royal entry long ago.

Tewodros rode a fine horse surrounded by his honor guard. The impassive face he wore flickered not one bit as he raised his hand to acknowledge the people, the nobility and the honored guests. Even the British raised an eyebrow and looked at each other with some appreciation of the moment.

The sound died quickly and the crowds dispersed as Tewodros passed on to the small church where the Abuna would set the crown upon his brow. Though that ceremony was restricted by lack of space to only the vassals whose exclusion would be an unforgivable slight to their promised loyalty, feasting was promised for all at the many stations through the city. Trafford, Johnson and Boyle found themselves hemmed in by the crowds with an exhausting, dusty fight to find their way back to their lodging and the sacred gin. Tomorrow would bring Glendon's mission and a chance to see in close quarters whether there was some substance behind the majesty they had witnessed today. Tonight, they would be drunk at cards.

* * * * *

Haymanot sipped the last of her drink, wanting to taste their precious Moonie's milk one last time. The candles cast shadows against the wall and her profile was straight and proud, almost regal. "It's a good thing you didn't go for the coronation," said Grandma in her cracked voice. "That prince would have been too busy to pay attention to you."

"You know I had to help with the harvest, Grandma. But maybe I shouldn't go to Magdala after all." Haymanot felt such an attachment to their rough kitchen table, where she had scratched her name as a girl under the side nearest the oven, and around which the family sat every night to eat their bread, play their games and talk of many things, that she felt to leave the village would mean dragging it with her.

"Haymanot, Haymanot," her father said gently. "We will miss you terribly but you are too good for this village. You have too much ability, such a fine mind, to waste it here with us old farmers."

"Besides, if the prince doesn't like you anymore you'll be back stuck with us anyway," Grandma cackled.

Haymanot had seen the way Tewodros looked at her and knew there was no danger of coming home. "Let's save our farewells for the morning, and I'll be back to visit before the seeds need planting."

## Chapter Fifteen

The first morning after the coronation, Tewodros was in the throne room and his next set of guests had just arrived. There was an awkward silence while they were kept waiting a proper time in the anteroom to be received.

"Thank goodness the coronation ceremony is over. Never have I felt so out of place as when all those people watched me put on a silly crown, as if I am better than the next man," the king whispered. Yohannes stood with him but they could not talk freely like before, as in the court at Magdala several obligatory nobles and other sycophants lined the walls of the chamber. Tewodros had to continue suffering them his patronage, however, if only to protect the feudal system from falling apart, by which he controlled the people up and down the empire. Even as he had wound his way through the parade yesterday, soaking up the energy of his people, he had been keenly aware of the weight of tradition that would dictate what he must do in his new role.

So it was that his mind was more keenly focused on the place where he felt he could make some change, and that was beyond the borders of his lands. While the king was bitterly disappointed (though he admitted this to no one, not even Yohannes) that England's regent herself was not in attendance, he regarded her emissaries as among his most special of guests. Tewodros was glad they had come, for he had a feeling about England, and there was hope of great things to be had through a relationship with Victoria, the ruler of the greatest empire on Earth. Perhaps she was too busy to leave her homeland, but would invite him to London, where even Yohannes had not been; where untold grandeur and wisdom must reside. How did its people with their education and pride comport themselves? What gleaming wonders of technology could be seen amidst its massive industries? His reverie was interrupted as Trafford, Johnson and Boyle were ushered in.

Tewodros maintained his impassive face while the three Englishmen openly ogled the court and the exotic king. Perhaps this was the English custom, Tewodros told himself, unwilling to let go of the picture he had painted of this powerful people. "Welcome to Ethiopia," he began. "If there is anything I can do to make you more comfortable as my guests, please do not hesitate to ask." The interpreter gave Tewodros his first impression of the English language, with its lack of fluidity and strange syllables, the weirdness only accentuated when the response came from the native speaker, Boyle.

"We are most grateful to his majesty for the excellent welcome," said the interpreter, flushing. Tewodros could tell that the interpreter was trying to shield the lack of humility in Boyle's discourse. Boyle continued, less roughly with this prepared statement, and the translation came, "Her Majesty Queen Victoria sends her best wishes on the occasion of the coronation of King Theodore."

Victoria – the name held a power for Tewodros, and he leaned forward as he heard Boyle, and then the interpreter say it. Not hearing Boyle express any regrets at the inability of Victoria to attend in person, he shrugged this off and was prepared to inquire as to the best means of delivering a gift to the English monarch. However, Boyle did not stop talking.

"I have here," and he pulled out a smooth, polished case of oak, thin yet hefty and a full cubit in length, "a gift from the British sovereign," Boyle waved the case about, and Yohannes deftly stepped forward to receive it, handing it to Tewodros with decorum.

As Tewodros looked down and ran his fingers over the wood grain showing on its varnished surface, the court fell silent, remaining so as the click of the latch was heard and the king opened the case. The green felt inside cradled an old dueling pistol, over half a foot in length, with several bullets, powder flask, rods and flints in their own compartments. The wood and iron were plain and simple, but inlaid on the handle was a piece of exquisitely carved ivory.

"It is the twin to a pistol remaining in the collection of the Prince Consort," proclaimed Boyle, drawing the king back out of his engrossment to look at the speaker. "Along with the wishes and the gift of the Queen we have come bearing an opportunity for the Ethiopian people – an offer of treaty with the British Empire."

"A treaty with Britain – this could be an important alliance," said Tewodros, his mind flitting to the Turkish threat. Some relationship with the Royal Navy, the most feared mistress of the seas, would cause the Ottoman Empire to think twice about leaning in his direction, or arming his Mussulman subjects against him.

Boyle continued while Trafford pulled out and brandished an official document, impressing the nobles lining the court. "As detailed in the treaty which my colleague Mr. Trafford now holds, Her Majesty will establish a formal legation and chamber of commerce in Magdala to incorporate Ethiopia into the East India trade routes, with accompanying protection for the port of Massawa, on an exclusive basis."

Tewodros had felt his expectations inflating as Boyle was speaking, but a sharp puncture had come as the interpreter concluded. "What does this mean, exclusive basis?" asked the king, raising his hand to quell the murmurs that began to circle the room.

Johnson cleared his throat. "It means, that Britain would not suffer other trading nations to engage in the same commerce with Ethiopia." Johnson paused, looking around to take in all the eyes that now bored into him. "Britain offers the broadest array of goods and markets in the world and no other partner could offer a treaty of such value."

Tewodros' hand remained raised, and he boiled to retort with a cutting reminder that Britain held a reputation as the foremost bastion of free trade, making this exclusive treaty the apex of hypocrisy. "We thank you for this offer from Her Majesty and will consider it promptly as a matter of state. It would be more palatable, however, if the exclusive aspect could be removed. We would of course treat Britain as a preferred trading partner."

"We have been given no authority to negotiate the terms of the treaty – it is Her Majesty's only offer," Trafford piped up.

"I see," said Tewodros, done with the meeting. "I hope that you will take some rest and perhaps the time to enjoy a tour of our fine churches, since you have come so far." Trafford, Johnson and Boyle shuffled out, Trafford still clutching the treaty. There was Klaus again, sitting in the anteroom for his turn at an audience, and Trafford felt the urge to hide the treaty behind his back. The Germans always made him ill at ease.

His court waited for the king to break the silence after the closing door. "Surely this Queen Victoria does not know how these subjects of hers conduct themselves?" Tewodros often found himself the only one talking as his courtiers had not yet developed the confidence to voice opinions. "I must admit, I had to cut the meeting short to remove any temptation of hasty speech. No matter, as I am sure any diplomatic niceties would be lost on these particular emissaries. This far across the sea and no time for formalities – I would have no time for them if not for the great importance of the opportunity they bring."

"Sire, perhaps you can communicate with them through a representative, in that case. You need not meet with them again," said his Minister of Trade, Henok, hoping to be selected as the messenger. A bright young man with a mastery of languages, his rugged features and athlete's build almost made one underestimate his intelligence.

"What would I say, minister?"

"Sire, perhaps we should review the treaty in detail – while we have the attention of such a great nation, we could take advantage," but Tewodros cut his waffling off there.

"If we do not have free trade they will charge us whatever they want for the goods they peddle," said the king. "I will not even look at an exclusive treaty. Further, we have not yet heard what our visitors from Germany, and France have to say."

Yohannes spoke up to support the king's line of reasoning. "We cannot know what this treaty might lead to. The British will offer protection for Massawa, but we know well what news comes from the dhow captains who sail east – they begin with trade, and will support its growth, but they did not stop in India until they governed the whole land. God help us if they find something they want in our mountains, and we have no other allies to play against them."

"I had not even considered that," said Tewodros. "However Henok is right. We cannot let these envoys go, lest we lose Britain's attention and our chance at concluding a beneficial treaty." Henok swelled up. "As they have no real authority, Henok will be my messenger to them while I communicate directly with Queen Victoria, who we know has received at least my invitation to the coronation." Henok deflated somewhat.

Mulugeta spoke, "very clever. Since I am sure these envoys have no desire to remain in Magdala indefinitely, they will agree that the fastest way to divine the ultimate British position is to write to the Queen."

"Surely, once she decrees an alternative to this 'exclusive' arrangement, or sends someone with authority to negotiate, their nobles will effect her wishes promptly," offered Henok. And Henok it was who went on foot the next day to the foreign emissaries' pleasant side road.

Interpreter in tow, he was pleased to again see Trafford, Johnson and Boyle in their guest quarters, where the visitors from various countries had occupied rooms up and down a long, low whitewashed building. The British had the first suite at the end nearest the gate, where the air was still tinged with the smoldering remains of last night's cooking fires.

The dry season lay waning, but the rains would not come to wash away the capital's haze for some time. The guest quarters were above the worst of it on the mountain slope, with an abundance of jacarandas for shade. The purple blooms framed a view of the verdant fields in the valley outside the city limits, and the distant river catching flecks of light beyond. No wonder, then that Trafford, Johnson and Boyle seemed open to the idea of staying a few more months. "There is no need for King Tewodros to write to London," said Johnson, having heard Henok's explanation. "We will compose a missive to Her Majesty and request authority to negotiate a non-exclusive treaty."

"This is most gracious," replied Henok through the interpreter, already resolving to learn English himself in short order. "His Majesty will be very pleased and we will ensure your every comfort while the reply waits."

"Go on, wait outside then. We'll give it you in a minute."

"Ah, right now?" Henok and the interpreter were ushered from the rooms and stood outside, patiently waiting while the envoys composed a reply.

"Here, here it is," called Trafford, passing a sealed envelope to Henok. "See this is sent to the High Commission in Aden." Henok did not see the curtain move slightly two rooms down the line as Klaus Zimmer watched him walk away.

## *Chapter Sixteen*

Henok dutifully delivered the envelope directly to Tewodros and his core council. "Did they really think we would not read their communiques?" marvelled the king. "Break the seal. Don't worry, we will be delivering our own letter, and now we know to go through Aden – much faster than Cairo."

"Yet another of the arts of diplomacy lost on them," observed Yohannes drily as they waited for the interpreter to prepare his translation. The man was flushing again, reluctant to let Tewodros take the sheet from his hand and begin reading aloud.

"To the Foreign and Commonwealth Office, Africa Desk. Mr. Glendon. Arrived in Ethiopia, witness to coronation parade and delivered offer of treaty directly to King Tewodros. Appears France and Germany here to observe only. People generally backward, most dressing in rags and feathers or even naked as monkeys, and we fail to see what our nation stands to gain from relations with this isolated barbarous place. They fail to see the gift we offer in the exclusive treaty and expressed a wish to negotiate its terms. However they, particularly the King seem very impressed with our Queen Victoria and will no doubt follow her wishes as they know she is a mighty potentate. Please send a letter styled from Her Majesty making clear there is no other offer than exclusive treaty, possibly also some token beads and sundry to entice them; they will sign and we can return forthwith. Yours Trafford."

"These mongrels, how dare they," began Makonnen, as the king was too furious to speak for a pause.

Tewodros shook his finger. "We cannot let these men return to Britain with this the only impression of Ethiopia," he said.

"They have agreed to stay in their quarters until the response arrives," Henok reminded him.

"I'll be damned if I let them stay where they are staying now."

"Where will you put them?" asked Tekle-giorgis. "If you move them it must be swiftly, and some place secure as they will know that something has transpired."

Tewodros looked around the room and his eyes came to rest on Yohannes, a small smile dawning. "I will keep them under lock and key at the monastery of Saint James while we write to Queen Victoria. It will be no worse than the cave I lived in my whole life – their physical and spiritual needs will be attended to, but they will be kept from the outside world. Besides, it was a good life there, wasn't it, Yohannes?"

"Not too barbaric or isolated at all," smiled Yohannes.

But only frustration showed on Tewodros' face when the council had broken up and only Yohannes remained. "Why won't the foreigners engage with me?"

"Your actions were perfect diplomacy, Tewodros. It is nothing you have done."

"All I want is make my country greater," he complained, as back to the envoys' quarters went Henok, with the interpreter and this time a squadron of soldiers.

"These buggers can't leave us alone for a day, can they," said Boyle as he opened the door a crack.

"Gather your belongings," said Henok, his tone and the spears behind him wiping the leer from Boyle's face even before the translation came.

"Yes," replied Boyle evenly, "we will come out as soon as we have made ready," and closed the door, leaning back against it while his companions, and the French emissary who was as usual their fourth at cards, looked aghast.

"Pierre," whispered Boyle in his rusty French, "you may be our only chance and you must get out now. By God, let's hope you make it to the coast before they can put their hands on you as well. Try and send a message from here in case they come for you next, that we are taken under armed guard. What will happen to us, I don't know."

The British packed their things.

\* \* \* \* \*

On the Red Sea it was many moons from that day when British engineers had crossed from Aden to begin driving pilings at Massawa, without so much as a by your leave from Tewodros. In the king's chambers he could discuss the situation with Yohannes away from the posturing of the official court. "I would like to take this as a positive sign that the British prepare for some commencement of trade, but without an official reply from their Queen I cannot trust what they are doing."

"I am sure they will send a negotiator in due course and all will be fine," said Yohannes, not quite trusting his own words. "If we expel these port-builders by force, then we are in danger of closing off the negotiation altogether."

"You are right, we cannot show more aggression on top of detaining their useless diplomats. But even if their army comes and there is no negotiator, we cannot show fear, we cannot back down – then they will surely take everything from us."

"How would they be so foolish as to risk war, without even trying to reach a peaceful solution?" Yohannes was still trying to convince himself.

"It is war we must be prepared for," rejoined Tewodros. "Remember the German fellow – Klaus something or other? He is due to arrive soon, with the two thousand rifles he promised us."

"For ten thousand thalers," recalled Yohannes. "I suppose he will be a useful friend to have."

"If we had kept the money, I probably would have spent it on the wedding anyway," Tewodros kidded.

He had grown besotted with Haymanot, the girl from the mountain village, who had come down to be courted by the king. They had set a date to wed, and though Tewodros would have preferred a simple ceremony, perhaps even back at his cave or Haymanot's village, a royal wedding was required. He was impressed with how his betrothed handled the massive rush of detailed planning as the date drew nearer, and in truth preferred to focus on this happy enterprise rather than what the British might be doing at Massawa. In the end, he would stand at the altar and feel there was no one else in the world except Tewodros and Haymanot, so it did not matter where or how they wed.

# PART THREE:
# BARON OF MAGDALA

# Chapter One

*"On desperate seas long wont to roam…"*
*- POE*

A late summer day, and the fleet ferried across the Red Sea from Aden to the piers that looked so out of place at Massawa, extending from little more than a tent city into the water's intense blue. It was brisk in the wind, and Napier could see up the coast for miles; distant whitecaps touching dun cliffs with scraggly green amid the rough rocks. Now the expedition was truly real; the planning, logistics and comforting officers' quarters of his preparation in Britain's outposts were behind him. This was different than the campaigns in India; though just as rugged, there was no retreat to friendly soil; no reserve army to aid him in case of a misstep. The tension he felt when he saw the tiger in the tree would grip his stomach unexpectedly, at least twice a day since his boot touched Abyssinian soil. He relished it.

The British moved inland toward the beginnings of the great plateau, marching slowly and tentatively as each man looked about him for some sign of resistance from Tewodros, or some glimpse of the wild Afar tribesmen who were said to roam parts to the south and had thrown a spear through Burton's jaw. More than once a day Jeevan would look up at the sky, then down at the fetid, volcanic earth and wonder what the hell he was doing there. He missed the languid succor of home's stifling, sweaty air, where the chai wallah had sweet tea for sale and the clack of the carom board offered an afternoon's lazy pursuit. He trudged on, telling himself that every step brought him closer to finding some water supply and ending the short rations of that one thing a man cannot do without.

It was not to say this country had nothing to recommend it. Alfred found himself leading Jeevan's company, and knew he could always count on his friend from the ship for a bit of light conversation and to show his connection with the men under his command. "Still, this country is as beautiful as any place, no?" he inclined his head at the perilous, broken landscape that forbade them to deviate from their route.

Jeevan stopped his trudging momentarily to look all around. "It is more terrible than beautiful," he declared and looked at his feet, one in front of the other, again.

Talk lessened as they began the ascent to the highlands; the column snaking in single file up and around the twisting switchback paths to higher ground; the Gurkhas laughing at the lesser lungs of the other battalions as they scampered up and down the steep slopes with ease, sent ahead to scout and able to climb the same incline twice in the time it took Jeevan or Alfred to climb it once. Just when it seemed they could go up no more, and Jeevan's legs burned in the day and throbbed to swollen gingerness in the night, it was the plateau, and a blessed green carpet laid over the rough terrain to mark where the rains had been the month before.

The new landscape felt lush after the desert crossing from the coast, and the yellow meskel flowers were everywhere, proud against the green. Napier had chosen to ride his elephant Goliath only after they reached the top – he did not want his men to think he could not manage the steep climb under his own power. He was told there would be many days of marching across the plateau, navigating steep defiles and crumbling terraces, and it would be good to have a change from foot, to elephant and perhaps to horse, to give one set of muscles a rest while he used another.

When the days of traversing the highlands turned into weeks, and the repeating patchwork of cultivated plots at first a beautiful quilt had now turned dull, to break the monotony of small village after small village he cajoled his senior officers into trying the ungainly mode of transportation along with him. It tickled him particularly to see Colonel Smithers terrified at every lurch of the elephant's back. The convoy took a break for lunch in the shade of a great, lonely tree, with baboons for attendants at a respectful distance, and Smithers was glad, knees knocking, to get down from atop his animal.

"Where do the guides say we have come?" asked Napier, stretching his legs out, knowing very little from the crude maps at his disposal. "Are we near to the city of Lalibela?"

A translation of his question flew back and forth before Smithers cleared his throat. "There is a Gurkha that went there to scout, and came back to the column," said Smithers.

"Bring him!" cried Napier in his excitement. The temptation to see the famed, rock-hewn churches at the ancient site of Lalibela was too much for him, and it showed in how boyishly he pursued the inquiry.

The Gurkha was brought. "He measures distance somewhat strangely, sir," explained Smithers. "He says the time it takes a fresh sprig from the tree to wilt, is approximately how far he walked from this city with the churches."

"Damn it, Smithers, how far is that?"

Smithers consulted. "He says, about the time it takes a wetted handkerchief to dry on a sunny day. I would estimate three to five leagues, sir. It is not on the planned route, it seems – it would be quite out of the way."

"Have we had any word in the villages of how this Tewodros has reacted to our arrival?" tried Napier, seeking some pretense for the detour. "It is disquieting, this lack of engagement, or even an acknowledgment that we have arrived. Perhaps we had best make inquiries in a larger settlement, like this Lalibela, now that we come so close to Magdala."

"Yes, perhaps there are some representatives of the court there, that must be interrogated," agreed Smithers.

"It is no point the army forging on recklessly with no intelligence of what might lay ahead," said Napier to himself as much as to his officers. "We go to Lalibela," he ordered.

They marched most of the way there the following day, and camped that night with anticipation. In the morning a small group of officers and men walked silently to Ethiopia's holy city, its new Jerusalem, past green terraces staggering upwards around them to flat mountaintops, broken by the exposed black ribs of volcanic rock where the slope was too steep for soil to cling. They came upon the churches as the earth filled its lungs full after waking up, and the sun was just warming the tops of the stone structures. Napier was almost in a daze as they passed each one, the names translating to those he knew so well from Sunday school, the churches of Michael, Golgotha, there they pointed to Mary, and finally the most incredible, the church of England's patron, of Saint George.

At Westminster the abbey imposed by seeming to lean its great bulk over you, by the myriad intricacies of Gothic elements that were too much to compass in one frame. Here Napier was drawn down, down into the depth that opened before his feet to cradle the church, where his breath shortened as he saw the burnt umber color of the stone that was all one continuous extension of the very ground that held him up, and the church that was part of the earth itself. The sanctuary was carved into a square cross three stories high, as if God himself were the sculptor, building his castles made of rock and not of sand; the top just level with the ground on which Napier stood at the edge of the pit that surrounded the church.

He descended by a stone stair and then through a short tunnel into the canyon that man had made, chiseled blow by blow to leave the sheer walls that did not seem to close in, but opened the way to the sky above. Now the church made him feel insignificant with its massive, immovable presence reaching up, now he saw the beautiful detail of the stonework around the windows on the exterior. As he entered the dark sanctuary at first all he could make out were those same small bright windows cut through to the outside, patches of salvation streaming down, by which light he could soon see the painted images of brown-skinned saints with wisdom in their eyes. He stood dumbfounded until an aide sidled up and whispered, "sir, the locals say it is the feast day of Saint Raphael and there will be a celebration at his church beginning shortly. Would you like to witness it?"

Through a tunnel again, this one longer and more roughly hewn, Napier was led in a single file as his officers scrambled to ensure this church of Gabriel and Raphael was secure. Napier emerged from the tunnel and waved away their concern as he saw the simple white robes of the priests and deacons gathered on the ramparts of the solid shrine – these men were here for God and peace and he even felt embarrassed to have his pistol at his waist. The columns of Saint Gabriel-Raphael framed pointed arches and windows of almost Moorish design, while below the rampart a massive stone moat was mere inches from the feet of the outermost ranks of white-clothed and head-dressed men. Some bore silver crosses, some wood and some were bare-handed, as they took up a chant to begin the ceremonies with jangling sistrels for accompaniment. Of the British delegation, there was space for only Napier and Smithers to enter the church itself with their interpreter, the guests ushered across two crude planks over the moat and into the crowded, thickening air of the nave that oppressed as the glory of God.

The unknown smells assailed him and the shoulders of strange men rubbed his, but the structure of the liturgy was familiar, and the foreign words that flowed over the massed pilgrims were clearly to Napier his same holy scriptures. The faces of the men around him were not those of barbarians, but of proud sons of God, in awe at His presence in their midst; displaying a true reverence that had been somehow missing from Napier's dry childhood experiences in the parish church. In the pause between readings as more censers were swung and more suffocating smoke dispensed, Napier leaned to his interpreter and asked what the reading had been. "It is the story of Saint Stephen martyr, when his face looked like the face of an angel."

Napier told Smithers the incense made his eyes water, but admitted to no one that he was profoundly moved. Upon their return to camp, he instructed the officers not to let the rest of the army explore the churches, lest they too come away with any sense of spiritual kinship with the people they were here to subjugate. He passed the night in deep slumber and heard nothing of the hailstorm that came through.

It woke Jeevan up as the stones pummeled the thin fabric of his tent, but when he stuck his face outside the stinging particles drove him back in. In the morning a blanket of white, made of pebbles of ice was piled ankle-deep throughout the camp, and in some places where the wind had swirled it made crazy patterns or built up a small tower to rise above the plain of hail. The army-issue tents were white as well, and Jeevan was easily picked out as a dark speck crunching his way to fetch a ration of tea.

"No need to fetch water today, we can just melt the ice, no?" smiled a friendly Gurkha in line.

"Do you see this kind of strange weather in the mountains where you come from?" asked Jeevan.

"Not like this, no," said the Gurkha. "The hail may come but not so much, and the snow will stay on the ground but it is different. This I never saw," he shook his head.

"When a new thing comes from the sky it must be an omen," mused Jeevan. "What can this mean? We are covered in white as if being washed pure. It must be the gods that bless us."

"We need an omen," laughed the Gurkha. "I heard them say there was no news of this Tewodros-Sewodros in the Lalibela town." He used the rhyming alliteration that Jeevan had noticed sometimes among the Gurkhas. "We have no inkling what we are in for."

"Have you seen nothing when you go out scouting?"

"I have seen no sign of any soldiers, but there are too many valleys. I don't know what is waiting for us even in the next one," admitted the Gurkha.

For the first time it occurred to Jeevan that the Ethiopians may be waiting for them to come too far inland, and then cut them off from ever leaving this foreign country. "We have come a long way from the ships," he said out loud.

The Gurkha shrugged and took his tea – they had reached the front of the line.

## Chapter Two

"I know we expect them to weaken the longer they have to eke their way through the highlands, but now they are close - they have passed Lalibela," said Yohannes, speaking to a moody Tewodros, the other Rases in the council chamber and Klaus the German who sat quietly by, twirling his thin moustaches and sometimes leaning over to his interpreter when he sensed something important was going on. Ten thousand silver coins had gone back to Germany with Klaus, the face of Maria Theresa on each one with its bouncing curls and haughty look, unable to show any emotion on her return through the old country from her long sojourn in southern lands, and the mute lips not able to reveal what secrets the Empress had seen.

Klaus was an honest soul and had returned along with the purchased rifles upon Tewodros' invitation to provide advice on European military tactics. The weather seemed always to be good in this country and he had felt no desire to stay home in the cramped and cold streets of Berlin, where he was nobody. Here, he sat with the king, and his few years of experience as a German army engineer were sufficient for men to take his word as command.

"Klaus, when will the cannon be ready?" asked the king. Tewodros had ordered the casting of a mighty mortar when Klaus had stressed the importance of artillery, and confessed to some knowledge of how to forge it.

"The ore has been collected and we have sufficient fuel, so we can begin immediately – with nearly seven tons the weight, we needed quite some materials," replied Klaus, sitting up extremely straight. "Then the testing with just one or two shots, and we can build the wagon very quickly."

"We may have some advantage of numbers but they will slaughter us if we cannot match their weapons," declared the king to general assent. "I will not sacrifice my people unnecessarily, as other rulers on this continent might – I would prefer to have this great cannon on my side before I engage the enemy." Tewodros looked around at the aggravating room where nobody spoke, surveying the men he had been given as his council, who wished they could help him just as much as he yearned for someone to guide him.

There was the Qenazmatch, Ras Mulugeta, commander of the right, an old and solid presence whose ambition had burned out but whose sunken eyes held much wisdom. The Dedjazmatch Balcha, keeper of the door, who never held Tewodros' gaze for more than a moment before looking up at the ceiling, or away. Now Ras Makonnen, commander of the left, the Grazmatch was always quick to speak his mind and Tewodros knew where he stood. Finally, strong and bold in spirit and appearance, the king's favorite, his Fitaurari who led the vanguard, Tekle-giorgis the true.

"Well, what would my generals recommend? I need ideas! Even if they are foolish, let them be weighed by the council. Tekle-giorgis, let us begin with you; I know you have thought of how we might defeat this foe."

"My first recommendation," said the Fitaurari, "is that you make yourself scarce from this place. The enemy will look for you in Magdala, but if you move through the countryside it is likely they can never catch up to you, and eventually they must grow tired and go home."

Mulugeta leaned back and spoke, "but while they stay, an army of that size will impose dreadfully on our farmers. I do not wish to sound weak, but would it not be wisest to simply give them the diplomats they have come to retrieve? We no longer need their treaty, we have our friend Klaus," he nodded at the German, "and how can these British stay any longer if we no longer have their men? Once we fight, however, they may win, and in that case the British may not leave without forcing this treaty upon you, or some other infringement of your sovereignty – I think we all know what some of these European powers are apt to do."

Tewodros shook his head, then leveled his gaze at the two men. Though he knew they only had his safety in mind, he felt he was chiding them, "I will not be a fugitive in my own lands, and I will not yield my principles simply to avoid a conflict. Nothing but the enemy's force may remove me from the capital, or take these men without an apology. And who is to say they have sent an army all this way simply to be satisfied with the freeing of a few buffoons? We must force a resolution and we must do it as men of courage and therefore from Magdala."

"May I speak, though not a military man?" asked Yohannes, from his customary seat just behind Tewodros. As usual, the room fell into a respectful silence to hear the words of the monk. "As always, my aim would be to avoid bloodshed to the greatest extent possible, and if letting the hostages go could achieve that aim, I would certainly do so. But the king is right; the stakes are now higher than the freedom of three emissaries, or even the pride of the nation that sent them. This is an army of subjugation, and if we now appear weak we risk sending a message that Ethiopians will yield immediately to force. This will invite further aggression from the British, or indeed from other quarters."

"In that case let us bring an end to this now!" Makonnen spoke up. "The new rifles are already here, let me take them and go to skirmish in the hills and valleys where they cannot use their cannon against me. Your mortar can stay in Magdala to protect you, but I think these dogs will turn tail and run when they get their first taste of a fight!"

Balcha was quick to plead, "King Tewodros, let me go out instead of Makonnen. He has spoken wisely, but I know the northern marches better than him. If we gain a victory or two by taking the initiative, we may well get the apology and withdrawal of the invader that you desire, without a drawn-out engagement."

Mulugeta was more cautious. "I think this army is too serious to be deterred by a few quick strikes, but instead they may become enraged if we hurt them. We may yet face a longer campaign, and have we the strength for that?"

Yohannes was not expected to speak again, and his suggestion was also strange as he looked to a corner of the ceiling, "it is true that Saint Paul in his weakness found God's strength, but it is also true that God's strength was given to the Israelites in war through that ancient box of wood and beaten gold – a box we now possess."

"The Ark of the Covenant?" scoffed Balcha.

"Yes, was it not said by some that the weapon may even have been used by Galawdewos to defeat the left-handed Imam?" said Tekle-Giorgis.

Tewodros knew the legends, of the Ark and what fearsome power lay within, that lightning would flash forth to strike men down; of its spiriting away from a burning Jerusalem to a monastery on the shores of Lake Tana some hundreds of miles away from his capital, and of the triumph of a past Ethiopian emperor, with help from the Portuguese, over the Turkish-backed invaders from Somalia. "But Yohannes," he reminded his teacher, "Galawdewos and his Roman Catholic allies had fought the followers of an entirely different religion. These invaders now are Christian."

Yohannes chuckled, "the King speaks true, we cannot use the Ark of God against a fellow believer."

"Then in this battle, what side is God on?" asked Tekle-giorgis.

To which Tewodros simply responded, "justice."

"And what is justice?" Yohannes could not help pushing his former student.

Tewodros looked around at his advisors. "Justice," he spoke, "will be when the people of Africa are treated with respect by those who seek to make our acquaintance, no matter if their cities are built higher, their coffers are limitless, or they carry a bigger stick. If the only way to teach this respect is by our own force of arms, then let us begin the lesson. Tekle-giorgis," he barked, "though your rank tends to the front, you will stay behind with me and garrison the city. Mulugeta, Balcha, my commanders of the right and the center, you will take the central and the northern passes between Lalibela and Magdala by which this army might come, and hold them as long as you can so the invader does not come to Magdala at full strength. You will send skirmishing parties down from the passes to sting this invader like the tsetse fly of the south – but fall back before you are drawn into a full engagement, as we must rely on our advantage of the high defensive positions. Makonnen will remain here to reinforce either of you that needs it, or move quickly to another front if the British try to outflank us. Klaus will divide the German rifles equally among you," Tewodros wanted no general with sole control of the better arms, "and when the cannon is ready, we will send it to where it can make the biggest impact."

Tewodros left the chamber to see Haymanot, while his generals went to do his bidding. He walked along a cool corridor to where the queen now spent her afternoons, the chambermaid letting him through the door and then leaving to give the couple privacy. The king sank down on the embroidered cushions next to Haymanot, letting out a long, slow sigh.

"What is it, Tewodros?" asked Haymanot, taking his hand in both of hers. "You are going to worry yourself sick as long as this British army is out there – perhaps the sooner they come to Magdala the better and we can have an end to this."

"I have sent Mulugeta and Balcha to hold the passes. If the British meet some resistance, then maybe we will receive some message regarding their demands. We have had no communication thus far, and I cannot make the best decision with so little to go on."

"I am sure you are making the best decisions under the circumstances," Haymanot patted his hand.

"Unfortunately the best thing for me to do is to be trapped in Magdala." He looked at Haymanot and kissed her forehead, "although in some ways most fortunate since you are here with me." Tewodros leaned back against the wall, some light trickling in the windows around the curtains that were drawn to allow the queen some peace. "I thought I had left the cave, but now I am in another cavern, grander though it is."

Haymanot moved his hand to rest on her stomach, which six months ago had begun to grow and now seemed to be another being attached to the queen. "We will make sure this one has all the freedom and more that was taken from you growing up," she smiled, and the king smiled too.

## Chapter Three

A frustrated Mark Glendon sat in London drumming his fingers on his desk, with no clue what was going on in real time half a world away. Matthews had already moved on to other problems, and looked exasperated every time Glendon wanted to talk about Ethiopia. "Look, Mark, the pieces are set in motion. There really is no part for us to play except to massage the story however the action turns out," was all he would offer.

Glendon again flipped through the most recent cables reporting the fleet's arrival at Massawa and departure inland, but there had been absolutely no news since. He scribbled a message to the Aden station ordering them to report the latest developments, and then scratched it out. If something transpired, he would hear of it. He had to get out of Whitehall, and he made for the crooked streets to walk until his nervous energy was spent.

Down below the palace window in Magdala, Tekle-giorgis' lieutenants were already walking out from the briefing to pass out the new duty assignments in camp.

"Eshetu? Alemu?" said one, lifting the flap of the first tent in his quadrant.

Eshetu recognized the slim, grim face of the lieutenant Dawit. "Haven't seen you since back in the other camp, when we were waiting for Makonnen to come," he said, rubbing his stubbly beard. "Now it seems we're waiting again. What do you have for me now?"

"Your brigade is being reassigned to Dedjazmatch Balcha's division, and you'll only have today to report in and get situated. His troops move out tomorrow."

"What? I'm sitting for weeks and now we're all supposed to fit in with a new commander at a moment's notice?" snapped Alemu. "Same thing is happening in each division – seems the Fitaurari was adamant on mixing up the troops. Loyalty insurance, I think he called it."

"Nobody needs to question our loyalty to Tewodros," grumbled Eshetu.

"Yes, but are you more loyal to the Fitaurari than to the king?" grinned the lieutenant. He pointed the way to Balcha's camp and told Eshetu and Alemu what supplies to take with them, and what they would be rationed once they got there.

Eshetu saw the new German rifles being handed out in Balcha's division that afternoon, but was not surprised that Tekle-giorgis' "loyalty" brigade did not receive any. He would still follow his own captain who was to take orders directly from Balcha, and did not have to mix with Balcha's men, who regarded his faction with a combination of disdain and curiosity from across camp lines.

"When we march tomorrow, let's show these Balcha bastards how it's done in a real army," Alemu said at his side.

Eshetu nodded. The next morning came too soon, with bleary eyes and stiffness in all the legs that had been too long squatting in one campsite. Eshetu felt like an ant, dwarfed by the rocky promontories to his left and right, following the trail set by the column that scurried in front of him as they headed for the northern and more difficult of the two passes by which the British might approach Magdala. All routes to Tewodros' capital were rugged and perilous, but the central approach from the east was wider and Mulugeta had gone that way while Makonnen camped just outside the capital.

Eshetu carried more than he should be carrying for their mission, but Dedjazmatch Balcha had not wanted his men to leave their equipment in Magdala lest the fighting commence there before they could return. "I hope we don't meet these British dogs on the march – I'd much rather take them from the high ground," he puffed to Alemu, whom he now considered a fast friend in this new and strange army.

"I hear their skin is white like our cotton garments – at least we will see them coming!" laughed Alemu.

Eshetu grunted, and focused on keeping up with the fast pace. "At least we're used to this thin highland air."

That afternoon, for the first and only time the hills of Abyssinia rang with the cry, "Aayo Gorkhali!" and Eshetu looked up from a wooded section of their trail to see strange brown men, short of stature and painted with mud, leaping from soldier to soldier at the head of the column with heavy, curved knives that took men to their death with a single blow.

The ambush was so unexpected that Balcha's men ahead of Eshetu milled about chaotically, running into each other and crushing the column back into Eshetu. He managed to unsling his rifle but there was no way to fire without hitting his own men, and the spears and knives of the soldiers closer to the front of the trail that took no more than four abreast were waving uselessly as if at shadows. Though it seemed that there were two Gurkhas to every Ethiopian, it was a scouting party of less than twenty that had burst from the trees and killed no less than fifty men before collecting for a coordinated volley of gunfire into the mass of confused soldiers. After the first fusillade, the Ethiopians expected a pause while the enemy reloaded. Four more shots from each Gurkha followed with no pause from their repeating rifles, throwing any man hoping to fire back into confusion. There were few screams from the wounded as the Gurkhas had aimed deadly and true, then turned as quickly as they had come and vanished up the wooded slope.

Eshetu was breathing heavily though he had moved little, and the army fell into a stunned silence for what seemed like a full minute before orders were shouted by the captain of the vanguard to form a defensive perimeter and clear the bodies. Word was quickly sent to the back of the column where Balcha followed, that the enemy was scouting the northern route.

"What invaders are these that fight like this?" breathed Alemu in Eshetu's ear. "If all their troops are of this quality…"

"We must get to where the pass opens up and establish ourselves before these British come at us in numbers," said Eshetu, looking back to see if orders were yet coming from the Dedjazmatch. "They simply caught us unawares - we had expected to be the ones that would strike first and then retreat."

"No," said Alemu, "did you see how accurate were their rifles, and how they fired without reloading? We cannot fight these British alone – we need Makonnen to come to succor us if we are to defend the pass. Better yet, we should fall back to Magdala now."

"That is not for us to decide – here comes our captain now, he must know something."

The orders were to camp at the pass, and Eshetu and Alemu spent the next hours walking in paranoia through the shadowy trees, and the sleepless night not knowing what the morning would bring.

## Chapter Four

Napier had arrived at the Djidda, the last river to cross before the final climb through the pass and on to Magdala. He stood on the bank in the quiet afternoon, the clouds moving slowly in one direction and the river in the other, God's light on the trees and His spirit twinkling in the reflections from the eddies. The history of the Djidda was not told much in the world, and never would be. There were far greater rivers, but for Napier this was the most significant of his life; his Rubicon. From the corner of his eye, he saw Smithers signaling furiously to join the colonel for a palaver.

A Gurkha was there, looking jaunty, his square face framing a broad white smile. "Make your report, man," snapped Smithers. To Napier, Smithers said in more ingratiating tones, "sir, his squad has met the enemy." Napier felt a thrill – this was their first real excitement since they began slogging their way through the rough Abyssinian territory.

"We climbed that ridge there," the Gurkha indicated a direction, "then we found many men marching on a narrow path. We hid in the trees, then we jumped out and killed maybe fifty, very quick. They don't have the repeating rifle like we have," he noted. "We come straight back to camp, nobody followed us. No Gurkha was killed," he continued matter-of-factly.

"Did anyone give you orders to engage the enemy?" Napier looked sternly at him and the Gurkha deflated.

"No, no, just observe and report. But…"

"That is all. Dismissed." The Gurkha left, bowing his head several times.

"I apologize for their insubordination, sir. Won't happen again," said Smithers.

Napier turned to him. "Damn good job those men did. Taking initiative in the field and making the right decision – if all our troops were like this we could dispense with the sluggishness of central command and overcome the enemy with far fewer numbers. It helps to have the better weapons, of course," he added.

"Yes, sir."

"Why didn't you give them orders to sting the enemy if they could make a clean exit? I thought we discussed this very tactic in Bombay. Undoubtedly they have sown a seed of fear through our first contact with the Ethiopians," Napier actually rubbed his hands together.

"I...I wasn't quite aware of their capabilities, sir," stammered Smithers.

"Now, they mustn't think we lack the courage to fight them toe to toe, without jumping from behind trees. Find me a good man in the ranks," Napier was enjoying himself now there were real happenings afoot. Alfred happened to be at the mess nearby and was brought.

"Alfred, isn't it?" said Napier, and Alfred was pleased that his general addressed him as a friend.

"Yes, sir."

"We need a drum."

"A drum, sir?"

"The biggest drum you can find. The Abyssinians are going to know we are coming the next time we meet them."

"I'll see what I can do, sir."

"They will learn to run when they hear that drum," laughed Napier. "Dismissed, Alfred."

Alfred had finished his dinner and decided to attack his task straight away. Stalking through the camp he found an idle interpreter, then recognized Jeevan and beckoned him to join the mission, in case he needed an extra man to help carry any drum they might find.

"A drum, sir?" said Jeevan. "Why would we want them to know we are coming?"

"The major general thinks it will strike fear into the nativ- the Abyssinians," Alfred replied, leading the way along the dirt path that wound through fallow fields to the nearby village. The earth was dry and cracked in places, and one could see over the fences made of thorn bushes where the irrigation ditches had been stopped up while the land recovered. "I say, how are you? I mean, how has it been, since we came here, d'you miss your home? Alfred tried to continue the conversation.

"As soon as I joined the army, even in India I already missed my home."

"Fair enough – so it seems we are in the same boat again," mused Alfred.

Up the path in the opposite direction came four Gurkhas leading two men in white clothes, almost like Indian lunghis but worn in a strange style. Alfred, the interpreter and Jeevan stood aside to let them pass, the Gurkhas saluting and grinning but saying nothing.

"Must be messengers," said Jeevan, his head swiveling to watch them go.

"We'll find out the news soon enough if we've finally had word from this King Theodore," said Alfred. "Come on, then, let's keep moving." The three men passed the outskirts of the village, and knocked at the nearest tukul while the villagers looked on and swatted the incessant flies.

"Come on out," called the interpreter, then to Alfred said, "the villagers are scared of army men. Many soldiers from the king's army come through here and they are not always...kind."

The farmer came to the door. "A drum?" he said with a mixture of incredulity and relief warring on his lined, sun-darkened face. He shrugged and called to his wife in the dark hut, whom the men could not see as the goatskin instrument was brought.

"Is that as big as they come?" asked Alfred.

"We'll have to go to the church to find bigger ones," said the interpreter.

Alfred sighed. This was turning into a fool's errand, and even in this far country he really did not want to start levying any of the army's needs on the house of God. "See how loud it is, and we'll see if all the ones in the village add up to enough racket to please the general." He fumbled in his haversack for a few twists of English baccy, which he had found generally to be good compensation to the locals, but a blight on his own troops' lungs in the mountainous air.

The farmer gave the drum to Jeevan, snatched the tobacco and vanished before the visitors had even left his threshold.

In Napier's camp, the senior officers had gathered again to receive the men in white that now crossed their threshold. The two messengers were handsome men, just as tall as the Englishmen though somewhat slighter, and looked supremely uncomfortable as they cast their eyes around at all the white faces. They held their palms out above their waists to show they were unarmed, but Napier could see they were not sure if the custom of the British was to deal gently with messengers in war. He quickly called for camp stools and water to be brought – the more he could make these men feel at ease to speak, the more intelligence he could gather.

"They have come with greetings from the Dedjazmatch Balcha," the interpreter conveyed.

"You mean these messengers have not come from the king?" Napier was clearly disappointed, but before he could speak further one of the men had stood up and blurted out the next part of their message.

Napier saw the interpreter pause, and leaned forward to catch what came next. "The Dedjazmatch wishes to meet with the British general to offer his services, on the understanding that he would be the best partner for Britain as Ethiopia's leader."

Napier leaned back into his chair, smirking. It was a bold move by this Balcha, to lay such a card openly on the table. He respected it. "Who is the Dedjazmatch Balcha?" he asked.

"The title means keeper of the door – he is one of the king's top generals," answered the interpreter.

"Ha! Perhaps this man is indeed the keeper of the door to Ethiopia. It is always easier to divide and conquer," said Napier. "Ask the messengers what Mr. Balcha proposes for a meeting."

The interpreter gave the reply, "He is camped in the pass by which you must go to Magdala, the capital – he will meet you there."

Napier chuckled. "We will come to the pass, but he will not meet us there. They will tell Mr. Balcha to decamp to below the pass, to show he is no threat to us. He will give his assurances in writing that the treaty desired by the British government is approved pending his replacement of Mr. Theodore. Then we will go to Magdala together, but he will go first, to pave our way to the capital. If these terms are accepted, we will meet in the pass – but in my camp, not his."

At each pause for the interpreter to relay the terms to the messengers, their faces grew more drawn, and they were undisguisedly agitated at Napier's last sentence. They hurried off, casting many a backward glance as the clouds built steadily over the mountain pass to which they returned.

## Chapter Five

In Balcha's camp, a light rain had been steadily falling and the men were in the main confined to their tents. Alemu had dozed off and with the air inside now stuffy, Eshetu poked his head out to breathe. Through the drizzle he saw something was amiss, as a group of elite soldiers were making their way down the last few rows of tents in the neighboring sector, where a company of troops originally from Balcha's army were housed. He could hear murmurs of discussion but could not make out what was being said. "Alemu," he nudged his companion, "look outside, there are fully armed men. What do you think is going on?"

Even as Alemu's head poked out alongside Eshetu's, some of the armed soldiers broke off to begin forming a perimeter around the camp sector where Tekle-giorgis' men stayed. In the tents that had been visited already, men were making preparations to stand to. The remaining soldiers that were already armed were making a beeline for Eshetu's row of tents, and two fanned out to menace him and Alemu, the two heads comically peering up from the tent flaps.

"Look, you, here is the deal. Balcha is no longer answering to King Tewodros until this affair with the British is over. If you will pledge your loyalty to this army, you will not be considered an enemy."

"So I am to swear an oath to Balcha or die?" asked Eshetu. "By all means, we are loyal to Dedjazmatch Balcha," he raised his hand and tried to keep his voice from being droll, while slack-jawed beside him Alemu dumbly raised his palm also.

"Good. You are to surrender arms in the meantime and wait here for further instructions," and the two men handed over their rifles, cartridges and bayonets to be piled in a makeshift armory. There was very little sign of resistance from anywhere else in the camp. The tent flaps closed again and the men sat in silence while the hours passed slowly.

No one spoke at mess time, but there were sideways glances and raised eyebrows aplenty. Eshetu regretted giving away his weapon, but a vulnerable feeling was better than a dead feeling, he reasoned. He still had a knife tucked away, and if they came for him he would not go quietly. When darkness came it was strangely easier to sleep, as the rain and the fear of going abroad dampened the usual rowdiness of camp life. The night passed quickly.

In the morning again there was hubbub. "Strike the tents! Pack your things! We are moving. We are moving the camp," the orders were heard before breakfast. Tekle-giorgis' soldiers were herded down the slopes towards a sort of dell where the camp could spread out again, below the treeline but clear of the thicker forest that guarded the path back to Magdala. Ahead of them they could see a detachment of Balcha's men who had gone before to block the way down from the dell.

"I don't like being surrounded by men with guns when I don't have a gun," mused Alemu.

"The real question is, why are we leaving the heights?" said Eshetu, looking behind him to the pass they were supposed to be defending. "Balcha must be in cahoots with the British. It is the only explanation."

"What does it matter anyway?" asked Alemu. "We are on Balcha's side now, whatever side that may be. Maybe I would rather fight with the British than against them, you saw what those devils did to us the other day."

"Shh," warned Eshetu. "You don't know who will hear you."

Before Alemu could look around for eavesdroppers, there was a loud hee-hawing just ahead in the clearing, and all eyes snapped to where a mule had trod on a fallen tent-peg and was kicking out in rage. The animal had already knocked down two men, and several more hustled over, shouting and pressing on each other as they tried to dance in and secure the mule's bridle.

Eshetu glanced over at the trees ten feet to his left. If he could skirt the clearing in the woods and stay high on the slope, he might be able to evade Balcha's men. The soldiers escorting his squad had clustered forward to get a better view of the commotion below, and now was his chance.

He darted into the forest, behind the first bush, now down to the ground where he could no longer see Alemu, or anyone else, but that must also mean they could no longer see him.

"If they just give the mule some space it would calm down," was Alemu's advice, but when he turned back to his friend, Eshetu was not there. Alemu's mouth opened and the urge welled up inside him to shout Eshetu's name, but the sound died in the back of his throat as a whisper, and instead he pursed his lips to blow a stream of air, and shook his head. If his friend had managed to slip away, he had better act nonchalant. Alemu eyed Balcha's men who had now returned to goading him towards the clearing, and they did not seem to twig that anything was amiss. He suppressed a smile, and trotted on.

"My only chance is if they didn't see me at all. If they saw me they will come now and I'll just say I went for a pee," Eshetu said to himself. He counted to thirty in his head, but he lost track of whether each count was one moment, or ten moments, as time seemed to expand and contract while he was frozen behind the bush. He counted again, almost unwilling to believe they really weren't coming to tramp through the woods in a line of men with spears and find him. "I can't sit here all day – I must get away," he whispered, and dropped to the earth on his elbows to crawl deeper into the woods, slowly and painstakingly, trying to keep the most foliage always between him and the column he could still hear passing by.

The pebbles dug into his forearms and the dirt made his clothes filthy, his neck itched and he could see the earthworms all across his way, but all his urges had to be suppressed. He kept counting in his head, each time to thirty, just to give his mind

259

something to do as he crawled, lest he panic and move too suddenly.

It seemed he had counted thirty a thousand times when Eshetu stopped to breathe the fragrant humus beneath his nose, and could hear the men behind him no more. He turned his head to look back and could see nothing but trees. Carefully, he stood up and sought to gain his bearings. The slope to his left must lead up to the peak above the pass where he had been this morning. "Magdala must be to the right," he was still whispering to himself.

He started at a slow trot through the pines, thankful for the carpet of needles that cushioned his steps; though every time he heard a twig crunch he thought it might echo in the valley for Balcha's men to hear. He turned his head from side to side imagining phantoms all about, as he quickened his pace. Soon he was careening, a pinball between the trunks, and every so often he nearly stumbled, or turned his ankle on a root, and wondered how the British dervish soldiers had moved away so fast up the slopes. His breath became labored, and he slowed, realizing his panic was silly. "I must be far beyond the camp now," he reasoned, "and will move faster on the path." Eshetu cautiously made his way down the slope, and peered out from the wood back up the path to where Balcha's camp would be settling down. There was nobody to be seen, and he had sunlight for a few more hours at least. He would make Magdala on the morrow if he kept going, and could maybe last without food or water for just that long. Would they believe him when he returned? Would Tekle-giorgis, or even the king, welcome his tidings and reward him for unmasking the traitorous Dedjazmatch?

It was much easier going on the path, and soon he fell into a rhythm and felt he could run all day and all night, each stride flowing smoothly from the last, his mind eventually devoid of thought, his flight inexorable and inevitable, the sunlight turning to moonlight and a shadow still passing over the stony ground.

## *Chapter Six*

A dusty man shambled towards a sentry post, saying to himself, and sometimes out loud, "Magdala...Magdala...Balcha...Balcha..." Eshetu had reached a point of exhaustion where he could barely focus on the ground in front of him, and let his legs give way when his arms were grasped by two of Tekle-giorgis' men.

"What is this? A deserter?" one of the sentries shook him, and Eshetu's eyes rolled around to meet the sentry's accusing look.

"I need...water," Eshetu licked his lips. "I need to speak to the Fitaurari Tekle-giorgis."

"A crazy man," concluded the other sentry.

Eshetu stood up again on his own legs and shook off the sentries' hands. "I have escaped! The men of Balcha have turned; they have all deserted the king...they are the deserters. I must see the Fitaurari!" and he collapsed to the ground.

"Get him water and bread," scoffed the accusing sentry. "Send for the lieutenant as well – Dawit will know what to do with a deserter."

Eshetu was too tired to care about the accusation just yet, and grateful for water as he slurped it down, but was careful not to drink too much lest his body reject it. He looked up at the slim face of Dawit, who arrived at the sentry post soon after the bread.

"I know you," said Dawit. "You were sent to ensure Balcha remained loyal to the king, yet you have deserted?"

Eshetu spread his hands, "I have been telling them, I am loyal to Tewodros. They asked us to swear to Balcha and desert the king, they took our guns, all I could do was run back to warn the Fitaurari..." Eshetu's voice trailed off as another wave of exhaustion hit him.

Dawit raised his eyebrows. "That is serious talk," he said. "It will be for the court martial to decide." He turned to leave.

Eshetu rallied himself. "There is no time for that! I fear they will join the invaders. There is no time."

Dawit stopped and looked back at the earnestness in the soldier's eyes. "The court is sitting this afternoon – the Fitaurari is the judge. I will try and fit your case in." With that he strode away and Eshetu was satisfied.

"No need to tie my hands," he told the sentries, "I am too tired to run away," and he slumped into a nap on the hard earth.

He awoke to see the Fitaurari Tekle-giorgis standing over him, and sat bolt upright. It seemed silly to salute from a sitting position, but he did so awkwardly, anyway.

"You ran from the pass without stopping," mused the Fitaurari, more of a statement than a question. He smiled at Eshetu. "And I placed the court in recess and came here without stopping. Tell me everything that happened."

His eyes were fixed on Eshetu and the soldier knew that his leader was one of those men who could see a lie forming in the mind before it came out as speech. Thank God he had nothing to hide – he told Tekle-giorgis his story, filling in details he had not even realized he had observed, when asked to give more regarding the number of troops whose weapons were taken, and the way the camp in the clearing stood in relation to the ridge.

The Fitaurari stood up to leave when Eshetu was done. "Thank you for your loyalty, soldier. And I assure you, this traitor Balcha will pay. I go directly to the king." He turned to the sentries. "The watch is changing - get this man to his bed with some hot food, then you may rest yourselves."

There was no rest for the Fitaurari. Word of Balcha's treachery had brought the members of the king's council that remained in the capital to a tense emergency meeting. Most of the men, including Tewodros, had no time to change into their court clothes and were dressed in the same simple white garments – an outsider would not be able to pick out the king from the group.

"We know now that the invader comes through the northern pass – do we pull back Mulugeta to the city?" asked Yohannes.

"How can we talk about Mulugeta? He is more than a day's march, and every minute counts," blurted Makonnen. "We must focus on Balcha."

"Yes, time is short," Tewodros raised a finger, "but we cannot make any rash decisions. Mulugeta must stay where he is or the central path will be totally exposed."

"Yet we must take care of Balcha," Tekle-giorgis struck in.

"Very well," said Tewodros. "Let us think of how best to win his soldiers back. How can they be loyal to a turncoat such as the Dedjazmatch? Surely he has confused them – let us send a decree that I am stripping Balcha of his office...or do they knowingly desert me, and we need to offer an amnesty?" Tewodros' head began to spin, and he lowered it into his hands to rub his temples and let his council do their job.

"The invader is cunning, but not in a way that can be admired – he has found a way to turn Ethiopian against Ethiopian, to hide his conquering army behind a human shield made of the very men he came to conquer. Surely he will send Balcha to attack us first, I see it now. Is it better that those he has tempted to treachery would thus perish on a field of battle, weakening us and strengthening him? Or that they perish justly by the king's hand, as traitors by the sword of your loyal army sent to execute them in the camp where they now sit? This would send a message that no other man shall dare seek his own aggrandizement over his country's fortune, by allying with this British devil."

Tewodros looked up to see that Yohannes of all people had said this, and to make sure there was no smile on his tutor's face – but Yohannes was not joking. The somber faces of his generals spoke their assent, and Tewodros had to give the orders. "We strike as lightning, a concentrated force will cut through the camp directly to Balcha. He must be killed as quickly as possible – surely his men will return to my side if the head of the snake is cut off. If that force fails we have no choice but to take more life until those men surrender."

There was a small silence, and Makonnen spoke. "Death to traitors."

It was the Grazmatch, Ras Makonnen, who was diverted up the pass to sack Balcha's camp. "I will lead the force to Balcha's tent myself," he had said on taking his leave, gloved fist over his chest in a gesture of loyalty. Every available horse was used to give his men all speed on their mission – there was no need for cavalry in the planned defense of Magdala, as no mounted brigade could effectively charge up or down the near-vertical slopes surrounding the capital. Those who could not ride followed behind to begin preparing the way for a slow, hard-fought retreat when the British eventually came, for all knew that they would come, and that the best chance of victory would come in a final stand at Magdala.

There was a balcony on the upper level of the palace where Tewodros stood with the Fitaurari Tekle-giorgis, from which they could see the stream of horses winding up into the defile towards Balcha. Tewodros placed a hand on the Fitaurari's shoulder.

"As long as you are here I feel safe, my friend."

Tekle-giorgis gave a wry smile. "I will not live to see any British lay a finger on you." The light dimmed and he looked up to see black clouds rolling in, on the tide of a stiff breeze from the north.

"What omen is this?" laughed Tewodros.

"A good one, my king! Let the thunder mask the sound of our horses' hooves – and neither Balcha's men nor the British will move from their tents in the downpour."

## Chapter Seven

Makonnen rode in the first rank of the cavalcade; he knew each footfall of his mount was marking history; the ride of Ras Makonnen. They could reach Balcha's camp as night fell if they kept a good pace; the timing was perfect and the horses were well rested for the challenge. The first drops of rain struck his face, one, two, three at first, and then too many to count as the water became a wall through which the riders must constantly breach, and the trees to the fore melted into a dull pastiche of their former green.

"Spears only!" the word was passed back through the column, "we cannot trust the guns when they are wet." The increasing resistance of the wind-borne drops and steepening trail only served to goad the riders into pushing onward, upward, and faster.

"We are an unstoppable force," Makonnen shouted to the weather, and to no one, and to everyone. "We will cut through Balcha's camp before they know what came out from the mists. We will ride him down before they can raise a rifle or spear to stop us. Long live the King!" and he heard it echo next to him, then behind him, and all the riders took up the chant, "long live the King."

\* \* \* \* \*

It was evening and Alemu was tired of waiting, tired of the incessant raindrops that slopped against his tent, and he didn't care if he got wet or Balcha's men shot him. Maybe there was news to be had of new orders, and the rain was refreshing as it doused his upturned face the moment he left the tent. Nobody was stirring in the camp, and the sentries around it were shrouded from his view.

Now he heard a yelp from down the valley, and a muffled thunderclap; yet the thunder rolled on for too long, and there had been no lightning. He straightened and peered into the gloom. Something was moving, and some voice in his head told him to crouch down near the earth that was turning to muck and mire.

Like a line of ghosts he saw them pass, the riders of Makonnen's army, a spray of mist flying up around them as they fanned out to ride through and over the tents of Balcha's camp. Here and there a shot, a scream, but with the storm and the suddenness it was chaos and Alemu saw many men around him scramble from their tents only to stand dumbfounded, or crawl back to sit with their hands on their heads, not knowing what to do.

"In the center – the Dedjazmatch!" he heard a faint call, and saw others rally to its source, and he knew that Balcha would die.

Four hundred feet away, the guards around the Dedjazmatch's tent yielded their arms and Makonnen dismounted with twenty others. "Come forth, Ras Balcha! You are surrounded, it is finished!"

The flap opened and there was the Dedjazmatch, his hands raised and his face impassive.

Makonnen did not hesitate. He thrust his spear into the center of Balcha's chest, and the man staggered back into his tent and fell to the ground.

Great shouts went up from Makonnen's riders, "Balcha is dead! Return to the King! Death to traitors! Return to Tewodros!" as they circled the camp and found none that resisted.

Makonnen's men entered the tent to secure it, and their leader followed. The Grazmatch placed a foot on the traitor's chest and yanked the spear free in a fount of blood, but saw Balcha's eyes flutter open. He knelt by the body and inclined his head – the traitor was trying to speak.

"Makonnen..." he rasped, and a hand rose to grasp the Grazmatch's shoulder in a clawlike grip. "Tell the king..." and Balcha coughed horribly.

"You are not worthy that the king should listen."

"I am guilty!" Balcha continued. "I must confess my deeds. Tell the king it was I...at Sodere, it was I..." and his hand slipped from Makonnen's shoulder.

"What did you do, traitor?" asked Makonnen.

Balcha focused his eyes once more and held Makonnen's gaze. "I am the one who killed Kassa. Tell Tewodros...let him feel no guilt at taking my life, or the lives of any Ethiopian I turned against him. Mine is the evil, I am the one. Is there no priest?" his eyes rolled around, and darkened.

"There is no time," Makonnen replied, and to himself he continued, "Such is the grace that Tewodros has, I feel he may even have forgiven you all this before he put you to death; you his betrayer, you his father's murderer. I am glad you did not have the chance to face him and receive his forgiveness, for you are not deserving of the heart of our king." Makonnen closed the dead man's eyes. "It will only sadden Tewodros further to hear of this, but I will not deserve his trust either if I do not tell him."

The Grazmatch straightened, and turned to Balcha's honor guard. "You will bear the body back to Magdala, if you dare – or bury him in the trees as you see fit. But before you go, tell me what you know of the dealings with the British. What was promised, by you and by them?"

Balcha's captain looked at his fellows, and when they nodded, he spoke. "The Dedjazmatch offered his services to the British if he would be made king upon their victory. The British requested a written agreement, that he would follow their instructions if they placed him on the throne."

Makonnen interjected, "Ha! We prepare an ambush for this British so that when he comes to seal his pact with the traitor, he will meet instead with the ire of my forces – on top of Balcha's, whom he thought had surrendered to him!"

Makonnen sneered in triumph, but the captain went on. "The British arranged that the Dedjazmatch was to meet in their camp to sign the agreement, and required that when the British ascend the pass, they would see us camped below as a token of good faith."

"Blast!" said Makonnen. "This British is devious. If we establish the high ground again we will lose any surprise, and who knows if we have time to prepare the defenses before he arrives at the pass." He clutched his chin, and turned to peer through the tent flap at the still-drumming rain. "Blast. We can do nothing in this dark and rain. I will inspect the camp while we wait. Sleep is for the weak. At first light I want scouts atop the pass to see if the British are coming."

## Chapter Eight

The pitter-patter of the rain slowed as Ras Makonnen waited for the light, until the only drops that fell were those shaken from trees and tents, and the stars appeared in faint farewell before the unyielding sun snuffed them out. Before the scouts could make the pass Makonnen, and every man in the camp, heard the rat-tat-tat of drums, floating down with the morning into the dell. There were figures on the skyline, and the Ethiopian scouts had wheeled and rode back down almost as quickly as they had been sent forth.

Goliath had brought Napier up, and the other elephants had brought the guns. The Major General smiled into the teeth of the updrafts from the valley below. "The fools actually moved their camp off the high ground. I wouldn't have believed it if I hadn't seen it with my own two eyes," he laughed, clapping an Indian soldier on the shoulder.

The soldier was Jeevan, and he looked uncomfortably around at the officers with him as he shrank from the touch. His English was the best among the scouts who had been on the ridge since the day before, and he alone had been chosen to brief his commander. There had been no glimmer of recognition on Napier's features, though Jeevan remembered clear as day the morning far away and back home when he had seen the same man take a tiger skin as trophy.

"Smithers – those horses that started up the pass, but turned and went back down a quarter of an hour ago. Were not the arrangements made that we would inform this Door Keeper chap when to meet in our camp?"

"Yes, yes," responded Smithers. "Perhaps they saw us arrive and thought to come, but then remembered to wait for your invitation."

Jeevan coughed. "Sir, if you please."

"Yes, what? You have something to say?" Napier's head snapped around at the native accent, and he glared at the soldier whose place it was not to speak.

"Sir, yesterday we saw not so many horse." Jeevan indicated the camp below, where it was difficult to make out one smudge from another.

Smithers had the benefit of field glasses. "The baggage trains and camp followers appear to be making preparations to leave," he said. "Yes, yes, they are definitely beginning to move out."

Napier stood silent for a full two minutes, and none spoke. "Enough horses arrived in the night that even from here, a scout with his naked eye could tell the difference. They must have come from King Theodore - and yet there is no discord in the camp where Theodore's general has promised us his allegiance."

"But why did they leave the pass? And now, why does their camp begin to depart?" asked Smithers.

"Irrelevant," snapped Napier. "There are only two possibilities. The Door Keeper is with us, or he is against us. If he is with us, do we need his men and guns to defeat the Ethiopians?"

"I should think we have brought enough of our own," said Smithers rather smugly, surveying the British artillery and looking to where ten thousand men had his back.

"If he is against us, we will never have the fool in a better position to best him – before he gets away into this bloody ravine." Napier took the field glasses from his colonel, saw for himself the Ethiopian army beginning a retreat, and passed the glasses back. "Kill them all."

The dawn was thunder and darkness under palls of smoke from the guns on the high ground. Makonnen felt more and more helpless as he shouted commands – "leave everything! Get the men to the trees, and let the camp followers go first!" Could his men even hear him amidst the ear-splitting noise?

"Sir, we cannot keep the chain of command – we do not know which are Balcha's officers to organize them." Nobody in the camp had experienced shelling of this kind before, and around him Makonnen could see half the soldiers standing dazed and still, looking about, while the rest scattered to the forest to risk falling trees rather than the direct strike of shrapnel. The smooth bore of the British guns lessened their accuracy, and made it haphazard where the next volley would land.

The horses were no better than the men, whinnying as they reared, but Makonnen found his mount and signaled his cavalry to converge towards the ravine. The shelling became heavier in that direction, and Makonnen realized the guns were sighted to cut off their retreat. Some of Balcha's men were now looking to push their way into the ravine, creating even more of a bottleneck as Makonnen screamed to let the camp followers go first, for they were not soldiers.

"Balcha's men will not listen," said the Grazmatch's lieutenant.

Makonnen looked back to the pass. "You are right, we can accomplish nothing here except to get in the way of the infantry's retreat, and to get shot. If we go towards the hill, we will be underneath the flight of the ordnance," and he led the cavalry charging back through the camp clearing, shouting at the men he passed, "To the trees! Get to the trees, and then retreat!" The line of horse re-formed at the head of the clearing, and the slope beckoned upwards to where the British stood stoic, patiently letting the blood of those beneath with only the frantic gunners betraying any exertion.

"To attack will be suicide," reasoned the lieutenant, seeing the glint in his commander's eye.

"So will retreat," rejoined Makonnen. "Perhaps we can distract them long enough that the rest of the men can escape."

Napier was still on the heights, fascinated by the scene below. "Our boys are really letting them have it!" he heard Smithers say with glee at his side. He could make out a line of horse that had not scattered like the rest of the Ethiopians, pawing at the slope as the riders struggled to control their mounts; a splendid, living war machine. A kind of memory, not of mind but of heart and body, flooded his being, and it was the feeling again of being high on his elephant, looking down at the wounded tiger before the killing shot. "There is no glory in this," said Napier to himself.

"What's that, sir?" asked Smithers.

Napier snapped out of his thoughts. "Cease fire!"

Smithers gawked.

"Cease fire! Cease fire!" Napier shouted. "We will march on the Door Keeper's camp. Form the lines, they're already on the run and we're wasting shot." The memory of the tiger hunt was replaced by a strange emptiness, and he sought out Goliath to carry him with his army into the valley.

Below, Makonnen relaxed his grip on the reins as the ear-ringing silence washed over him. "Perhaps we live another day," he grinned at his lieutenant. "Let us follow our compatriots down the ravine before these British change their mind." He turned his horse and looked back at the ridge. "We will fight them in the plain. We return to the King!"

By the time Napier had made the soggy march down to the clearing, all living things had evaporated like the rain. The British paused amid the smoking craters to gather up whatever useful had been left behind in the carcass of the camp.

## Chapter Nine

As the rain cleared in Magdala, Tekle-giorgis stood again on the balcony where he and Tewodros had watched Makonnen depart. The same horses now led the companies of Balcha as they emerged from the northern valley in disarray, and Tekle-giorgis fancied he could see their tails swishing between their legs. The council would meet soon and Tekle-giorgis shook his head, for their options were shrinking fast.

Inside, Tewodros sat with only his old tutor in attendance. "Why am I here, in this room, Yohannes? The action is out there," he waved at the window, "the blows are traded while I cower in my palace. Is there nothing I can do? Is a king so useless?"

"It is far more difficult to sit patiently and order a kingdom than to ride around with your warriors and shoot at things. To dispense real justice, not rough justice, to move men in the right direction and build the foundation for your subjects to grow a mighty nation around you – that is the true work of a king."

"And look what work I have accomplished," replied Tewodros. "This invader looks to divide and conquer, and I have aided him by setting my own generals to fight each other. Now Ethiopians have died without even fighting the British, and even now this invader leads his army to Magdala, unopposed since he landed in our country. Perhaps that is justice – I have spilled my own people's blood for nothing, and this man will be vengeance for the wrongs I have committed."

"My king, what wrongs? You are as pure as the hail that falls on the mountain," Yohannes said sincerely. "All your choices have been made with a true heart – it is not for you to control the results."

"Yet I now regret my choice of months ago that led to all this," said Tewodros with a wry smile. "I acted with anger when I locked up those rotten men – look at all this trouble, this insanity they have brought about."

"It is a choice that was made also out of a hope for your country," Yohannes reminded his student. "It will not profit us to cling to any past decision, just to agonize over what hindsight shows us."

"Yes, I must let it go. And indeed, why should I even hold on to these prisoners? It changes nothing if they stay in Magdala, or...or go to hell!"

"If they have served their purpose, it will matter greatly to the captives if you let them go."

Tewodros sighed. "You are right – I have been distracted. Let us send Henok to check on our British and make sure they have behaved themselves. Let him confirm that they can give us no further information regarding their countrymen who threaten us with destruction, and we will release them to the north – it may even buy us a day or two to reorganize our defenses while the invader puzzles out why we have let them go."

"Speaking of defenses, the Fitaurari comes," said Yohannes, as Tekle-giorgis stepped in from the balcony."

"My lord, Ras Makonnen enters the palace; shall we convene a council? Time does not wait for us," Tekle-giorgis seemed to be visibly under stress for the first time since Tewodros had known him.

"Yes, there is no time to lose. Just the three of us and Makonnen need meet – any more will only bog us down with interminable sophistry," Tewodros replied.

"They are coming down the valley. We don't have much time," were Makonnen's breathless words as soon as he entered the room, hair still windswept and face streaked with dirt from his ride.

"Mulugeta serves no purpose guarding the central pass, then. We will recall him to make our stand at Magdala," Tewodros found it easy to make decisions now that he was simply reacting to urgent realities.

"And we know where to place our great cannon," smiled Tekle-giorgis, the prospect of action sweetening his mood considerably. "Let us see what that German contraption can do to the British in the valley."

Makonnen shuddered at the memory of the artillery shattering his position the morning before. "Let us keep my cavalry and Balcha's men back for now – they are sore winded after our rush back to Magdala."

"Of course," said Tewodros. "You have earned your rest – but you still have not told us what became of the Dedjazmatch, whose men you have brought back from the pass."

"Forgive me, sire, it seems so long ago that we moved against Balcha, after the events of yesterday.

As you know, he had yielded the pass before I arrived, and the British had the high ground – there was no choice but to retreat."

"Yes, there was no other choice, Ras Makonnen. And if Balcha met his end, how did it come?"

"At the end of my spear," said Makonnen.

Tewodros looked down. "It is a sad thing that I had to turn on my people in this way."

"My king, it was as planned, we had the element of surprise. Less than ten men fell in the encounter."

"The lives of few sacrificed for the lives of many," observed Yohannes.

Makonnen interrupted, "and Dedjazmatch Balcha, he had a message for the king." The Grazmatch met Tewodros' gaze, and though he had resolved to share Balcha's words, he paused before continuing. "He confessed – he confessed to the murder of your father. It was Balcha who killed Kassa!"

"I knew it! The snake!" cried Tekle-giorgis, while Yohannes motioned to silence him, and Tewodros lifted his eyes to the ceiling.

"So in a way we have justice, at the end," said the king, and stood up to leave the room, for he knew not what his mind and heart would do next.

Henok soon after left the palace and wended his way toward the compound where the captives were behind high walls, playing cards in the fresh sunshine. He stood at the gate and watched the methodical slapping of worn jacks and queens on the table, punctuated by the odd grunt, and interrupted when the guard let him and his interpreter in. The appearance of the British envoys had certainly declined, a ragged beard ravaging Johnson's face, Boyle's shirt greasy and collarless, and Trafford not wearing a shirt at all as he squinted up at Henok.

"Look, it's the chap who brought us here. Haven't seen you in a while," said Boyle.

"Blimey, can't even remember when that was. How many days have we been here?" Trafford shook his head.

Long enough for me to learn a bit of English, thought Henok.

"Are you here to let us go? What news?" asked Johnson, glancing at the interpreter and motioning to pass on the questions.

"Have you been treated well?" was Henok's response, his accent quite good. "Perhaps we should clean them up," he observed to the interpreter.

"Bloody savages, left us here to rot!" The vile expression on Boyle's face was aimed directly at Henok, now he realized the interpreter was superfluous and could not soften the translation.

Henok sighed; it was a fair enough accusation, and he felt no inclination to argue that the blame might lie in part with the government that had sent these fools to the coronation. There would be no cleaning up what was inside the prisoners' heads. "His Majesty wills your release, and you may join your countrymen who have decided to pay us a visit. Gather your things; you will be escorted from Magdala at first light, ready or not."

The envoys normally slept in, but the next morning there was no need to rouse them – a mixture of fear and wonder had kept them starting awake throughout the night, anxious for freedom and even more fretful thinking of what might happen next. England did not seem a particularly near prospect.

Once the luggage was assembled, none were particularly happy at the prospect of having to carry their own. Due in the main to Henok's generous disposition they were able to negotiate an old mule to accompany them out of Magdala. Provisions were tightly rationed, however, and they were given no more than two days' food to load up before a detail of six spear-carriers goaded them out of the compound. Passersby in the town paid them little heed, but once on the outskirts the ranks of soldiers glared at the passing British; most of the Ethiopians getting their first look at the foreigners whose brethren had come to fight.

"Perhaps we should go back to our old digs – they really weren't so uncomfortable," offered Boyle to his companions.

"They say our boys are just up this valley," rejoined Trafford. "Would you rather be behind or in front of our gunners when they blow this awful place to kingdom come?"

"If they're not there, we'll be at the mercy of whatever waits in that wilderness," observed Johnson.

He looked back to see the spears of their accompanying detail seeming to incline slightly towards him, as if to prod him onwards and out of Magdala. "Little choice we have in the matter."

"Worst choice I've ever made was to join this embassy," muttered Boyle. The weather seemed to imitate his mood as the clouds rolled in and the three men were released into the darkening beyond.

## Chapter Ten

Napier was loath to leave Balcha's camp, but he had delayed long enough. The Ethiopians could afford to wait, but he could not and eventually, he would have to put his men in jeopardy if he was to see his mission through. The main camp would stay in the clearing, as they had come close enough for a quicker, leaner strike force to make the assault on Magdala. The elephants would lead carrying the guns, and would set up the artillery where the trees petered out at the base of the valley. From there he would shell Magdala, and provide covering fire while his army formed ranks and made their charge.

They started down the valley where the high ridges loomed to either side and made Napier feel small even atop Goliath, and he smelled danger though the air was pure and clean. He had deployed the Gurkhas forward to sweep the forests, and a small vanguard to protect the gunners who marched in front of the elephants; nonetheless he became more and more uneasy with his army strung out over two miles on the narrow track. At some point, the Ethiopians must attack.

"Finally, in the next few days we will sack Magdala," he told Smithers, hoping to pass off his anxiety as excitement. "I feared that boredom might become the death of this expedition!" but his eyes still scanned the trees.

Now, there, to the front he could see some activity, a platoon of Gurkhas hustling against the flow of the march to return to Napier. Bewildered, in their midst some sort of ragamuffin men, whose skins looked white, and one white officer, Alfred, whom the Gurkhas appeared to have recruited to mediate with their charges. "Smithers, have we had any deserters?"

"Not that I know of, sir."

"Good Lord, could that be..." Napier signaled to let him down from his elephant, and temporarily halted the march to set up a post to receive the returning hostages.

"Shall we hold the march for now, sir?" asked Smithers.

Napier felt the sore spot on his tailbone where he had thumped against his seat one too many times. "No, send Goliath on with the other elephants and start the march again while I debrief these men. We cannot hold up for this – I will rejoin the column when our caucus is done."

Ahead of Napier the soldiers had all seen the reason for the interruption of their forward progress. Behind the elephants, Jeevan was among the troops who were called to a halt, simply shrugged their shoulders, and sat down on their packs. "What's different? Walk, don't walk, nothing ever happens. Why did we come here?" Jeevan muttered to nobody in particular, but saw a few nods of agreement.

In the midst of more people than they had seen since Tewodros' coronation all those months ago, Trafford, Johnson and Boyle kept their eyes locked on the head of the man in front, unable to meet the stares, and sometimes even whistles of the Indian and English soldiers they passed, whose kempt appearances somehow made even the least of them more respectable than the envoys-turned-vagabonds in that moment.

The envoys were ushered to camp stools where they had to fight back tears, as the joy of rescue that they had dreamed of, with cheers and hugs and hot tea with biscuits, was absent. No emotion could yet be vented as the steely eyes of Napier showed that he was not pleased to greet them. Alfred was not dismissed, so he stood to one side.

"You were treated poorly?" asked the British general.

"I wouldn't say mistreated," admitted Boyle.

"Well...it was not the most comfortable of lodgings," offered Johnson, seeing Napier's disappointment.

"The food was rather unsavory," Trafford chimed in.

"They gave a reason for releasing you? A message, perhaps?" Napier moved on, probing for a reason, any reason to maintain the justification for his expedition, now that the hostages he was sent to rescue sat chatting in front of him with nary a chain about their persons.

"No sir, they said we are free to go and so, we went," Boyle concluded lamely.

Napier rubbed his hands on his stubbled cheeks for a pause. "You must be tired, but we cannot delay our march any longer, or draw you a hot bath – you must return to our camp followers, and take what they can provide. We have all been in this country too long, but I promise we will go home as soon as we can. You there, my good fellow, Alfred. You've seen action before and have no need to witness more, I'm sure – take these men back to the clearing and see they are made comfortable."

Alfred obeyed, feeling relieved and at the same time disappointed he would miss the assault they had come so far to make. He resolved to go back down after his task was done to be there for the ending.

As he led Trafford, Johnson and Boyle up the valley to the camp, the envoys became the interrogators after being starved for the society of other Englishmen for so long. "Did the old boys back home really send all this just for us?" asked Boyle, swelling up a bit as he gawked at the column of military might that never seemed to end. "Elephants and everything?"

"Yes, it appears so," replied Alfred, "and so far not a man lost in the effort, as not a soul has dared attack our force."

"We're free now," it occurred to Johnson. "Why aren't we turning around and going home?"

Trafford rejoined, "we've got to teach them a lesson – you can't go around kidnapping British subjects. A punishment of sorts, if you will."

Alfred mused. "Perhaps a bit vindictive, but yes, I think the message is that our empire is not to be trifled with. Although, if we continue the endeavor it seems to me that we may have ceded the moral heights."

"As long as the army keeps the high ground in the real world, what does it matter?" scoffed Trafford. "Certainly back in civilization, we will write the stories and it will be understood that one must treat savages, well, savagely."

As he spoke, at the base of the valley Eshetu was climbing the western ridge. Behind and below him Tewodros' army was encamped in numbers too great to count, the lazy smoke of cooking fires rising from between the rows of white and grey tents towards the palace above them, looking like a mighty fortress. Eshetu had been relieved from duty as a soldier in the rank and file as a reward for his actions in warning the king of Balcha's treachery, and assigned to the special unit newly formed to man the artillery piece completed by Klaus Zimmer's forge only weeks before. Klaus himself led from the front, shouting instructions that nobody understood, but his gesticulations seemed to slowly but surely usher his masterpiece towards the vantage point over the ravine that they must reach before nightfall.

The mortar was the most monumental piece of iron Eshetu had ever seen, squat and hulking with a wide mouth that seemed to yawn at the men and mules straining to pull the wagon upwards, one step at a time. Its sole purpose was to destroy, to spit fire and metal and disregard the weakness of soft things, and

Klaus' few tests had shown it could at least do that. Between the massive gun and the legions of men waiting in Magdala, Eshetu found it difficult to imagine how any force could challenge, let alone defeat his King.

There was a movement near the mouth of the ravine and Eshetu rubbed his eyes and squinted. Something large was making its way into the valley – nothing could be that size except an elephant, but this was not the usual range of the great beasts that usually roamed in dusty herds farther to the south, and east. "It must be a lone bull," Eshetu said to himself, and indeed even at this distance he could make out massive tusks, white against the dark skin of the animal and the contrast growing as the evening advanced. Perhaps it had lost a fight for a harem and wandered off course. The elephant disappeared into the forest, and Eshetu turned back towards the King's gun, which was almost in place.

He scrambled up past the mortar, Klaus making adjustments like a wife preparing the house for guests, and found a stony perch where his job was to note any sign of the British approaching under the cover of the trees flanking the path to Magdala. Eshetu glanced at the sun and judged it to be around an hour from twilight; thankfully he would not need to focus for too long, as the uneven rocks he crouched upon already taxed his muscles. "If it is those little mountain men that come first I will never see them, they are as ghosts," he mused, but then the treetops began to sway around where he knew the path to be. Something was shaking the forest, and far closer to the mouth of the ravine than he expected. Eshetu waved his hand frantically to catch the attention of the gunners, lazing around their death machine like nursing pups about their mother.

In the defile below, Jeevan looked up at the jittery pines as the elephants jostled for position on the narrow path ahead of him. The mahouts cursed each other as one beast would shoulder a sister into a tree trunk, then back up into the face of the unstoppable column behind, leaving a slow ripple of men coming to a halt in its wake. One of the guns slipped from its harness and Jeevan could see it rolling some twenty feet to the side of the path. He sighed and simply unshipped his pack, knowing the delay would last at least long enough to give his aching shoulders a rest. By the time the Gurkhas set up the pickets and the guns were deployed, it would be well after dark and he would be stuck on this heinous path for hours. "What is the rush? We wait all this time to get this far and now we hurry, for what?" he muttered.

The response to the question he asked of the air was an ear-splitting whine, followed by the dreadful noise of a massive ball crashing into the forest somewhere on the ridge to his left. The entire column froze in stunned silence for six heartbeats – Jeevan counted them. Like the men before and behind him he stooped involuntarily, and scanned the sky, waiting for the remainder of the fusillade. A full minute passed and small titters began to nervously sprinkle forth from the column. "Have they only one gun?" Jeevan jeered, as the men stood up to their full heights.

"One gun, and if they still haven't reloaded yet, maybe only one ball!" said his mate, who had spent enough time with the gunners to be impressed only if a crew could fire again in under sixty seconds.

As if on cue, a second shot sailed over the tops of the pines and again struck the left side of the valley, somewhere between Jeevan and Magdala. "There it goes! One gun, haha!" cried Jeevan.

"They have missed the column completely," his fellow soldier chimed in.

On the slope to the south, the ball thudded into solid rock, showering splinters around before it rolled down the incline, triggering a small avalanche of debris. The ball skidded over a ledge and a rain of dirt fell on the African bull elephant's right ear before the eighty-pound hunk of metal smacked him on top of the head. The elephant shook his head, flapped his great ears, let loose a trumpet blast and launched a dead run down the slope.

Every elephant on the path below ignored the cajoling of its mahout and strained to hear in the direction where an elephant had spoken, but not in any language the Asian beasts could understand. Goliath at the front turned to face up the slope, and each elephant in the column followed suit, stamping and heaving, shoulder to shoulder with its forty-three brethren. As one, they and the mahouts gaped in awe as a magnificent animal burst into view, shedding pine branches over the shuddering ground. He was taller than any elephant they had ever seen, and his tusks longer; his ears were fully extended to each side and his charge was unstoppable.

The sight and smell of a herd of strange, fetid cows, when he had seen no elephants since he was driven from his harem by a dominant male many days ago, confused and enraged the bull even further as he bowled into the line. The noise of blaring trunks was deafening as the mahouts lost control, and their animals scattered into the pines, and twirled away trampling over the men who were packed in on the path.

Eshetu was transfixed by the massive commotion he could see and distantly hear. Could the king's gun be so powerful as to cause such a reaction from the invader's ranks? Even the gunners could see the target clearly now and Klaus' arms windmilled about as he lapsed into German expostulations regarding elevation and angles. The pale man pushed the Ethiopians aside and took the ramrod himself, the fuse was lit and the gun fired a third time, arcing lazily on a higher trajectory before accelerating down, speeding ever faster towards the British column and this time finding its mark.

Jeevan saw a man struck twenty yards in front of him, and as the sounds of the elephants began to subside, the screaming of a wounded soldier rose in their place, and then the rapid peppering of rifle fire from further ahead where the repulsed vanguard retreating up the ravine again sent a wave through the column. Makonnen had set a small ambush, his men firing from the trees as he had been told the Gurkhas had done; but the enemy had quickly formed into defensive squares. The British casualties were few, and Makonnen's men melted back into the forest as the day went down, lest so small a victory yet turn pyrrhic. The Qenazmatch had been tempted to mount a full charge up the valley, but with the path so narrow and the lack of visibility, he would risk too much to inflict too little damage on the enemy. Klaus meanwhile had reluctantly calmed down, and deemed it wiser to save his ammunition than to have his crew of novices operate the great gun in the dark. The Ethiopians' first salvo ended almost as suddenly as it had begun.

As the moon rose, Goliath stared into the trees where the strange bull elephant had disappeared, and thought back to his youth, with memories flooding back of elephants stamping and moving free before the herders had come to take him away. Men would write of what Goliath had seen in these strange lands, then this generation would pass, and another man would write of his kindred, still wild, and still dancing back in the hills of Meghalaya. He moved his foot to test his chain, and turned to his fodder. The British had bivouacked in place as orders were passed up and down the line by torchlight.

Up above, Eshetu could see the winking flames winding far up the valley, and made his mental calculations of the distance, and the probable numbers of the enemy, for the report to be sent back to the king. His confidence from earlier in the day was waning with every new torch he counted. With all his men, the king would not be able to overwhelm such an army as had come over the pass toward Magdala.

## Chapter Eleven

From a room upstairs in the palace Tewodros could look out upon the soughing trees and find a transient peace. The movement of the branches hypnotized him for just long enough that memory was driven out, and the anxiety of the meeting in an hour with his generals was kept at bay. Floating into the clearing of his mind, the first face he saw was his father's, and then Haymanot's. His father, and Haymanot – the only two faces he had seen in his life whom he could call family, and all that truly meant in this dreadful hour; and of the two he could only call for his wife to come and join his lonely waiting.

She entered the room with her hair piled high in round braids like hyacinth above her classic face, gently smiling as always, but Tewodros could not smile until he placed a hand on her rounded stomach and felt the kick of his unborn child. Haymanot understood that he did not wish to speak of war, and held his hand. "I think it will be a boy."

"It matters not to me," said Tewodros. "And if my being king allows me to make any difference, it should not matter to Ethiopia that a woman is my heir. Are you ready to leave this evening?"

"I would like to stay with you," said Haymanot.

"I should like that very much, but you must go to a safe place, if only for the little one." Tewodros meant for Haymanot to stay in his cave, where he knew the monks would keep her from harm until the crisis of the British was resolved. "You know, if we can reason with the man who leads this army, and a better man they must have sent than the other British we have seen, it may be that their country and ours can conclude a proper treaty."

"Yes, I know you believe the trade we can conduct would be beneficial for our people."

"But I want to exchange more than just goods," Tewodros looked at Haymanot. "There is knowledge and learning these people have, that we do not have. I wish to send more than just caravans to England."

He had not taken his hand from Haymanot's stomach, and her face clouded. "You ask much if you mean to send a child so far away from its mother."

"If anything happens to me, I have told no other one of this plan – you must arrange it, for my sake," Tewodros was earnest.

"Nothing will happen to you!" she scolded, but it caught in her throat and Yohannes had come to bring the king to his council.

In the council chamber Tekle-giorgis could not sit down, and paced back and forth as a racehorse chafing at the bit, but not permitted to run. "My men sweat in daily exercise to prepare for battle. When will they have a chance to fight?" he challenged the king. Gesturing at Makonnen, "some of us at least have tasted action," he said.

"Yes, and my taste was a bitter one of gunpowder and smoke," said Ras Makonnen. "We cannot fight them in the ravine, it is too narrow for a full engagement. We cannot fight them under their great guns, or they will rain hell on our men before a rifle can be fired, much less a spear put to use. And if we can engage them in a real fight, their rifles are superior to ours – I was told that their men who melt in and out of the trees can fire more than once without reloading. Even the new weapons that Klaus has brought, though they load from the breech, can fire but a single bullet."

"I will not have your men be slaughtered in the field below Magdala, in any vainglorious attempt to protect me," Tewodros said to Tekle-giorgis, with finality.

The Fitaurari was exasperated. "My king, you have said you will not run from the invader, and this I understand – it proves you are no coward. But now you say you will not fight them either, so what are we to do?"

Makonnen chimed in, "If they establish their guns at the base of the ravine, they can shell our men. If they come any closer, they will be able to shell the palace, I am sure of it."

"I have surrendered before," offered Mulugeta. "And I am still here."

"Let them have the palace," Tewodros spoke sharply. "I will yield the city; it is the people that are my concern."

"Ras Mulugeta's question still stands," Yohannes observed. "We have already given them the hostages and a reason to turn around, yet onward they still come."

"Let him come and see me face to face," said Tewodros, looking down and chewing his lip. "Move our forces back, allow them into the city, and we will reason like civilized men," he looked up. "Then, if they cannot listen to reason, we will storm the city from the south and fight them in the streets of Magdala."

"They will not expect us to destroy our own capital," acknowledged Mulugeta.

"They will have the king hostage," warned Yohannes.

"Give me fifty handpicked men and we can fight our way out with the king if need be," claimed Tekle-giorgis. "We know the city best, and they will not know to cover the escape route from the palace kitchen. It can be done."

"This invader has no compunction," said Makonnen. "You did not see his vile action at the pass – I cannot think he is civilized, and he may kill the king before he has a chance to speak."

They all looked at Tewodros. "I am not afraid," he said.

In the early morning, in the hours of deepest sleep when quiet reigned and the dark was not yet troubled, the shelling began. A thunderous burst roused the city from their beds, or for those like Tewodros who would sleep through an earthquake, the touch of a wife's, or brother's hand. The sound of shouts or screams was worse than the noise of crumbling mortar, worse than splintered wood. "Let us wait in the kitchen, we are too high up here," urged Haymanot, and the king went down to join his scullions, while Tekle-giorgis' picked men spilled about the corridor and postulated whether the palace walls would hold. The king saw Tekle-giorgis seated in the doorway, his headdress on his lap, carefully brushing the dun and golden strands as the sputtering candlelight played across the lion's mane.

"Your courage is about your head even when you wear it not," remarked Tewodros with a kind smile. "I see it there, and we both know it is no saintly halo that glows!"

Tekle-giorgis returned the smile. "I fear we have more need of patience, than bravery, in these hours."

"As it has been since the invader came – and you have shown plenty of that too," replied the king as he took a station by the old clay ovens.

"They will be here tomorrow," said Tekle-giorgis.

"I am ready."

"Soon it will be over," said Haymanot, closing her eyes and resting against Tewodros. Though her eyes were closed, it was a fey look that crossed her face.

Napier had had them train the guns before nightfall, so their shots would fall indiscriminately across Magdala, unexpectedly, and in the dark. It was a nice touch, he told himself; a creative tactic. He thought it would be even better when the day broke, and he could see the missiles find their mark, with satisfactory puffs of smoke and toppling edifices. Instead, in the morning he felt the emptiness again, while Smithers clapped with glee beside him.

"How much ammunition have we left, Colonel?" Napier asked in a clipped tone.

"I suspect we could keep the bombardment up for another hour or so at this rate, sir," said Smithers. He trained his field glasses on the plateau that lay across the valley. "From what I can see, we've done quite the job on their city. Do you think the Theodore fellow is waiting in what's left of that palace?"

"He must have run off by now," said Napier. "Shame, really. We've come this far without a real fight; I thought the natives would at least have a go before we took their capital."

"They know they can't stop us," said Smithers.

"After all those weeks of slogging on the march, we will conquer the country in one day."

"We'll have to find another one of them to run the colony, now the Door Keeper chap is gone," remarked Smithers.

"Who told you London wants a colony?" barked Napier, and Smithers flushed.

"I...I'm sorry, sir, it's just...this is quite the conquering army," he waved his hand over the British company.

"London has given us a mission. First, retrieve the hostages - done. Second, punish the Ethiopians – well under way; and third, get that treaty signed since those buffoons we rescued were not able to." Napier saw Smithers' discomfort at his terseness, and thought to throw the poor colonel a scrap of

301

magnanimity. "Though, once we've got a treaty and the trade starts, I'm sure as soon as the Suez opens London will send someone back this way again, and we'll colonize this blasted land in no time. You're thinking ahead, eh Smithers?"

Gratified, the colonel had another incisive question occur to him, and thought to press his luck with the general by asking, "If Theodore is not there to sign the treaty, what will we do?"

"It is simply a matter of how convenient our task will be, Smithers. Various degrees of convenience. If Theodore is on the lam, or suffers an untimely end in Magdala, as you said we will have to find another Door Keeper to submit to us instead. Either way, the seat of power will belong to us, and Ethiopia's resources will belong to Great Britain very soon."

"Very good sir. Shall we move along soon then?" Smithers looked at the smoldering city.

"Finish the ammunition first," said Napier. "We're going home after this, and we don't want to have to carry it all the way back to Aden."

With that, Napier went to dress for the march on Magdala.

*Chapter Twelve*

Jeevan moved with a caution to his step, peering up at the lee of the Magdala promontory. An eerie silence had been ringing about the whole sky since the shelling had stopped. He knew the destruction wrought by the great guns of the British had likely stamped out any real resistance in the city, but nevertheless expected some kind of opposition to fling itself from the plateau upon his head at any moment. At least the elephants were not in front this time to cause chaos on the narrow path, and the Gurkhas would take the brunt of any frontal assault.

"We will walk from the Red Sea all the way up to the palace steps without me even unslinging my rifle," he muttered. "And yet they have shown no sign of surrender."

He peered up again, as if a white flag might now appear fluttering down the rocky slope, but still nothing. Jeevan shook his head. "A soldier with no enemy to fight – what then is my purpose here?"

The Gurkhas were near the top of the path where it rounded the corner up onto the plateau, and widened past a few homes, then open fields to the gate in the palace wall. Yohannes had wandered to the guardhouse, needing a respite from the tension that was the king's council chamber, where Tewodros was left with just the guard of Tekle-giorgis' picked men. Yohannes could see the veritable anguish on many of the soldiers' faces, but try as he might to empathize with the soldiers' emotions, the monk had not been able to dredge up a similar distress from his seasoned depths. "I used to feel life's pain more keenly," he reminded himself as he climbed the few rough steps of cobbled stone to see over the wall to the empty, reeling city.

Now it became real, as he saw the pointed bayonets of deadly men in sharp uniforms. He dashed back to the palace at once.

Tewodros looked up from his brooding to see his mentor burst into the council chamber, one of the few rooms in the palace that had survived intact. "My lord, the barbarians are at the gates," said Yohannes, at last a crack in his voice and a glimpse of unease creeping into his usually serene eyes.

Tewodros looked at him and held his gaze. "God is my only fortress," the king said. And a calm washed over Yohannes again.

The king seemed to mull something, then raised his head and spoke, "I will go out to meet them." As the guards scurried to escort him, he simply waved them back. "They will not shoot me," and he turned to leave the chamber. Yohannes watched his master's back pass through the door, and silently raised his hand in blessing over the soul he loved.

The Gurkhas fanned out to establish a forward perimeter while the rest of the vanguard trickled up on to the plateau and deployed, forming several squares that left a lane along the path to the palace, where no defender yet appeared along the walls as a small Gurkha detachment burst through the gates before waving their fellow troops on. Jeevan found himself inside the compound, while the unnerving quiet continued, and up the lane came his commander. Napier halted before the palace steps, in formal dress and burnished face to go with his copious medals and glinting scabbard.

Dressed all in white, in the unembroidered cloth of his people, Tewodros emerged from the palace doorway into the soft sunlight. At the top of the stairs that led up to the imperial palace, his bearing was unmistakable. The British troops below knew this was the king, and Napier shouldered his way to the front of them as Tewodros raised a piece of wood and silver aloft.

He slowly pulled the trigger, and the musket ball entered his temple, lodging exactly in the center of his head and ending the life of Tewodros the great, the King of Kings. There was no exit wound, and no drop of blood to stain his white vestments. The light left his eyes as the figure at the top of the staircase pitched forward, alone in his majesty.

To those below he looked as if a falling leaf, gently floating down the stone steps.

No one had counted the time that the men in the palace, and the men on the grounds outside, stood still; but the sun had moved when Napier at last dropped to his knees by the prone figure at the base of the steps. The king's arms were spread and his head tilted back, where Napier took his hand to the already cold brow and brushed the brown eyes closed. "Peccavi," he whispered.

305

"Bring a stretcher!" he shouted, and the medics shuffled furiously through the broken silence to bear the body back into the palace, Napier striding up the steps alongside while his troops milled behind and the Ethiopian soldiers gave way with stricken looks.

In Napier's head repeated the line he now composed that would end his report to Queen Victoria, "thus fell Tewodros, by no hand but his own. Thus fell Tewodros..."

The king's face looked so solemn, so handsome and young. A monk was waiting in the throne room, and another tall, vital man who commanded respect. Yohannes took Henok's shoulder and asked him tersely, "who shot the king? Translate for me."

All eyes turned to the one who had spoken, and then to Henok. "The king's advisor has asked," and feeling the awkwardness of Yohannes' direct question, changed the words, "how it came about that the king has passed."

"Well, he's bloody committed suicide, hasn't he?" blurted Smithers, and saw Napier raise his hand for silence. Napier saw the tall old man, Alfred, who had left the freed hostages to join the final attack, and now entered the room carrying the weapon that had slipped from Tewodros' hand.

"Bring the gun to me," said Napier softly, and Alfred obliged.

"Sir, Mr. Johnson had told me they brought a pistol as a gift from the Queen to Theodore's coronation. I believe this is it."

Napier turned the piece over and over in his hand. "I've seen this pistol. Or its twin, perhaps – it was displayed by the Prince Consort at a state dinner."

"What are they saying?" Yohannes squeezed Henok's shoulder.

Henok translated. "It is fitting. The bullet came from Albert's gun," spoke Napier, "the gun sent by Queen Victoria to precede her army. It is I. It is all of us; England, we have pulled the trigger." He turned first to Smithers, and then looked around the room. "This is no suicide. Let no one cast dishonor on this man." He fixed now on Henok. "Tell them to bury your king. The English will give you three days to mourn. Make it a proper burial."

As Napier walked out of the room, he touched his cheek and found it wet.

*Chapter Thirteen*

Three days had passed, and Tewodros was in the ground. At the funeral Yohannes and Haymanot held hands, each thinking they supported the other, and both being supported. "I told him to send Ghannatu with the message at Sodere; I told him to kill Balcha; I taught him to admire sacrifice," said the monk, anguish on his face. "Is it my fault?"

Haymanot squeezed his hand. "It is not your fault. He could not have had a better teacher and guide than you."

"And no better wife," said Yohannes.

After the funeral Mulugeta had taken his army towards Lake Tana, and Makonnen was further south towards Shewa when Napier sent riders from Magdala.

"Do the British require my capitulation?" Makonnen asked the messenger. "They can have it, and leave me in peace. I want no part of what they do next."

"Ras Makonnen, the British have a wish to end the interregnum promptly. Their commander, the man Napier, wishes to offer you the kingship. You would have the full support of the British, and a large sum of silver thalers for your personal fortune."

"Tell your master the answer is no," said Ras Makonnen, and he knew Mulugeta would say the same. He moved on sedately for the pastures of home, his fealty intact.

By now Napier had determined that Yohannes was the wisest man available to him, Ethiopian or British, and often called the old monk in to harangue him with questions about one or another idea. "These are all the three generals, then, and each one to a man has declined my offer?"

Yohannes nodded. "There is no other nobleman at the level of the Rases Mulugeta, Makonnen and Tekle-giorgis. They all know you will force the successor to sign the treaty that Tewodros opposed, and none will be the blackguard who gives away our sovereignty."

"Does nobody want to be king of this awful country?" railed Napier. "You!" he pointed to Henok, privy as the translator to all the interactions of state, "what if I make you the king? I have terms of surrender, and I need a king to cede them!"

Henok dutifully passed the sentiment on to Yohannes, though Napier had not meant the outburst to be conveyed.

"You cannot appoint a king, Mr. Napier. According to the law that was instituted under Tewodros, only God, through the Patriarch in Alexandria and his agent in Ethiopia the Abuna, can make the appointment."

"When I set a king on the throne, he would change this law," scoffed Napier.

"He will not have the power to change it, unless he first becomes king by this law," and Yohannes could not help but smile at Napier's frustration.

"I could put every man-jack of them to the sword," said Napier, knowing that to chase down even one of the scattered armies would mire his forces down in unknown country until they succumbed to any number of horrible risks.

"Your profession is to kill, but killing cannot solve your conundrum," Yohannes put to Napier boldly.

"I killed your master," replied Napier, cruelly.

"Perhaps you drove him to kill himself. And in this weakness of his, he has defeated your strength," rejoined the monk.

Napier turned his gaze away. "These fools in London. They send you to the ends of the earth with a simple mission, but nothing is ever that simple," he fumed. "They want their Westphalian system but they want me to bring them an exclusive trading arrangement at the same time. Guns and money are not enough anymore," he declared to Yohannes. "Next time I will bring lawyers too."

Napier's tirade killed the conversation for a spell, until Smithers ventured, cautiously, "so...shall we send for the Abuna?"

Napier directed a benevolent smile to the Colonel, who did usually try his best, after all. "Yes, I think you are right; that is the next step, and I have an idea for whom we will appoint to rule. You must have paid attention in your politics course at Sandhurst."

Smithers beamed.

"Bring me the king's widow," Napier ordered, and Haymanot arrived just moments before the Abuna. "We have a Queen in England," he began. "Is it not your custom here, as Pliny the Elder and others wrote of Ethiopia, to have a woman to rule from time to time?

"We have had queens," Yohannes informed him, "though we are not Pliny's Ethiopia."

"I submit that the king's successor should be his wife," said Napier, looking for the first time at Haymanot, who did not flinch from his gaze.

"Do you think that a woman would be easier to bend to your Queen's will?" Haymanot shot back.

Napier cracked a smile. "Now that you mention it, I don't think I've ever been able to make a woman do anything she didn't want to do."

"Then, what are you offering me, to take on this role that all the king's generals have refused?"

Napier raised an eyebrow. "I see – there is something you want. Is it money? Weapons? I want my treaty, and what is that worth to you?"

Haymanot looked down, and all in the room could see how tired she was. She raised her eyes again to Napier and spoke softly, as Henok translated. "You will never have an exclusive treaty. My husband died to prevent it. But I know you cannot leave empty-handed, after all the long way you came; and taking your countrymen home with you is not enough. What say you if you take a treaty that will let us begin to trade as equal sovereign nations, and..." Haymanot paused, as the request caught in her throat. "And you take me with you, so my child can go to England, and gain an education there. This way, when we return, no other power will have such a connection to Ethiopia, and the bond between our nations will surely flourish, more than if you had the treaty you say you want."

Tewodros had not shared this hope with anyone else, even Yohannes, and all were taken aback before Napier replied, "I understand. With each new thing I see on my voyage, I understand better that this is a Christian nation and more worldly than we had presumed. What makes you think I can grant this, to bring your child to England to be raised?"

"Are you not a man with power?" Haymanot asked, innocently.

"Ha! Here, my word is followed by ten thousand men, without question. When I return home, I will be lucky if my valet brings my pipe when I ring for it."

"Sir, I am just a simple woman from the hills, and I cannot even imagine the places in this world where my child might go; but you, I know, have been there and can take us to those places."

Napier was still amused, but even his heart was touched by Haymanot's earnestness. "When the child is old enough, send word and I will see to it that he receives the finest education even an English gentleman could hope for."

"And if it is a girl?"

"I should hope the English can offer just as fine an education for a lady." Napier found that he was expressing this sentiment for the first time, but it was a genuine one. "My dear, I cannot bring a pregnant woman back to England with me. Will you accept my promise instead as granting your request? I assure you my promise can be trusted, madam. And if you accept, do I have a ruler of Ethiopia?"

Before Haymanot could answer, the Abuna burst out with what he had been steeling himself to come out and say ever since Napier had summoned him. "I will not bless any that have the taint of your appointment!"

Napier glowered at the interruption to his banter, and even more deeply when Henok conveyed what the Abuna had said. "We are getting nowhere with these people. Tell them all to leave, and you get out too!" he raised his voice at Henok. When just the British top brass remained in the room, he continued. "So, tell me, what can I do? Do we put this Abuna to the sword, and have our boys in Cairo encourage them to send another, more pliable fellow?"

"Sir, I believe the situation in Egypt is quite sensitive at the moment," said Smithers. "They may not feel they owe us any favors."

"Cripes, man, I was joking – I'm not about to kill a bishop," grumbled Napier. "And even if I were that callous, 'Queen Victoria, Defender of the Faith, burns the Coptic church' doesn't make for quite the headline we want to see. It'll be my career that burns."

"Shall we wait, then, for instructions from London?" asked Smithers. "If you just follow orders, they can't hold anything against you."

"Sit here for months? We haven't that time, and the longer we stay, the more likely something goes wrong. We've been lucky enough this far; let's leave while we still can."

"Do you think they would be so crude as to trouble us on the way back to the sea?" was Smithers' next question.

Napier looked at him. "Are you worried, Colonel?"

"Sir, I have been worried since we set sail from Bombay. I believe that is my job."

"Then I put this to you as our plan. We won't get the exclusive treaty the pencil-pushers in London want, agreed?"

"Sir, we have been foiled."

"We've nonetheless built port facilities to land our army, and we've seen good potential in the country for some kind of trade, of which non-exclusive is better than none."

"Agreed."

"We'll offer a non-exclusive treaty in the meantime, in exchange for safe passage to the coast. When they eventually sort out a new king, they can formalize the treaty on their end. In the meantime we'll tell the chaps in London to send a better ambassador than the jolly fellows we came all this way to rescue. Does that ease your worry, Smithers?"

"Certainly. One request, if I may?"

"What is it?"

"Let us wait and send word from Aden on the day we depart for Bombay, so that when it reaches London they cannot make us turn back. I've had enough of...wandering, in wild places. And I haven't had a decent cup of tea since we ran out in Lalibela."

Napier chuckled. "Very well, Smithers. It shall be so." With that it seemed their mission was over, and the moment that had brought them all to Magdala dispersed.

## Chapter Fourteen

*"And did those feet, in ancient time…"*
*- BLAKE*

The British went back the way they came, out the same ravine, and even Eshetu was there watching again. He had climbed up to his old vantage point, this time a slow and melancholy toiling up the ridge, no fear and alarm, no adrenaline to fuel him. Similarly from afar he had watched the king's funeral, too unimportant to get close to the Abuna intoning the interment, feeling aloof but somehow part of the whole patchwork of what was happening, and remembering the king's face the times he had had the honor of speaking to Tewodros, as clear as day.

He marveled again at the sheer force the British column projected, and even more that at its head was a small detachment of Ethiopians – Yohannes and Tekle-giorgis had volunteered to accompany the foreigners to the edge of the desert; to give credence to the promises of safe travel that had been made, and to flee the place where their beloved Tewodros might haunt their steps too often. Without being conscious of it, Eshetu raised a salute – to the passage of the Fitaurari, or the army, or of history, he knew not which. All he knew was that he was done soldiering, and a quiet life with food, and family, and perhaps a little music, would satisfy him now.

In London, there was only hollow satisfaction for Glendon when he got the news. This time, Matthews had called him in, as the matter of Ethiopia was now too weighty for messages to go directly to Mark Glendon. The waiting had been interminable, Glendon dreaming of huge accomplishments and expansion of empire, but knowing how unlikely it was that such might come to pass; and being completely unable to focus on any of his other mundane work.

"Didn't go the way you planned it, eh?" said Matthews. Glendon's face was so glum that Matthews felt compelled to add, "not much we could have done, sitting back here in England. Never wanted to go to the field myself. Can't get shot in Whitehall," and now he felt he was rambling, as Glendon still didn't say anything.

"Look, Mark, the good news is when they spend that kind of money they will find a way to make it a success. We didn't get much out of it for a treaty and all that, but we still beat the buggers, didn't we? Hostages home safe, not a scratch on them. Glorious victory for Her Majesty's troops."

"I suppose I will keep my job, then, sir," offered Glendon awkwardly.

"Haha! And how. They'll give that Napier chap a title, you watch, and they'll probably let you come up with it as the Ethiopia expert, you know."

"How about Baron of Magdala?" came instantly to Glendon's mind.

"Topping!" said Matthews. "Mark, you'll do well, never fear. You, or Napier, or all of us together, somehow managed not to cock this up. In this government that's about all we can hope for, and call it a fine career." Glendon shrugged, attempting a weak smile. "Buck up, man. Dismissed." Matthews began rifling through his China papers.

On his way out through the heavy oak doors, Glendon thought he could use a friend to talk to, and realized now that he had none. He yearned to his surprise for the dull steadfastness of his father's simple silence, and the comfort of mother's cabbage soup to soothe him. Though he kept telling himself he had missed all the excitement being stuck in dreary Whitehall, the stress had taken its toll. Perhaps some time away would be the thing, and he surely needed the rest. I've finally had success, he thought, my own war, I met two men who are likely to be Prime Minister, and I spoke to the Queen, and now I just miss my family, my people who were just as good as the whole lot of them all along.

He caught a train to the country where the clear air might clear his mind, chugging through the outskirts of London and staring out the window at the passing industry that had made his nation great.

And the windmills turned, and the land was old and tired.

In Glendon's thoughts too was the general who made determined progress northward each day, the tramp of feet and cadence of the march disturbing jackals from their dens and sending starlings skittering from the trees. The dry season was coming on, and the dust billowed to the rear, so Napier rode in front, and by his side came Tekle-giorgis and Yohannes in a place of honor. The Fitaurari did not speak much, but Napier found Yohannes to be the best conversationalist he had encountered since Bombay.

"No need to stop at Lalibela, for you have already seen the churches, I understand," was today's topic as Yohannes knew they were passing the area. "The true church is God's people, but when they make such a monument to their Lord it is worthy of appreciation."

"I did see the churches. All of them together might fit in St. Paul's, but it was a different kind of majesty," reflected Napier. "Like the old stones at Durham cathedral, perhaps, that have stood for hundreds of years and make one feel the church is immovable – but again, different."

"Perhaps I would also see the churches in your land as different – but just the same, they would remind me that the church is immovable, and that God reaches to the ends of the earth."

Napier was silent for a time, glancing over to study the old monk's features, and wondering at how he felt such a kinship with someone who was not an Englishman, and not even a European. Indeed, when the Ethiopians turned back at the edge of the highlands, for they would not descend to the desert where the king's power had never held much sway, he felt a sense of loss like when he had left school, and knew he might not see some of his chums for quite some time.

"You know the English chief said to me, 'I will miss you, old man,'" chuckled Yohannes as he and Tekle-giorgis took an easy pace through a gently sloping patch of scrub.

"And what of you, old monk, have you missed your cave?" smiled Tekle-giorgis. "I will accompany you there to see it before I go on my way."

Yohannes looked around at the pale blue sky stretching endlessly over the carpeted hills, a white day moon looming large above a solitary tree on the ridge ahead, and no people for miles. It was beautiful and he would remember this picture always, but it was no place to stay for long. "My abbott Gebrewolde will need help keeping the young ones in line," he said. "I have done plenty to fill a lifetime, but it seems I still have some usefulness back in my cave at the end of it, and that is enough for me. But for you," Yohannes turned to the Fitaurari sitting straight and tall in his saddle, "I think you need a country, and a king to serve. That is what you do, and better than any other man."

Side by side they rode, the friends talking little and thinking much as they made their leisurely way through their land, and to their purposes.

Behind them in the English camp, Jeevan stretched his legs and felt their new, wiry strength from all the weeks of marching, as he made his way towards his tent. There was Alfred, the English captain who was his friend, and who gave a cordial nod. "Ready to get back on the boats, sir?" Jeevan smiled, but Alfred looked over Jeevan's shoulder and straightened as Napier came up to the two men.

"Something of a last campaign, eh, old man?" the general said to Alfred. "Nearly home, and I hope you enjoy your salad days."

"Yes, sir," said Alfred, and could not help beaming at the thought of England, and the wife bringing him tea by the fire after a long stroll across the moors.

"You, I know you as well," Napier turned to Jeevan. "You gave me the tiger pelt back in India, didn't you? that day when this whole business started. And here you are at the end of it too. Good man, good man." Napier took Jeevan's hand and shook it vigorously, and sauntered on.

For the rest of the day Jeevan puffed up his chest a little more, and felt a part of the whole world like he had not felt before.

Napier for his part sat on a rock early the next morning, thinking about the Danakil desert stretched out below him, that they would cross once more on the way to the Red Sea; their own exodus of sorts beckoning. He had heard there was a lake of fire somewhere to the east, a living volcano that breathed tongues of flaming lava, but his men needed to go home and in truth he hoped he might never see such a sight.

With no more to plan and naught to do but ride his elephant, it was a time for reflection. He had asked Smithers, "why do you think we are here?" and the answer had come nonchalantly, and matter-of-factly, "for Queen and country," before Napier had asked his assiduous colonel to leave him alone. It was true, that was the ultimate end that drove Napier's decisions, but he now wondered if those decisions might have been different if he had another, higher purpose to serve. He felt respect for how nobly the Ethiopians had faced the invader, and how Tewodros had held his position until the last; but something else, that he had not felt after his conquests in India, tickled at his conscience. He knew it was not the Christianity of the Ethiopians that was to be credited for the difference, but his own lack of Christian charity in India, and his new sense of it now, that accounted for why he could not be satisfied with the victory at Magdala.

He knew there was a stirring within him for some new and greater challenge, that was neither the excitement of his past exploits, nor the cognizance of the adulation that waited for him in England; and he knew it could not be compassed in this one moment, but the mere beginning of knowing it was enough for now. So he looked at the scenery, back at the towering mountains where the cruel rocks lay defeated below the timeless ramparts; at the sunlight peeping into hidden green valleys where springs of water trickled into life; at the silhouettes of men and tents and goats and the shadows of birds in the dawn that passed along and left little trace, but the earth knew they had been there.

He turned anon and left the highlands to serve his one true master, Christ the King.

## Afterword

A tale could be told that hewed to actual events and personalities, of the rise of Kassa Hailu during the Age of Princes to unify modern Ethiopia and become the Emperor Tewodros II, of his decline into a cruel and paranoid figurehead, and of his fall through various intrigues and invasion to ultimate suicide. This is not that book. Rather, this novel takes a skeleton of historical snapshots and names, and builds on it without fetters on the imagining. Thus, the telling of events and their context leaves out most of what existed and what took place, and the details are on the whole quite made up. To anyone who knows Ethiopian or British history, this weaving of meaningful strands into a totally different tapestry may be jarring, but I hope will be seen as a tribute to a unique past. To others without such background knowledge, I hope this book will inspire them to read more veritable accounts, both contemporaneous and modern, of the fantastic stories that come from Ethiopia.

## About the Author

Ravi Faiia is of Italian and Indian descent but lived in both Ethiopia and England as a child. He studied international relations at Stanford University before his postgraduate work at Harvard Law School, where his thesis in comparative constitutional law focused on Ethiopia. During his thesis research he came across a footnote that referenced and reminded him of Napier's elephants, planting the seed of this book in his mind. There it remained throughout his corporate law career, when he was involved in the dynamics of shareholders and business acquisitions rather than geopolitics and nation-states. Eventually, the book grew into an escape from the present day that he hopes others, as readers, can share in enjoying.

## Acknowledgments

Foremost thanks to Graham for his wonderful support, several readings and astute editorial input. Thanks to my mother for her belief and encouragement; to Gabrielle and Lawrie for their generous gifts of time and expertise; to my wife and children for their inspiration; to my father, sister and other readers for their participation in the process. Above all thanks be to God, the potter, the strong foundation, the source direct and indirect of all that we draw upon to express our true selves.

P186 BRITISH ARMY ADOPTED THEM IN
1866    used until 1874

∴ 1866 TO 1901,   FIRST TRIALS 1853
THEY WERE CONVERTED FROM 1853
IN ALL USED

P5 "THE CAVE WAS NOT A "PRISON"

P7 "SANDALWOOD ARMS" = SON TRAPPED

P16 GROUNDSKEEPER or GROOMSMAN?

P171 "RAMPANT" SLEEP?

P16    SLOW POKE / COACH
              USN        UK

       PECCAVI = I HAVE SINNED

P146  RAPE SEED SEEN IN
FIELDS FROM A PASSING TRAIN
WINTOW EARLY 1960's GS

P150  A FANNING SERVANT OF A      <·007 TO
PUNKA WALLAH?

P188 KENDAL 'MINTS' ARE KNOWN AS
CAKES

P206  OBSIDIAN = TIPPED SPEARS NOT OBSIDIAN   SPHD

286  CAUCUS. AUCLD USED IN US by
POLITICAL BODIES - UK not used

P293  EXPOSTULATIONS WRONG BECK   RIGHT WORD

196  "HAIR BRAIDS" LIKE HYACINTH ??

297  CARAVAN = A LARGE CIRCUP OF people

300  SMITHERS GOOD CHOICE FOR A GAY MAN
HAND PICKED FROM "THE SIMPSONS"

317  "TOPPING" BUCK UP 'CHUMS' OLD MAN
'GOOD MAN

313  "CRIPES" FROM "DANDY/BEANO SCHOOLBOY
SUBSTITUTE FOR CHRIST  CHILDISH

314  I cannot believe that SMITHERS would have
risen in the Ranks to
become a (clone).

Printed by Amazon Italia Logistica S.r.l.
Torrazza Piemonte (TO), Italy

176 LANGUOROUS 177 CRIMINY  CRIKEY
CRIPES

238 "SOUTHERN LANDS"